Reign of Change

Reign of Change

Book 2 of The Ripple Affair Series

Erin Cruey

Acknowledgements

To God, who is the author of love and second chances.

To Dale, thank you for being the father figure in my life. I appreciate your faithfulness and support more than you'll ever know.

To Papaw, my other father figure, and Mamaw; thank you for your love and encouragement. You inspire me to be the best that I can be.

A Cast of Main Characters

Arden Engel VI, the King:
Tough, strong, and loyal to his people, Arden is the king of Audlin and father of Edward, the heir to the throne. Unsure of whether his son is ready for the kingship, Arden is prepared to do anything to ensure the progress of his country.

Maria Engel, the Queen:
Loving and loyal to her family, Maria is hopeful her son Edward will be ready for the throne of Audlin. Supportive of who he will become instead of who he is, Maria has hope in her son's future, unlike the rest of the family.

Edward Engel, the Husband:
Strong, rash, and completely broken, Edward returns to his country with a new wife and child on the way, betraying the family and friends he held so dear. Desperate to weather the storm of his mistakes, Edward turns to isolation in hopes to never hurt a loved one again.

Malina Engel, the Wife:
A clever woman with an eye for deceit, Malina enters her new home with confidence and stamina, ready to take charge. Alongside her lover, Malina plots her rise to power as her husband Edward unwillingly becomes a pawn.

Marcus Peterson, the Knight:
A bowman in the royal guard, Marcus is the closest friend and supporter of Prince Edward after his betrayal. Sincere, honorable, and a product of a familiar past, Marcus is determined to stay loyal to Edward even if everyone else goes astray.

From the Kingdom of Edeland...

Susanna van Echt, the Mother:
The queen of Edeland, wife to King John and mother to Antoinette, Caspar, Bernette, and Robert. Susanna is determined to marry her daughters off so as to prevent shame on the family, but after Edward's betrayal, her plans are all but ruined, forcing her to act quickly.

Antoinette van Echt, the Bachelorette:
The former fiancée of Edward Engel and eldest daughter of King John and Queen Susanna, Antoinette is lovely, beautiful, and utterly devastated. Shocked and confused, she turns to the only man she feels truly cares, much to the dismay of her mother.

Bernette van Echt, the Planner:
Called Bernie by most, she is the youngest daughter of King John and Queen Susanna and sister to Antoinette. Clever and plagued by guilt from her sister's cancelled wedding, Bernie is determined to help her sister find true happiness.

From the Kingdom of Hugellia...

Aldaric van Ketten, the Ambassador:
The father of Emmerich and husband to Anna, Aldaric is an ambassador from Hugellia who works hard to build alliances with other nations. Wise and loving, Aldaric is determined to be a more supportive father to his son than what his stepfather was to him.

Emmerich van Ketten, the Friend:
The only child of Aldaric and Anna van Ketten, Emmerich becomes furious after learning of Edward's betrayal. In love with Antoinette since childhood, Emmerich vows to comfort and support her despite the controversy it may cause.

From the Kingdom of Liegen...

Arnold von Liegen, the Charmer:
The youngest prince from Edeland's neighbors to the south, Arnold is a sweet talking businessman set to become Edeland's new financial advisor, and possibly more.

From the Kingdom of Verloris...

Vacius, the Velori:
A skilled warrior and spy, Vacius is a member of the mysterious Velori. Aiding Malina in her rise to power, Vacius proves himself as a most loyal companion.

Chapter Index

Chapter 1: The First Wave   17

Chapter 2: A Hasty Departure   26

Chapter 3: Saying Good-Bye   41

Chapter 4: The Ripples' Effect   58

Chapter 5: The Prayer of the Godless   75

Chapter 6: Playing with Fire   86

Chapter 7: Calla and Chocolate   94

Chapter 8: A Date in the Apple Orchard   107

Chapter 9: Antoinette Day   123

Chapter 10: The Treaty   140

Chapter 11: The King and His Son   152

Chapter 12: The Next Heir   161

Chapter 13: The Feast of the Edellwood   170

Chapter 14: A Reason for Everything   183

Chapter 15: A Man Named Arnold   194

Chapter 16: The Last Decree   206

Chapter 17: A Departure Too Soon   216

Chapter 18: The Next King of Audlin   227

Chapter 19: The Friend or the Stranger   238

Chapter 20: The Funeral   245

Chapter 21: A Play for Power   262

Chapter 22: The Birthing   271

Chapter 23: The Proposal   279

Chapter 24: A New Plan   289

Book Two: Reign of Change

"In love, there is loyalty."

The story continues...

Chapter 1: The First Wave

When Edward saw Antoinette run towards the carriage, his heart stopped. Not out of awe in her beauty or in love from seeing her after so many weeks apart, but out of despair...and disappointment.

Because Antoinette wasn't alone when she walked down the steps to meet him. Emmerich van Ketten was with her.

Why is he here? he wondered to himself through gritted teeth. For a moment he thought that somehow Emmerich knew of his secret marriage and had come to Reigal to warn Antoinette, but seeing her reaction to his arrival, the joy on her face and the hope in her eyes, he thought otherwise. She didn't know what was coming. Emmerich was there for other reasons-or coincidence.

Or maybe it's fate mocking me.

Edward supposed he should be thankful. He was about to break his love's heart. At least Emmerich would be there to pick up the pieces.

He just wished Emmerich wasn't there to see him fall.

The carriage came to a stop and Malina gripped Edward's wrist. "Are you ready, Edward?" she asked, pointing out the window. "And look! Is that Antoinette? It must be, from the green she is wearing. Typical forest land garb. But oh, the

Edelandian girl is happy to see you! Perhaps you should say hello."

It was the part Edward was dreading the most. He didn't want to hurt Antoinette. He'd rather cover his mouth to keep his hurtful words inside, to keep her from hearing his voice confirming betrayal. But it had to come out. She couldn't feel any remorse for him. She couldn't love him like he loved her. He was worthy of Malina. He was never worthy of Antoinette.

And it was time she saw the truth.

He hardened his face to stone when he stepped out of the carriage. There were barely any greeters; the family must've been busy and weren't expecting company. They would arrive within the minute, though. It didn't take long for word to reach the household, and Antoinette and Emmerich had to have seen him coming. Perhaps they were in the garden or taking a walk and saw him from the road.

A pang of jealousy crept through Edward's heart at the thought. Why were they together in the gardens, the place where Edward and Antoinette shared so many memories alone?

When Antoinette approached, calling his name, the Verloris guards that traveled with him stepped forth and blocked her touch with spears. She looked confused, almost frightened, yet he kept his face hard. Emmerich came to her defense like the noble lion he was, and his face contorted into a snarl as he tried to pull Antoinette back to him.

"You *dare* brandish weapons to a lady of the court?" Emmerich spat. He clung to Antoinette's arm, looking as if ready to strike. His words were meant for the guards and went unnoticed, and as Antoinette stood there, still silent and processing the events around her, Emmerich turned to Edward, his eyes piercing.

"What is the meaning to this, Edward?" he demanded. "Tell these men to lower their weapons *now!*"

"No." Edward's voice was low, but Emmerich heard it as if it were a scream.

Emmerich's face soon matched Antoinette's and they both stood there, befuddled. Emmerich tried to pull Antoinette back again, but she remained firm. She didn't change at all until Malina peaked out of the carriage, taking Edward's hand as he helped her off.

Malina squinted at first, looking around and gazing at her surroundings. "My, what a quaint palace you have! So majestic with the mountains. I think I shall love it here, Edward." She turned to Antoinette as she took off her cloak. "Here," she said, holding the cloak out for Antoinette to take. "Feel free to have this cleaned. It's so dusty from the journey and I can't afford to get a cold in my condition."

Edward held his tongue. He wanted to take the cloak himself and burn it, scattering the ashes over Malina's head, but his anger was quenched as he saw Antoinette's lip start to quiver and her eyes fill with water. She held it together, the dear woman, as she was starting to put the pieces in place. Edward could only turn away. He didn't have enough strength to meet her estranged gaze.

"Darling, we'll have to talk about hiring new help. I think this girl is dumb," Malina said as she took the cloak and tossed it to one of her guards.

Emmerich's anger flared at Malina's words. "You *dare* speak to Lady Antoinette in such a disrespectful manner?"

"Who?" Malina asked as she turned to Edward. "My, he's defensive of his lady friend, isn't he?"

Defensive, indeed. It made Edward's stomach churn.

His eyes managed to look up and finally meet Antoinette's. She looked as if she was trying to hold her breath but having a terrible time with it. At first Edward thought she wouldn't be able to speak, that somehow the shock was so great she would become mute, until he heard her voice-soft and quiet like a summer breeze.

"Edward...who is this?" she asked.

Whatever projection Antoinette lacked was made up by Emmerich. "I wish to know that as well, *Cousin*. Who is this wench you have soiled your land with?"

"*Wench?*" Malina seethed, but Edward held his hand up. He hated what he was about to do. Hated every being in his body for it, but it had to be done. He had to drive Antoinette away from him because she deserved so much better.

"This," he began as he took Malina's hand in his. "Is my wife. She is Malina, daughter of Calimus, princess of Verloris."

Silence passed between them save the gasp Antoinette gave. Her breathing became erratic, her hands shaking as she crossed her arms, trying to hide the shock. After the moment of silence, she could only look away.

"What madness is this, Edward? You had no wife when I saw you in Kettensburg!" Emmerich sneered as he put his arm around Antoinette in a protective gesture. Edward cringed at the sight of his cousin holding his greatest love, making him sneer back.

"I should ask you the same, *Cousin*. What business brings you to Reigal when you had none?"

"You know why I'm here, you sick and cruel wretch!"

"Boys, boys!" Malina held out her hands. The door to the palace opened and out came Arden and Maria, along with

Queen Susanna and Bernette. They all looked confused at the sight of Edward with another woman, but Malina ignored them as she put her hand on Edward's chest, caressing it. "Darling, I'm unsure if all this commotion is good for the baby. Please, can't we go inside and have this discussion in a more private setting?"

"She's pregnant?" Tried as she could, Antoinette was able to keep the tears at bay save the one that suddenly fell down her cheek. Edward felt as if the water had been acid and was slowly eating him away. He bit his tongue to keep himself from apologizing. In the end, the hurt she had now would deliver her from so much more in the future.

"Edward!" King Arden's booming voice echoed in the air. "Is this some sort of joke? Who is this woman?"

"Who indeed!" Susanna echoed.

"Apparently, Edward's hunting trip was of a different sort!" Emmerich huffed as he glared at Malina. "Though I daresay he's found himself a dog!"

His words were ignored as the entire group came together in an uproar.

Edward could barely understand all the words that came to him. "Liar!" he heard someone say. "You've betrayed us all with your fornication!"

The insults and questions came as if in a whirlwind.

"Do you realize what you've done?"

"How could you have been so blind?"

"You promised you'd be faithful to my daughter!"

"Stephen would have *never* done this!"

"My son, you've broken my heart..."

In the midst of the commotion, amidst the screams of his father and the weeping of his mother, amidst the sneers of Susanna and the threats from young Bernette, Edward stood there, silent, taking it all in. Malina offered no remorse or explanation-in fact, she laughed-and Sir Peterson could only stand there as some of the Reigal guards tried to question him, wanting an answer to "mad Prince Edward's" lapse of judgment. But Edward only kept his eyes on Antoinette as she met his gaze back.

He couldn't hear her, but he understood the last word she spoke to him before running back into the palace. "Why?"

If he could speak, he would answer her.

Because I deserve this and you don't.

Anger. Searing, pulsating anger. It was all Emmerich could feel as he watched Antoinette's heart be ripped out of her, shredded to pieces, with Edward and Malina gloating before them. In his mind, Emmerich knew this day would come, knew that Edward would one day betray his fiancée as he once betrayed his cousin, but Emmerich prayed daily he was wrong...prayed to God that somehow, someway Edward would be good to Antoinette even though he was good to no one else.

But despite his prayers, he knew the Almighty granted free will to His people, and Edward made his choice. It burned Emmerich's soul.

Everyone was fighting when Antoinette ran off into the palace unnoticed except by him. They were all too busy arguing, too preoccupied with their own anger of Edward and their shock at his new whore, Malina. No one paid heed to

Antoinette, the woman who had been hurt the most, so Emmerich followed her in. His worry for her was more powerful than his anger, and he was drawn to comfort the woman he loved more than life itself.

She had stopped in a hallway, now empty from everyone gathering outside to see what the fuss was all about. She didn't notice Emmerich behind her as she bent over, clutching her stomach and squeezing her eyes shut, grimacing as if in pain. She tried so hard to hold the tears back, to somehow seem like she was strong, but she soon broke. She fell to her knees, sobbing, unable to control her emotions anymore.

"Antoinette!" Emmerich rushed to her and she began wiping her eyes, trying to remain strong again. He put his hands on her arms, keeping her steady as her body shook so hard he thought she was going into shock.

"Antoinette..." he began, rubbing her arms gently to calm her. "Look at me. *Look at me.* It's going to be ok. Everything's going to be fine."

His words of encouragement went unheeded as they often did whenever he tried to comfort someone grieving. She began to sob again, burying her face in her hands. "Why did he do this...what did I do wrong?"

"It was nothing you did. It was all him."

"He got her pregnant. Has he been with her this whole time?"

"I don't know."

"I was so good to him...why? Why did he do this to me?"

Emmerich had an answer, but it involved names for Edward that were inappropriate for her to hear.

"I don't understand." Antoinette lifted her face from her hands, her cheeks stained from so many tears and her eyes bloodshot and puffy from crying. "We were supposed to be getting married and he runs off and marries someone else? What-am I not pretty enough?"

Emmerich took a handkerchief from his pocket and wiped the tears from her cheeks. "You're beautiful. He's blind if he cannot see that."

"Was I not good enough? Smart enough? Funny enough? What was it that made him want her more than me?"

"You are wonderful in every way. Don't belittle yourself because you are *better* than this Verloris wench. You are better than any woman in the world."

"Then why did he leave me? If I'm so good, why did he not want me anymore?"

His heart surged with pity as he wanted to do nothing but hold her in his arms. "Don't take his actions to heart, Antoinette. He is a fool for what he's done to you. He always has been a fool and he will always be one."

"No." Antoinette shook her head, her voice hoarse. "No, Emery. I am the fool. You tried to warn me and I didn't listen. I should've seen through the lies. I should've known he never meant it when he told me he loved me. I am a fool. I am a fool!"

She sobbed again, falling forward into his arms and clutching him like a child clutches her doll when scared at night. As angry as Emmerich was with Edward, as upset as he was seeing Antoinette hurt, holding her in his arms gave him such life as he had never felt it. Her heart beat alongside his and he felt the warmth coming from her warm his soul. He breathed in her scent and held her close, wishing he could hold her forever and never be separated again.

"You are no fool, Lady Antoinette," he whispered to her as he cradled her to himself. "You are the kindest, most faithful, most loving woman I have ever known. You are wise enough to see the error of his ways, and it is better to know this now than later after being bound to him through matrimony. But hear me when I say this."

He gently kissed the top of her head. Was it too soon? He didn't know, nor did he care. He couldn't contain his love for her when she needed it so, so badly. "You are not at fault in this. You never were. And though Edward leaves, know I will always be here for you. If ever you need a shoulder to cry on, I offer my own."

He felt her hands cradle to him and her face bury itself to his chest. He placed his handkerchief in her hand and she held it to her heart, never letting it go as she dabbed her weeping eyes. He rocked her gently, like a baby, and in between her sobs he heard her muffled voice say, "Thank you, Emery."

He held her for what seemed like an age until Bernette came into the hall.

Chapter 2: A Hasty Departure

When Bernette first heard of a carriage arriving at the palace, she wondered if it could be Edward. A caravan, the servants informed, was flying royal banners down the road as they approached the front door. It wasn't everyday King Arden and Queen Maria had visitors, and Bernie knew her father wouldn't bother checking on his wife and daughters in Reigal. That left only Edward coming back early, unless it was some other foreign monarch who wanted to stop by and say hello.

At first it made Bernie giggle, foreseeing a great fight between Emmerich and Edward that would most assuredly halt the wedding and cause a good deal of entertainment for any onlookers. Yes, Antoinette would be frustrated and upset, but it wouldn't be anything she couldn't fix later on. It was all about the extra time Bernie would get with her sister before her marriage. If she could delay the inevitable, she would.

But when Bernie stepped out the door with the other royals, seeing Edward with another woman-a *pregnant* woman, unless she swallowed a grapefruit whole-she felt her world come to a halt. She saw her sister, shocked... disappointed...confused. Never had she seen a look of such sadness and hurt on Antoinette's face, and Emmerich...he was *angry*. Not the type of anger you would see when you just finish cleaning a room only to find the muddy dog jumping on the couch, but the type of anger that you see on a man when his world has been crushed and he's got nothing left to lose.

And when Bernie heard what had happened-how Edward married Malina, princess of the Verloris people, and they were expecting their first child-she fumed.   Whatever anger Emmerich had was nothing to the fury boiling inside of Bernie. Edward broke her sister's heart, *made her so distraught she became mute*, and then he decided to flaunt his wench bride in front of his fiancée!

It was instinct that made her rush forward to Edward, fingers ready to claw his lustful eyes out for daring to look at another woman.   Faster than the wind she carried herself, jumping to pounce on her prey, until she felt two hands pulling her back away from the prince before she could turn him into a princess.

"Let go!" she seethed as she struggled to no avail, the young knight named Sir Peterson holding her tight to keep her from escape.   She turned, meeting his calm features before giving him a snarl.

He was unfazed by her anger and tried to gently reassure her.   "Your Majesty, please contain yourself! Violence will not help the situation."

She scoffed at his words, feeling a desire to smack his pretty boy face to show him just how effective her ability to hit could be.   She writhed and squirmed, resorting to kicking and headbutting as the knight's grasp was too steady to let her fists fly, and before she could do anything else, she found herself being led away from Edward.

"What are you doing?" she yelled at Sir Peterson as she watched the others circle Edward like lucky vultures.   Even Emmerich, in all his fury, was getting more action than she. Bernie glared at the knight, slowing in her struggles, as they stilled near the steps, her anger now pulsating towards him almost as much as Edward.   "*What gives?* How come you're stopping me and not the others?"

"With all due respect, Your Majesty," Sir Peterson said as he panted, still trying to keep her from running, "but it is my duty as a member of the royal guard to keep the prince and royal family free from physical harm."

"It's not like I'm going to kill him," Bernie seethed. "I'm just going to kick him where it hurts!"

"That still counts as physical harm," he replied.

"It's only physical harm if it hurts him, but if he's unconscious, he won't feel a thing!"

The knight frowned. "My apologies, Your Majesty, but my duty includes preventing the prince from being knocked out, too."

His answer displeased her. *Ugh! This isn't fair!* Bernie fumed as she began flailing her arms and legs more, desperate to be free so she could attack her sister's presumed ex-fiancé. She kicked and she stomped and she waved and she flapped, hearing "oofs" and "ughs" from Sir Peterson as he struggled to keep her still. She was about to unleash verbal fury once more, thinking it would somehow help her in the fight, until she saw Antoinette and Emmerich rush past her and towards the palace doors.

Her sister was hurting. The look of despair and devastation was apparent on her face. Bernie slowed in her struggles as her anger began to subside. Edward wasn't worth beating at the moment. Perhaps later, when Antoinette was more comforted, but now was not the time. Mending her sister's broken heart was more important than vengeance.

Bernie stopped in her struggle, becoming still as both she and Sir Peterson gasped for breath. "Fine. You win," she muttered as the knight loosened his grip on her arms. "Edward's not worth it. I'm going to see my sister."

She walked out of the knight's hold as he gently let his hands fall away from her arms. Bernie took a few slow steps away from him as he watched her head to the door.

"I'm sorry this has happened to her, Your Majesty," Sir Peterson called out as Bernie stopped to hear him speak. "I wish the circumstances could have been prevented. Please, give her my best regards and sympathy."

Bernie ignored him as she headed up the steps and into the palace, feeling that the knight had to be lying because if he truly cared, he wouldn't have let Edward marry Malina in the first place.

Men were such jerks. She said it in the past, she'd say it in the future, and if anything the day's events proved that Bernie's pessimism was more accurate than what she thought. She tried to warn Antoinette that true love wasn't real and never could be. This just proved her right.

Are you happy now? she heard her conscience muse as she ran through the halls. She tried to push the thoughts from her mind as she searched for her sister. Guilt wasn't an emotion she could feel right now. There wasn't time.

The wedding's off. You should be glad. This is what you wanted, wasn't it? To delay the inevitable…maybe stop it altogether. You should be happy you got what you wanted.

Bernie felt like cursing her thoughts, telling them to *shut up* and leave her alone.

You know it's true.

She found Antoinette down a hall near the parlor, sunk to the ground and in Emmerich's embrace. She was sobbing harder than Bernie had ever seen her before, and she was clinging to the Hugellian outcast as he was clinging back.

"Antoinette?" she asked, approaching them. Emmerich looked up, his anger gone and replaced with a thankful gaze upon Bernie's arrival, and Antoinette turned, wiping her eyes with a handkerchief. She tried to stand to her feet but struggled, Emmerich helping her up and holding her close.

"You okay?" Bernie asked as she hugged her sister. Antoinette sniffled, but otherwise her tears lessened. She was trying to get herself under control, and it pained Bernie seeing her sister wanting to seem so strong in her presence.

"I'm alright," Antoinette replied as she pulled away. "I'm...I'm a little mad, though."

Bernie frowned. "Only a little? Don't worry about being all polite and nice in front of me, Antoinette. If you want to call Edward a pile of stinky goat cheese, be my guest."

"More like he's a pile of cow manure," Emmerich muttered.

Antoinette smirked, but it quickly faded. "I'm not going to stoop to his level with name calling."

"I will," Bernie replied, making Emmerich suppress a light chuckle. "You want me to go to him now and tell him off for you? I tried to kick him, but some knight held me back."

The expression on Antoinette's face looked surprised, making Bernie huff. She put her hands on her hips and seethed. "You think I'm kidding? Just say the word and I'll kick him where it hurts!"

"If you don't mind, Lady Bernette, please leave room in your beating of Edward for me," Emmerich replied, his hand still on Antoinette's shoulder, caressing it. "I would like a...word... with him too."

"And what would you say to him?" a voice came from behind. Emmerich and Antoinette looked up, both frowning, and Bernie felt her frustration rise. She knew Mother's voice and the venom it threatened to spew when she was angry. She turned around, facing her, as Queen Susanna stomped towards them.

"I would think you'd be happy at this little turn of events, *Emmerich*," Susanna spat. She crossed her arms as she stood, glaring at her target. "What was it that you told Edward in Kettensburg that made him so hastily change his mind about my daughter? When Edward left, everything was fine, but when he came back, he was a changed man! What words did you give him to make him turn on my Antoinette, because you should be happy! Your plan has worked swimmingly!"

Antoinette's mouth dropped open and her eyes filled with tears. Not that Antoinette believed Mother in any way-Bernie knew better than that. She was only shocked that their mother would blame Edward's actions on anyone but Edward himself.

"Mother, Emery had nothing..." Antoinette began, but Emmerich rubbed her shoulder again, turning to her.

"It's okay," he said softly before facing Susanna. His eyes narrowed. "Your Majesty, you can accuse me all you want. I vow before God and man that I did *not* encourage Edward in his dealings with Malina. In fact, I knew nothing of the sort. Had I known about this affair, I would've confronted Edward and contacted Your Majesty of the event; but I knew nothing. Your daughter is very dear to me, but do not think I would be so cruel as to ruin her happiness just to fuel my own selfish desires!"

Bernie remained quiet as she looked towards the ground. *Are you happy now*? she heard her conscience prickle. She bit her lip as the answer became painfully clear. No, she wasn't happy at all.

"Clever of tongue, little Emery," sneered Susanna, "but not clever enough to fool me. It does not matter. Come, ladies." She turned to Bernie and Antoinette, pulling her away from Emery's grasp. He reached out for her, unsure of whether to let her go so freely to her mother, but Antoinette shook her head, giving him a warm smile.

"It's alright," she whispered, and Emmerich lowered his hand.

"It's obvious we must be going now," Susanna said impatiently. "Gather your things and be quick! I shan't stay another moment in this place after what's happened. What rudeness!"

Bernie felt her mother's hand push her forward and she saw Antoinette be pulled along. Emmerich started to follow, but Susanna glared back. "Not another step, Emmerich. Leave me and my daughters at least some privacy where we don't have you nosing about in our business!"

Emmerich looked to Antoinette, and she nodded slowly. "I'll speak to you soon, Emery. Thank you for..."

"We're leaving as soon as we're packed! Now let's go!" Susanna yanked Antoinette away and rushed down the hall. Bernie watched as her sister glanced back at Emmerich, her face sad and teary-eyed, before facing the front.

I'm sorry, Bernie thought as she and Antoinette were dragged into their room and handed suitcases. *I didn't mean for it to happen this way.*

But Bernie remained silent as she and Antoinette started to pack.

Edward had to guess only twenty minutes had passed since his arrival back home, but already it felt like days.

Yelling. He was surrounded by it after coming home…so much yelling he could barely hear himself think. Shock, disappointment, anger. Every negative emotion of the human existence was shown to him in such a short span that he wondered if anyone truly knew how they felt. Confusion seemed to be the one thing everyone agreed on, all asking the same question: "Why?"

It was an answer Edward wish he knew.

After twenty minutes his mind could take no more. He was used to conflict-his father scolded him enough over the years to teach him-but it didn't make it any more desirable. He wanted a break, *needed one*, and he felt like doing anything for some peace and quiet. No one would let him have it. He tried to move, tried to get away from the people who suddenly smothered him without air, but no matter where he went, they followed.

It suddenly became too much. He couldn't take the insults and questions anymore and he had to leave.

"Just get over it!" Edward snapped, making even his father stare in bewilderment. "What's done is done!"

He pushed his way forward and headed inside, ignoring whatever words they spat back at him as Malina snickered in delight. Not too fast lest he look like a weeping maiden, but fast enough where he could get away from them and hide for a moment to gather his thoughts. His room was nearest and he swung the door open, slamming it shut and locking it so they couldn't interrupt his time to recuperate.

But as he turned, he gulped, for there was one other person in the room with him.

Antoinette slowly put a chemise in her suitcase, her face firm, yet looking away. Why was she in his room? Edward wondered, but then it dawned on him. She had been moving her things in during his absence. His room was to become their room, and now she was taking her things back.

"I'll leave," she said, stuffing a few more of her items into her bag. "You probably want some peace after all of that."

In all accounts, he did, but he stood in the doorway, blocking her exit. It dawned on him this could be the last time he ever saw Antoinette and he didn't want to say good-bye. At least not yet.

"Leaving so soon?" he asked, and he pursed his lips together after he spoke, thinking the words more arrogant than what he meant them to be.

Her eyes never met his as he looked at her. They remained downcast, sullen, and it broke his heart to see it. "I'm thinking I should've left sooner, Edward. Three's a crowd."

He had nothing to say to that. What could he say? The truth would hurt too much. The truth would make her feel sorry for him. The truth would never bring them back together.

They stood there in silence for a moment until Antoinette looked up, her eyes teary. "I don't know why you've done this, Edward. I don't know why you've chosen Malina over me. I'm not sure if I want to know, but I do want to know this. Why tell me when our wedding was so soon? Why show up at the door with a woman you've claimed as your own?"

"It's complicated," he replied.

"Complicated." Antoinette gave a sarcastic laugh. "Complicated is the explaining I'm going to have to do when I get back home, Edward. Complicated is what you've made my life become now."

"I don't know what to tell you, Antoinette. Just trust me when I say it's better this way."

Her face turned from hurt to fury, and Edward wondered if he shouldn't have snuck a bit of truth in his lies after all. "Better?" she seethed. "How is this better? You've ripped my heart out of me, Edward! Do you not have any remorse?"

He had more remorse than she would ever dream of, but she could never know. "What do you want? An apology? Fine. I'm sorry."

"You're not sorry, though, are you?" Antoinette asked as tears started to stream down her face. Edward wanted to look away. He had seen her cry before at weddings, during a sad scene in a play, or when laughing so hard she couldn't hold the tears back. But these were sad tears; tears caused by him. It made his stomach sick.

"How far along is she?"

Edward saw she was looking back at him, her face harder now. The tears had stopped for the moment. "Who?" he asked.

"Malina. She's pregnant, remember? How far along is she?"

"Two months."

She nodded, fingering the bag in her hands. "You didn't waste time, did you? Sir Rikert said you stopped in Verloris on your way to Hugellia. Was that when it happened?"

Edward lowered his head. "Yes."

"Were there other women besides Malina?"

Edward's eyes widened. "What? No!"

"Wow. She must be special then."

She wasn't special. Just clever. So very, frustratingly clever.

But Antoinette's next words caught him off guard. "Edward," she began. "Did you ever really love me? Has all of this been a lie?"

Liar. He knew he was. He had been since the day Stephen died. But he never lied about his love for her. *Never.*

They'll never believe you.

"Antoinette, don't twist this into something it isn't. You know I love you."

Antoinette shook her head. "Your actions certainly proved your words, didn't it?"

"Just because this happened doesn't mean..."

"All this time," Antoinette interrupted, his words going unheeded, "you were lying. You never loved me. You probably met Malina before and was going to see her for one final fling. It wasn't the storm that made you stop. It was her. I should've listened to Emery when he said..."

"Emery?" Edward's heart burned at his cousin's name. "Here you lay the blame on me with Malina when you've been with my cousin! What honesty is there in that?"

Antoinette's voice rose in fury. "Don't create an affair where there was none! I have been nothing but loyal to you, and so has Emery! He came because you sent that letter sending him here!"

Edward was confused. "What letter? I don't know what you're talking about."

Antoinette laughed, rolling her eyes in sarcasm. Edward wondered what cruelty his cousin was up to. He'd sent no letter bringing Emmerich to Reigal. He wanted to keep his cousin as far away from Antoinette as possible. "Whatever trickery he's playing on you, Antoinette, I had nothing to do with it!"

"I don't believe you," Antoinette seethed. "Emery warned me, you know, about you. About what you did to him all those years ago. He told me about what he wrote, confessing his feelings and asking for my hand in courtship, and then he told me you stole it from him and acted like it was your own!"

Edward felt his heart fall to his gut. He had long forgotten about that; his first big lie, his first deceit. It was the day his cousin turned from friend to enemy. It was the day he learned lies could be so much better than the truth.

Oh, what a lie he told himself.

"What do you say to that, Edward? Is it true?"

There was no point in lying on this. Emery would be better for her. Emery would take care of her. "Yes. It's true."

The look on her face hurt him even more than when she first saw him with Malina. Her lip quivered, tears streaming once again, and she wrung her hands together to keep them from shaking. "I believed you..." she stuttered as she looked away. "I trusted you. I defended you...I loved you...I..../ was so foolish!"

Edward had to fold his hands to keep himself from reaching out, to taking her in his arms and kissing every tear away and telling her he wanted to take back every day of his past and do them right just so she wouldn't cry anymore.

"I'm sorry I disappointed you," Edward whispered, approaching her. "Emmerich was right. He's...always been right."

"I wanted you to prove them wrong, Edward!" Antoinette said between sobs. "Not me! *Not me...*"

He couldn't control himself any longer. He had to hold her, touch her, do something to comfort her. He reached his hand out and touched her shoulder, but as soon as she felt him, she jerked herself away, screaming, "*Don't touch me!*"

He pulled his hand back. To hear her voice so angry, so distrusting of him...it was the ultimate rejection.

But this was how it needed to be.

One day you'll be glad for this. You'll be spared from so much pain.

A still, almost eerie silence followed. The air was tense, like moving amidst egg shells waiting to be broken, and Edward knew his time with her was almost up. She would be wanting to leave soon, and once she was gone, she would never come back.

He watched her as she bowed her head, her back hunched over, moving up and down. She was crying softer now, yet the sight still ate at him heart and soul. "Why, Edward? What did I do to you that you would treat me this way?"

"Nothing," he replied. "You've done nothing wrong."

"Then why did you choose *her*?"

Edward turned his back on her, looking away and refusing to answer. It was an answer he couldn't give. *I didn't choose her. She chose me.*

Antoinette sniffled, her tears suddenly stopping. She stood tall and straight, her bag in her hand as she walked to his front. "Do you love her, Edward? Do you love Malina?"

Edward's head rose to meet her gaze and he sighed. He was so tired of lying all of a sudden. So tired of all the deception and having to craft every word to make every story fit. But he had to tell one more for Antoinette's sake. He had to push her away.

"Yes, I do love Malina."

Her face was emotionless, but her eyes were clear. Her soul was rattling, every feeling of love and trust and commitment she had with Edward suddenly ripped away into shreds and tossed to the wind. For a moment she said nothing and just nodded until she whispered, "Normally I would say you were lying, but I don't know what to believe anymore. I guess now you're telling the truth."

Edward exhaled slowly, his eyes lowering to the ground.

"Good-bye, Edward," Antoinette said, and before Edward could say anything in return, she unlocked the door and walked out of the room, leaving him alone.

Silence remained. That was it, then. Antoinette was gone and would never be in his life again. He staggered back like a man punched in the stomach, leaning against a wall and running his hand through his hair.

She's gone...

The thought pained him, ate him away like decay upon a corpse. His heart pounded and his breath became heavy, but he didn't make a sound.

She mentioned her heart breaking, but he felt his shatter, ground into dust and never to be put back together again.

You deserve this, his mind reminded him.

But how he wished for a drop of mercy…

He bent his head, his face meeting his palms, wanting to hide from the world forever.

His last words to his beloved echoed in his mind.

Yes, I do love Malina.

He never wanted to lie again.

Chapter 3: Saying Good-Bye

Numb. That was the best way to describe Antoinette's thoughts and feelings. Unable to think, unable to feel, unable to do anything but walk down the hall, oblivious to the world around her.

There were servants who tried to console her, guests of the king who just happened to be there at the right time to see the new gossip first hand and ask her questions as to why Edward did what he did.

She didn't know if she could give an answer even if she knew what it was.

Her responses were short, to the point, clear…but there were a few instances where she did know what to say yet remained quiet. She had never felt so conflicted in all her life and no longer knew how to act. She wanted comfort, yet yearned for privacy. She felt so crowded, yet also so alone.

The only thing she knew she wanted was to lock herself into a room and scream.

This isn't real. This hasn't happened. I'm dreaming, aren't I? I want to wake up…

But sometimes the worst nightmares happened when a person was awake.

She found herself in the hallway, wandering, not sure where she wanted to go. Mother mentioned gathering her things and getting a carriage together out front. She wanted to leave soon, as quickly as possible, in order to avoid embarrassment from onlookers or to make a scene.

Antoinette's feet shuffled forward, moving as fast as sorrow could carry her, passing the rooms of the palace on her way to the door. She glanced inside each room, memories of the past suddenly flooding back.

The parlor...

"Have you ever been to tea before?"

She could see Edward's eyes looking around, befuddled and nervous as if wondering what to do. They had barely known each other, perhaps a few weeks, and in layman's terms, they were on their first date.

"Of course. My mother's held tea time every day with her friends," Edward had said.

He tried to be so proper so he could please his young lady, acting like he was enjoying her request to tea.

"Do you not like pekoe?" Antoinette had asked.

"I love it," he said after taking a sip, his lips scrunching together from the bitterness.

She had laughed, so pleased that he tried his best to make her happy.

She should have known he was such a fake back then.

Antoinette passed the parlor, looking away, heading down the hall until she came to an empty study, untouched by everything except time. It was once Stephen's personal room where he could read and learn in peace.

"I can't believe he's gone," she remembered Edward saying as he sat on the floor, surrounded by books and parchment, his head in his hands and his face pale and clammy.

"He's in Heaven now," she soothed as she hugged him from the back. He put his hands over hers and held them close to his heart, his breath coming in short spurts.

"I could've protected him. I should have done more."

"It was an accident. You couldn't do anything to prevent it or save him."

Edward bent his head, hiding his face. It was the only time she ever saw him cry.

"I can't take his place. I'm not meant to be king. I can't do it."

She had kissed his cheek, hoping to calm him, but it didn't help. He continued to weep in her arms. She wasn't sure he would ever stop.

"I believe in you, Edward," she had whispered to him.

Funny how faith could die so quickly.

The door was nearer now. There was one final room between her and the foyer-one final room of memory. A drawing room, large and usually meant for visitors, stood empty and silent, light from the outside shining through the windows and onto the hardwood floors and sofas in front of a wide hearth. She remembered last spring, a week after their engagement, as she and Edward sat in front of the fire and everyone retired to bed.

"Mrs. Engel," Edward had whispered as he held her in his arms. His hand stroked her hair as he laughed. *"I really like the sound of it. Mrs. Engel...has a ring to it, don't you think?"*

She laughed back, snuggling close in his embrace. *"I like the sound of it a lot."*

"I wish it were summer." He sighed, his arm draping down her back. *"We'd be married already. We'd be together every day for the rest of our lives."*

"Summer isn't far off." She smiled. *"Besides, I have to go back to Staalberg tomorrow to start moving my things. That's going to take a while."*

Her words went unheeded as he looked to the ceiling. *"Let's get married now. You and I-we can find a priest and get married tonight. Let everyone else worry about the details."*

She looked up and lifted herself from his arms, facing him. *"You want to elope?"*

"Why not?"

"But our families...our friends. They wouldn't be there. Don't you want a wedding so they can share the day with us?"

"It's just a party," he muttered. *"Besides, I don't care about everyone else. I'm only there for one reason-you."*

She frowned. *"You're serious, aren't you? About eloping?"*

"Very."

She remembered fingering her hair, nervous as to how she should answer. She wanted a wedding. It wasn't just a party to her. It was a day that could be called special, a day that she could share with everyone and declare how much she loved her husband-to-be in front of them.

"Why the rush?" she asked, and Edward looked away, his cheeks looking flushed.

"It's nothing," he replied. "Never mind. You want a wedding and I shouldn't question that."

"But you did," she said. "If you have something on your mind, tell me."

He gave her a smirk for a quick moment before rubbing his forehead. "Do you really want to know? I'll give you a hint: every time I think I'm strong, you walk into the room and prove me a weakling."

She cleared her throat, trying to hide her blushing face. Well…at least he was honest about what he was feeling. Not that she didn't feel the same for him, of course. She had just apparently managed it more easily.

"So that's why you want to elope-just so you can move up the wedding night?"

Edward's smirk had left and he suddenly looked mortified. "What? No, I never meant it to sound like that. I just…you know…"

She crossed her arms, almost pleased she could put him in his place so quickly. He gave a chuckle as he exhaled, leaning back on the sofa and staring at the ceiling.

"…And now I'm in the stocks," he said.

"Not quite." She laughed. "But I think one day you'll thank me for sticking with our set date. Besides, if we eloped, our parents would be furious-my mother especially. Do you really want to face her wrath and deny her being 'mother of the bride' to the future queen of Audlin?"

He looked at her, his brows going up. "That's incentive enough. Never mind I said anything."

"And," Antoinette cooed, snuggling back into his arms, *"patience is a virtue. You and I have something to look forward to and the wait will be worth it. Trust me."*

Antoinette stared at the room as her lip quivered, the memory fading back into her mind. She had her chance to marry him. What would have happened had she said yes? Was her saying no to the elopement his reason for leaving, because his carnal desires overruled his loyalty to her?

Was that all he thought of her as? Territory to be conquered?

I waited for you. Why didn't you wait for me?

"Antoinette?"

She turned to find Emmerich van Ketten standing quietly behind her, his eyes full of concern. "Your sister is looking for you and your mother has the carriage ready."

She nodded in thanks, pressing her lips together to force a smile, but it didn't last long. Her lips started to quiver and soon she was crying again.

I don't want to go.

"It's alright," Emmerich said as he approached her, handing her another handkerchief. She laughed as she took it in her hand, wiping her eyes.

"Do you carry a dresser in your pockets, Emery, or are you just prepared for crying maidens?"

"I won't lie. I packed them more for myself." He smirked. "Allergies and all. But I'll content myself with something else if the urge to sneeze arises. I'll steal some of Edward's and put them back in his drawers when finished."

She smiled at the thought of Emmerich being so devious to his cousin, but her smiled faded as she kept the cloth to her face. "I…I don't want to go back to Staalberg, Emery.'

He nodded, and she knew he understood. The disappointment, the questions, the harassments that would doubtless come her way when she returned. He hugged her, holding her close and stroking the back of her head. "Do you want me to go with you for support?"

"Mother would terrorize you the entire time."

"I don't mind as long as you're happy."

She gave him a gentle squeeze for his words. Had he always been so willing to suffer and deny his own wants just for her sake? It was a quality she felt unworthy of. Was she so blinded by Edward that she never noticed others cared for her even more?

She wanted Emery to stay with her, to be the shoulder she could cry on, to be the one to hold her when she felt so alone. But she couldn't let Mother abuse him with her words. Besides, she needed time to think, to heal.

"You don't have to, Emery," she replied. "I don't want to burden you."

"You are never a burden, but you are carrying one, and I wish to lighten your load," he said, lifting her chin to face him. "I'll escort you home. It's the least I can do. Please."

She smiled, giving in to his request. "Thank you."

He smiled back as he pulled away. "I'll gather my things while you go on to the carriage. Aunt Maria wishes to say good-bye to you, as does the king. I will leave instructions for one of the servants to gather the remainder of your items to send back. I won't be long and will be by your side before our departure."

"Okay," she said. He held her hands for a moment, kissing her cheek and running off towards the guest room where he stayed. As she watched him leave, she gathered her arms to her chest and took one last look of her surroundings before heading towards the door.

It was so hard to say good-bye. She didn't want to. She wasn't ready.

But she had to go. There was nothing left for her except broken dreams.

With one last look she turned away and walked out the door to wait for Arden and Maria so she could fare them well.

"YOU'VE BROUGHT SHAME ON OUR FAMILY!"

Edward bit his tongue to the point of pain, remaining silent. He stood in the throne room, his head bent towards the ground as his father circled him in a furious rage.

"HOW COULD YOU BE SO STUPID, EDWARD?"

He knew he should have stayed in his room. He should've stayed there and locked the doors, never to come out for anyone ever again. Curse the servant who found him and drug him back on the king's demand.

"STEPHEN WOULD'VE NEVER DONE THIS!"

Of course Stephen wouldn't, and leave it to their father to remind him which son was the good one.

"I'm sorry I disappointed you," Edward muttered beneath his breath.

King Arden stopped, his face boiling with red heat. "You aren't a disappointment, Edward," he seethed. "You are a *failure*."

"Arden, please." Maria sniffled as she put her hand to her quivering lip. "Please, let's not say such harsh things."

"I don't care!" Arden huffed. He took Edward's chin, forcing it up so he could glare at his son eye-to-eye. "I thought you better than this, Edward. I thought you a man of self-control. All it took was one night in Verloris and already you have brought ruin and embarrassment to the crown! *What madness came upon you that would make you do such a thing?*"

Edward forced a gulp as he tried to look away from his father. He didn't want to fight. He didn't want any more lectures.

"*Well?*" Arden demanded.

"I got drunk," Edward said quietly, making Maria gasp and cry some more. "We spent the night together and she got pregnant. I married her because it was the right thing to do."

Arden scoffed. "Don't try to make this an honorable decision."

"What would you have me do? Abandon my own child?"

"You're still a child yourself!" Arden spat. "Do you think you're ready to be a father? Do you have any idea what type of responsibility that entails?"

Edward looked away. It wasn't that he chose to get Malina pregnant. He didn't want children yet. It wasn't like any of this was planned.

Arden gave a sarcastic laugh. "You're not ready to be a father, Edward. In fact I pity the poor child you have. Do you think it'll look up to you and respect you after all that you've done? You are selfish, you are vain, you are arrogant! A child being born to you isn't a blessing-it's a curse!"

Maria looked aghast. "Arden!"

Edward looked at his father, shocked. Arden only continued with fire in his eyes. "I weep for this day, Edward. I weep for myself as I have failed to teach you wisdom and purity. I weep for your mother that her heart has been broken by her own son. I weep for Lady Antoinette that you've introduced her to betrayal. You have given her a hurt that even time cannot heal."

His eyes narrowed as he stood in front of Edward, his voice lowering. "And yet I do not weep for you. Your folly will produce fruit and you must bear the consequences of your actions, but I doubt you will even learn from that."

Edward's heart was beating fast. Anger, hurt, sorrow, fury...every emotion that haunted him seemed to swirl about, and he found his speech mute. Surely there was a word he could give, a line of defense to tell his father, *I tried so hard to make things right. I tried to be the man you wanted me to be. I didn't mean to fail!*

He kept silent.

You deserve this. Every word.

Before anything could be said, a voice was heard at the entrance to the throne room. "Your Majesties, Lady Antoinette's carriage is readying to depart. If you wish to say your good-byes, now is the time to do so."

Edward didn't turn as he recognized Emmerich's voice from behind. Arden looked away from his son and nodded in thanks as Maria headed to the door. "We are not done with this conversation, Edward," Arden hissed quietly as he pointed to Edward's chest. "And don't think you will be exempt from my anger. You've not only embarrassed us, but the entire country as well. Edeland was our greatest ally and you've slapped their faces with your actions! This will take years to repair. *Years!*"

Arden stormed off, following Maria out the door, leaving Edward alone in the silence of the room.

"Are you not going to fare her well?" Emmerich asked as he stepped forward.

Edward turned, facing his cousin. "No." He looked down, noticing Emmerich had a cloak on normally used for travel. "But it looks like you are."

"I'm going to escort her home."

Edward's eyes beaded. "You don't need to. She'll be fine on her own."

Emmerich stiffened as he entered the throne room. "I know she'll be fine, but unlike you, I'm not fond of abandoning someone I care about when they're at their lowest."

"I *didn't* abandon her," Edward seethed. "You don't know what you speak, Cousin. If you think my caring for her is less than what you feel, you are *lying* to yourself!"

Emmerich gave a huff as he leaned forward, glaring Edward down. "*If you truly loved her, you would never have done this.*"

Edward stood his ground, teeth grinding. "Don't you *dare* question my feelings for her, Emmerich!" Edward's voice neared a shout. "Besides, don't pretend you aren't enjoying this in your own way. You always wanted her for yourself. You were always jealous because she chose me and not you! I'd think you'd be happy now that you finally have a chance!"

Emmerich clenched his fists. "Don't go there, Edward."

"What?" Edward laughed bitterly. "Are you not fond of the truth? Do you not deny it? Admit it! Her broken heart allows you to pick up the pieces and finally get what you want. You should be thanking me for giving you the chance to..."

But before Edward could finish the sentence, he saw Emmerich giving a swing of his fist. Soon there was pain, burning and radiating from his jaw. Edward staggered back as he tried to keep himself from falling, rubbing his face with a moan and wiping the blood from his busted lip.

Emmerich had punched him.

Edward wondered if he'd ever get the feeling back in his face. Though Emmerich was never a fighter, he certainly had the swing of one.

"You think me an envious monster, Cousin," Emmerich heaved, his breathing heavy, doubtless from the adrenaline pumping through his veins. "I won't deny I was jealous of you, because I knew you didn't deserve her. She was always too good for you. But *never* did I try to ruin her happiness. Never did I try to break you up or wreck your relationship. As long as you treated her with respect and love, I could accept her choosing you because I wanted her happiness over anything else."

Edward was quiet as he rubbed his painful jaw.

Emmerich looked away as he shook his head. "I didn't want to believe you were capable of hurting her, Edward. I wanted to believe that even though you betrayed me you would never betray her because you loved her so. But now that I see what you've done and have seen the kindest woman on this earth be subject to tears and sorrow, I no longer envy you. I *hate* you, because you have proven my fears true and have broken the heart of the person most dear to me."

Edward stood there, dumbfounded, Emmerich's words hurting worse than his actions. *I hate you...* His words echoed in Edward's mind and he felt sick at the thought of them. They were friends once. Brothers, when they were children. He never expected Emmerich to be on his side, but to have someone loathe him so much...Edward felt sick to the core.

"You deserve Malina," Emmerich said, his voice hoarse, "and you deserve every bitter deed she brings you."

Edward licked his lips, tasting blood and wiping it away with his sleeve. *I know. That's why I've done this,* he thought. He lowered his head, unable to look at Emmerich anymore.

Emmerich scoffed, turning towards the door. "Farewell, Cousin," he said. "I'm going to clean up the mess you've made and make sure Antoinette recovers from this hurt. Don't think I shall ever forgive you of the pain you've caused us both. You are a wretch, Edward, and I do not pity you or your decaying heart. I hope to never see you again."

He started to leave, the sharpness of his turn able to cut like a knife. Edward watched as his cousin stormed towards the door, calling out to him one last time before he left. "Just make her happy, Emery. For me."

Emmerich paused for a moment, almost looking back, but continued on into the hall and towards the front door where the carriage stood waiting. Edward watched as his cousin left, feeling guiltier than ever at how many lives he had ruined.

God have mercy on me...please... he pleaded into the darkness. The air remained silent until he heard the sound of footsteps coming towards him.

He looked up, expecting to see Emmerich once again, but calmed as he saw a limping Sir Peterson approach him and sit across from him on the floor.

The knight had bruises from head to toe and a swelling eye to match Edward's. Apparently his arrival in Audlin went as well as Edward's, too.

"What happened to you?" Marcus asked as he noticed Edward's face.

"Emmerich," Edward muttered. "What about you?"

"Antoinette's sister." Marcus sighed as he rubbed the back of his aching neck.

Edward nodded as the two friends remained in the throne room, silent.

Saying good-bye to Arden and Maria was harder than Antoinette thought it would be. There were tears, bitter and angry, and there were embraces, long and sad. Arden's face was red, his blood pressure up from a confrontation with his son, but he did his best to keep his composure, his apologies never stopping. Saying good-bye to Maria was the hardest. She was like a mother to Antoinette, a mother she could be close to and trust and love, but she would never get that chance now. They held each other for a long time and Maria cried the hardest.

"I don't know if it's proper or not, but please keep in touch," Maria stammered as she clutched Antoinette to herself. "I've never had any daughters. Despite what's happened, I'll always see you as one of my own. This Malina isn't family. You are."

Antoinette appreciated the gesture. She wanted to keep in touch but didn't know how feasible it would be. Any reminders of Edward would be painful.

But she didn't let Maria know that. "Thank you, Maria. I'll write often," she replied, and it made the queen smile.

The king and queen stood back as Susanna ordered her daughters into the carriage. She only gave a curt nod to the king and queen, muttering something about "talking terms later", and Antoinette could only shake her head at the meaning of that. Bernie had entered the carriage, plopping down next to the window, but Antoinette eyed the door before wanting to step in.

"Come, child, while we still have daylight!" Susanna snapped.

Antoinette pressed her lips into a frown. Couldn't her mother be sympathetic at least once? She shouldn't be surprised. Mother was only interested in how everything looked and appeared to others. She was probably angrier at what people would think of the cancelled wedding than how Antoinette felt herself.

"We can't leave yet. Emery's coming along," she said.

Susanna's eyes widened. "That boy isn't allowed in my carriage!"

"That's fine," Antoinette replied. "I'm sure we can find him another one."

"Well then there's no need to wait. Let's go!"

Antoinette looked back at the door. She watched as Emmerich rushed down the steps, a cloak on his shoulders and a small bag in his hand. He barely took time to pack, it looked like, but just seeing him arrive was good enough.

"My apologies for my lateness," he said, out of breath. "Are we ready to depart?"

Susanna beaded her eyes at him. "We don't need you, Emmerich. Stay here with your own family."

"If it pleases you, Your Majesty," Emmerich replied with a bow of his head, "Lady Antoinette *is* like family to me and I wish to escort her home so that I know she has made it there safely."

"There's no room for you in our carriage," Susanna said. "Besides, we don't need a caravan. It will only slow down our travels."

"I think I can keep up." Emmerich smirked.

"But..."

"Mother?" Antoinette asked. Susanna looked at her, her brow lowered. "I want Emmerich to come. Please? At least to the Edellwood?"

There was a pause, and for a moment Antoinette thought her mother would agree to her request until she saw the queen roll her eyes in disgust. "Absolutely not," Susanna scoffed. "We don't need anyone to accompany us. We have our guards and they are plenty. Now get in the carriage, Antoinette. Good-bye, Emmerich. Give my regards to everyone in Hugellia."

Antoinette frowned as Susanna stepped into the carriage, keeping the door open and waiting for her daughter.

Antoinette turned to Emmerich. "I'm sorry," she whispered. "I wanted you to come-really, I did."

Emmerich only gave her a grin as he hugged her, putting his lips to her ear. "I'm still coming. I'll follow you on horseback. Why do you think I packed light?"

He pulled away from her, the grin still on his face as he rushed off to the stables. Antoinette gave a quick smile as she watched him leave and then entered the carriage and sat next to her sister.

Susanna shut the door harshly. "Driver, take us home," she muttered, and the carriage began to move. Antoinette took a look out the window and waved to Arden and Maria, who stood at the door. She gave a sigh, giving one last good-bye in her mind, and looked away.

Chapter 4: The Ripples' Effect

It didn't take long for the city to catch word of Edward's new wife.

Between visiting nobles, gossiping servants, and scoffs between his own family and friends, any hope Edward had for keeping his "surprise" quiet was gone. When he entered rooms, people became hushed and stared. When he was among guests at the palace, he often went ignored. In the hallways he would receive glances-eyes beaded, nose in the air, a low "hmph" as he passed the person by. People were angry, and for once he couldn't blame them.

The only one not being quiet was Malina. She relished in her new role as wife and future queen, ordering the servants about and taking tasks of redecorating rooms once given for Antoinette's use. Though the people of Reigal were far from accepting at first glance, she made sure she put her best features forward. She sweet-talked them, telling them of the baby and how she hoped for a son that looked just like her beloved Edward. Most ignored her, their loyalty to Antoinette still evident in their disapproving stares, but Malina only smiled as she went on to her business. She didn't care what people thought about her. She only cared that they knew who she was.

It was on a warm day that Edward decided to leave the palace, away from all the gossip and stares, to attend a local jousting match. He offered to take Malina, attempting to be kind, but she shooed him away from her chambers, not wanting to admit that morning sickness was plaguing her and making her feel weak. Edward didn't mind leaving her to her wanted loneliness. She was beastly when ill, and he'd rather spend the morning in peace than in havoc.

He walked down the halls, the humidity making the palace feel stifling, and passed by his parents' sitting room, glancing inside. The king was at his desk, working on a letter, while his mother sat on the sofa and read. He thought it best to let them know he was leaving for the morning, and he peaked into the room, gently clearing his throat.

His parents looked up as he greeted them. "I'm going out for a bit. There's a joust over at the arena. Did you want to come?"

The room was silent until the king got up from his chair with a scoff, heading to the opposite door in the room and walking out. Edward watched as his father slammed the door shut, leaving his letters and work splattered onto the desk.

The queen gave a sigh as she bowed her head, her eyes falling back to the pages of the book.

"He's still angry with me?" Edward asked, frowning.

"And you're surprised?" Maria replied, turning the page. "It's only been a week."

"I apologized. I don't know what else I can do."

"There's nothing you can do."

"So is he going to ignore me forever? Never speak to me again?"

Maria sighed. "I don't know. Your father is an unpredictable man when he's angry, Edward. I won't lie... he's very cross right now."

"But it's been a week!"

"Edward," Maria began, closing the book and looking up at him. "This is something that won't go away overnight. Do you have any idea of the magnitude in what you've done?"

Edward crossed his arms, looking away. Of course he did. He hurt a lot of people-he knew that, understood it, *grieved* every waking moment for it-but it was his burden to hold onto the guilt and hurt, not theirs. Why couldn't they just let it all go and leave him to rot?

"I'm not in the mood for a lecture, Mother. I know what it is you're trying to say," he muttered. "It's been a week and it's all in the past now. So can't we just get on with our lives? Just let it go."

Maria's expression soured, her lips falling apart as she gave a slight gasp. "This isn't something we can all let go, Edward. Do you not understand that this isn't just about you?"

Edward rolled his eyes. Of course it was about him. It was always about him. He was the troublemaker. He was the failed son. He was the liar, thief, adulterer, murderer.

"I get it, Mother," Edward said. "I did the deed and I fully accept the consequences. I understand that. You don't have to remind me."

"Edward, what do you think your father was working on when you got here?"

Edward shrugged. "A letter?"

"And who do you think that letter was to?"

"I don't know," Edward replied. "Some dignitary?"

"He was writing to your grandfather in Kettensburg," Maria said. "He was explaining why you never came back from your 'hunting trip' and why everyone had to cancel their plans in coming to Reigal. Do you know how angry the family is going to be when they find out you've deceived them?"

"Of course. Everyone's angry with me right now. Have them wait in line!"

"Edward, do you not understand how terrible a thing this is?" she asked, her eyes filling with pity. "You have angered the people of Edeland with what you've done to Antoinette. You have angered your own people here for giving them a princess they did not expect or want. Now you are angering the people of Hugellia because you have lied to them and deceived them when they gave you hospitality! Do you think, when you become king, these matters will be forgotten?"

"Father won't make me king," Edward scoffed. "He never wanted me to have the crown, so what does it matter?"

"You don't know that," Maria said quietly. "Besides, who would the crown go to?"

"I don't know. Maybe Stephen will come back as a ghost so Father can crown him. It would certainly make him happier, wouldn't it?"

Maria's lip started to quiver, making Edward curse himself for overstepping his boundaries. "I didn't mean it that way, Mother. I'm sorry for my words and take them back with the deepest regret."

She put her hand to her lips, biting her nail. After a pause, she sniffled, meeting his sorry gaze. "Edward, what has happened to you? What has happened to the little boy I once knew who looked at life with such adventure and wonder and joy? Ever since your brother died, it's as if you've been slowly dying yourself. I thought I knew you, but now I'm not so sure. You don't seem to care for anything anymore."

"That's not true. I do care," Edward said. It was because he cared that he was pushing them all away.

"I hope you're right," Maria replied. "I really do, but I worry about the decisions you've made. I won't lie and pretend that I support you in them, because I don't. Deep down I wonder if you are happy with your decisions, too. But regardless of how we feel, you need to learn a lesson through this, and it will not be a pleasant experience.

"You wonder why your father is busying himself writing letters? It's because he knows small decisions carry a big weight. You think your elopement with Malina only effects you, but it doesn't. It affects all of us. You have not only damaged your life, but also the lives of your family and friends. Your decision was like throwing a rock into a pond. The rock's weight doesn't just hit its target. It also makes ripples in the water, affecting everything around the center that was hit.

"Because of your choices, Hugellia and Edeland feel betrayed. They question whether they can trust us and that lack of trust can push them away, harming our international relations and economy. Not only that, but now we must deal with Verloris. Are they allies? Do we establish trade?

"And let us not forget our people here in Audlin. You are their future, Edward. Your decisions make a mark on their lives as well. You give them a queen, the mother of their nation, and ensure the future of the kingdom through your heir. Are you giving them people who are wise and who will bring them prosperity? Or are you giving them ruin?"

Edward held his breath. His decision wouldn't hurt anyone else. He was making sure of that. "You worry too much," he said.

"And you don't worry enough."

No. He worried more than anyone ever knew.

"I'll be back after a few hours," Edward said after a pause. "Don't worry about waiting for me to eat lunch."

"Alright," Maria said softly, returning to the book in her lap. "Have fun, I guess."

He didn't bother saying good-bye as he walked out the door.

It was too hot for a jousting match; at least Sir Peterson thought so. How the competitors could even stand in their full-metal armor under a beating sun was beyond him, and he felt thankful he took the road of a royal guardsman instead of a common knight. The guard's uniform was lighter, often foregoing the use of plate armor as they rarely attended the front lines of battle, and Marcus was glad he didn't have to sweat too much in the blistering heat.

"It's not that hot out, is it?" Sir Rikert, finally back alongside the rest of the guard, asked as they followed the prince's carriage to the jousting arena.

Marcus smirked. "I've been in cooler temperatures in recent months. I admit this is a bit warm for my taste."

Rikert shrugged. "The days will get hotter, I'm sure."

"How can you tell?"

"Call it a hunch."

Marcus knew what Sir Rikert meant. Though Rikert returned to Edward's service, the prince and the guard had not had the chance to speak to each other. Marcus thought it more Edward's preference instead of the knight's, especially after the unpleasantness of the week before.

"How is he taking it?" Rikert asked quietly as they rode on.

"Who?"

"Prince Edward," Rikert replied. "How is he handling his new life?"

Marcus shrugged. "As can be expected, I suppose."

Rikert gave a nod. "And how are you handling it?"

"Me?"

"Yes."

Marcus sighed. "I feel sorry for him."

Rikert gave him a warm glance. "That's a rare opinion nowadays."

Marcus looked ahead at the carriage, noticing Edward had closed the curtains on the windows. It had to be stifling in there with the heat and air remaining in the cabin car, but Marcus understood. Edward wanted to be hidden not from himself, but from the people who were angry with him.

"I'm sure people will forgive him in time," Marcus replied. "That's what people do. They tag along with the latest gossip and as soon as a new victim comes along, they forget the old and go with the new."

"Let's hope it's that easy," Rikert said quietly as the carriage stopped. They unhorsed, Marcus getting the door of the carriage and opening it so Edward could step out. When the prince stepped forward, his face was red and beaded with sweat, and he looked exhausted from the heat.

"Did you have to keep the curtains drawn? You don't want to get heatstroke," Marcus whispered to Edward as he followed him into the arena.

"It wasn't that bad," Edward panted. "I'm fine. Marcus. Really."

Marcus only shook his head as he and the other guards entered the arena.

The jousting grounds were long and open, benches on every side for spectators to find their perfect spot to watch the sport. At the center right of the arena sat a shaded area where the prince and his entourage could sit, and as he entered, the herald beside him blew a trumpet and announced Edward's arrival.

Normally such an entrance before the joust would elicit applause and cheers from the people in the stands, but as Edward sat down in his seat, barely a clap was heard. Instead, another sound filled the air.

Men, women, even children booed and hissed. Some walked out at the sight of him while others turned away, refusing to acknowledge his arrival. Though the herald tried to calm the crowd, pleading for respect, the crowd continued on until the herald gave up altogether, shaking his head in frustration.

Marcus watched from behind Edward's seat as the prince took it all in silence. He only rested his head on his hand, staring out into the grounds.

"They shouldn't be this harsh," Peterson muttered under his breath. "Do they not know the prince is sorry?"

Rikert's face remained stoic. "Unless they understand, they wouldn't care."

Marcus pressed his lips together, keeping himself from saying any more.

Eventually the jeers lessened as the knights came upon the field to compete. The herald blew the trumpet again, announcing the names of the competitors and the games that would be undertaken. As the knights came forward, Marcus expected to see them do a customary salute to the prince before competing. The salute never came. Instead, the knights got on their horses and readied for the competition.

The herald cleared his throat, leaning over to Edward. "Did…did you want to say something to the crowd before the games start, Your Majesty?"

It was customary to give a greeting, but Edward shook his head. "I doubt they'd want to hear me talk. Go ahead and start the games."

"But Your Majesty, it's tradition."

Edward gave a sigh as he rubbed his forehead. Tradition should be thrown out the window at a time like this.

The prince stood to his feet, stepping forward to where the herald was and giving a wave of his hand as custom. "Good morning," he began, his face looking around nervously at the crowd. "I want to welcome you to the Reigal jousting grounds…"

But before he could finish the sentence, the jeers began again. Louder and louder they became, turning so deafening the prince could no longer shout without his voice being drowned out. The crowd booed and cursed his name, and soon onlookers began throwing items at him, like food and dirt from the ground.

Marcus rushed forward, taking Edward by the shoulders and pulling him back as he tried to dodge the hatred of the crowd. "Get out of here!" Marcus heard a man shout. "Prince of whores!" shouted another. "Go back to Verloris where you're actually wanted!"

"You failed us!"

"We want Lady Antoinette as our queen!"

"You'll never be our king! Never!"

Marcus led Edward back to the other guards as the prince took the insults in silence. "We need to get him out of here!" Marcus said to Sir Rikert. "We don't need a riot!"

Rikert nodded, leading the prince out of the spectator's box. Marcus took one last look at the jeering crowd and lowered his brow before rushing behind and following the prince and his guards.

The taunts followed them down the stairs and outside the jousting grounds. Even the guards were starting to be pummeled by food and items from the unruly crowd. "Get back!" the guards yelled as some of the people began to rush at them.

"Marcus, take Prince Edward back to the palace," Sir Rikert said as he looked towards the other guards trying to calm the crowd. "The people aren't ready for him to be out yet. Take him home and make sure he stays there until this frenzy calms down!"

Marcus nodded, rushing Edward towards the carriage. "I don't need to leave!" Edward muttered, but Marcus ignored him and thrust him into the carriage car. He turned to the driver, telling him to hurry back to the palace as Marcus went into the carriage car with the prince.

Edward stared out the window at the crowd cursing him as the guards went to calm them and return them to the arena. As the carriage moved towards the palace, Edward fingered the drawstring to the window curtains, drawing them shut in silence.

Marcus exhaled as he fixed the other window. At first he and the prince were quiet while Edward sat in the seat, looking off to the side, his arms crossed.

"Are you alright?" Marcus asked.

Edward didn't look up. "Aside from being covered in dirt and what I hope is cabbage, I think I'm fine."

"You're not hurt?"

"Just my pride."

Marcus breathed a sigh of relief. "At least it's just that," he said. "That crowd...I am sorry, Edward. I didn't expect them to be so disrespectful."

Edward shrugged. "I'm not surprised. It's not like I haven't been getting this reaction lately."

Marcus frowned. "I know."

"I was hoping to at least leave the house." Edward sighed, looking at Marcus. "I guess even that's out of the question now."

"They'll calm down in time," Marcus said. "They just need time to process things."

Edward shook his head, giving a sarcastic laugh. "In time," he muttered. "That's not the conversation I heard before I came here."

"What do you mean?"

"I mean you're trying to be encouraging, Marcus, but you and I both know this isn't going to go away anytime soon."

"You don't know that," Marcus said.

"And you do?"

Marcus lowered his head, looking away.

"I appreciate you trying to help, Marcus," Edward said after a moment of silence, "but let's be realistic. When people screw up-in my case, literally-things don't get better. They get worse. You don't understand when…"

"With all due respect, Edward," Marcus interrupted, looking back up, "I think I'm more understanding than you think."

"Marcus…" Edward paused. "You *don't* understand. You don't know what it's like to make mistake after mistake and live under this scrutiny to try and be perfect only to fail. You're the model soldier of chivalry. What would you know about being a disappointment?"

Marcus remained quiet.

Edward snickered darkly. "I thought so. Frankly, I'm surprised you're still talking to me after all this time. If it wasn't for that oath you guards take, I doubt you'd even be here, too. You'd be in that crowd like everyone else."

Marcus' expression saddened. Did Edward think everyone an enemy, that everyone he knew enjoyed watching him fall? Though the prince talked big and pretended not to care, Marcus knew the truth behind the façade. Edward was sorry for what he had done-he knew it, he saw it-and now Edward was trying to push everyone away.

"I knew someone like you once," Marcus said as Edward continued to pout. "I heard this story when I was younger.

There was this knight named John from the town of Bruswell, just north of Circh."

Edward rolled his eyes but kept quiet, clearly not interested in the story but polite enough to listen.

Marcus continued. "He was highly revered. Eldest son in the family, brilliant with the sword and bow, and the perfect example of piety and goodness. Everyone expected greatness from him-his family, his friends, even the people who didn't like him.

"While he was training in Bruswell he met a young noblewoman named Agatha. She was beautiful and came from a well to do family. She wasn't very polite, but her beauty was so great that John ignored everyone who told him not to pursue her. He and Agatha met in secret and began to see each other. Pretty soon their relationship became exposed.

"The townspeople began to notice Agatha had gained weight and was wearing loose-fitting clothing. After some time passed, rumors began to surface that she was pregnant. It didn't take long for people to guess who the father was. John's family was notified and the town brought John and Agatha together. They confessed to the affair, much to the surprise of John's family and friends, and soon the couple married so as not to be looked down upon by the city.

"The people were furious. John's family kicked him out of the house and denied him his family's inheritance. The knighthood he worked so hard to achieve was lost as the school removed him from the program. He was no longer considered a model of piety and chivalry. Though he begged for forgiveness, admitting he was unwise in the affair, his friends no longer spoke to him. His family no longer welcomed him. Instead, Agatha's family had to support him, and they provided him a job in the family business just so he and Agatha could provide for themselves.

"They had the child, but whatever joy from the birth they felt was soon dashed as Agatha's father died. The money being given to John stopped coming, and because the town was still furious over what happened with John and Agatha, her family soon kicked them out, leaving them to the streets. They were mocked, the child was threatened, and the family had nowhere to go.

"Things became so bad that eventually Agatha wanted to leave. She no longer loved John and wanted nothing to do with their child. She missed her money and her lifestyle, and John could barely provide for her. She soon found another man and left John to raise his young child alone.

"John felt hopeless as everyone turned on him. He thought there was no one in the world who could understand how sorry he was for what he did with Agatha, and he prayed night after night that God would have mercy on him for the sake of his child. Years passed by without any improvement, until one day John met an older knight named Sir Terrance.

"Sir Terrance had heard of John and what happened and took pity on him. He offered to send him to Circh and hire him as a craftsman, providing for his training and a home so he and his child could have shelter. John followed Sir Terrance to Circh and was thankful for his hospitality, but couldn't understand why Sir Terrance was being so kind. 'Why do you help me?' John asked the knight one day. 'Don't you know what I've done?'

"Sir Terrance smiled at him and nodded. 'I know exactly what you've done, but you're sorry and you're willing to make things right. That's all that matters to me.'

"John was confused. He didn't think it possible for anyone to be kind to him after what he had done. 'I don't deserve this kindness. Don't you understand?'

"And then Sir Terrance told him the reason for his kindness. 'I'm kind to you because I do understand,' he said. 'I was you once and when I had my daughter, I did not have a wife. I was mocked and mistreated and I begged for forgiveness, but I was never shown mercy except by God. So that is why I'm being kind to you.'"

Marcus paused as he watched Edward go from disinterested to fully engaged. The carriage stopped in front of the palace, but Edward didn't move to leave the car.

"Where did you hear this story?" Edward asked quietly.

"From my father," Marcus replied. "John Peterson."

"You mean?"

"Yes." Marcus nodded. "I've never told anyone this, Edward, but I tell you because you think I don't understand, and you wonder why I stand by your side. My father once told me he wondered why God never heard him pray for help and why God could never forgive him for failing so miserably, but after he met Sir Terrance, my father realized God was showing him mercy all along. God wasn't making him miserable. God was trying to bring him out of his misery. The only person who was standing in the way of my father's recovery was himself."

Marcus got out of the carriage and opened the door. The palace stood in the background and Edward followed him onto the steps. "You think you're alone, Edward, but you're not," Marcus continued. "I understand what you're going through and I won't pretend it will be easy.

"There will be consequences to your actions just like there was for my father. He lost his family, his home, his job, and reputation. But despite all that he'd lost, he gained faith in knowing he served a forgiving God who would not abandon him while everyone else had.

"Life will be hard. The people will jeer and curse, but don't worry about them. Forgive them. Just make sure you forgive yourself as well."

"Did life get better for your father?" Edward asked quietly.

"In some ways, yes, and in some ways, no," Marcus replied. "He never did get to rejoin the knighthood and we struggled financially. His reputation was still tarnished years after the affair and the people of Circh looked at us like we were beneath them."

"Us?" Edward asked.

"The affair didn't just affect my father, Edward." Marcus sighed, looking away as if remembering distant memories. "I promise, life will get better for you in time, but I'd be lying if I said there wasn't a ripple effect to my father's actions. My mother left town because she was tired of being labeled. I was allowed into the Circh knighthood only because Sir Terrance sponsored me. Even then it wasn't enough to keep me from leaving after my father died."

"So that's why you came to Reigal?"

Marcus nodded with a frown. "Yes. One can only handle gossip for so long."

Edward lowered his head, his expression furrowing with concern. "Do you think my child will have the same struggles?"

"I don't know," Marcus replied. "But I wouldn't worry over it yet; for now, take each day as it comes. Remember town gossip does not have to determine a person's destiny. Your son or daughter will still have a choice in how to live life. Though I grew up with ridicule, I can't deny I had a pleasant childhood. I had a loving and faithful father who was the greatest example of honor I knew, and he taught me well.'

The two men stopped as they approached the door, Marcus putting a hand on Edward's shoulder. "Worry not, my friend. Though you have fallen, you can still get up and rise again. You have an entire future ahead of you."

"I just hope it's a good one." Edward gave a weak smile as he and Marcus walked into the palace.

Chapter 5: The Prayer of the Godless

It was just after dawn when the bells rang from the tower, calling the people of the city to morning prayers. It was a tradition that was held the first day of every month for the royal family, and Edward stood by the window, watching as pink and purple sky overtook the horizon.

He sighed. Today was the last day he wanted to go to church.

Not that he wanted to disrespect the Almighty and certainly not because he didn't respect the church or revere it for all its holiness. He just feared the people. The stares, the whispers, the scoffs that would ruin whatever chance at a peaceful time with God he could muster.

"What is that racket?" He heard Malina stir from the bed, her hand shading her eyes as sunlight peaked through the window.

"Church bells," Edward said quietly. "They ring on the first day of every month."

"Why?" Malina groaned.

"It's the call to morning prayer."

Malina sat up on the bed and eyed him. He didn't stir, keeping his eyes on the skyline of the city and mountains. "Is this tradition? Does everyone go?"

"Unless they are ill, yes."

Malina slid back into the bed. "Well I am most certainly ill. Morning sickness."

He turned and looked at her, noticing she seemed well. Not that it mattered. "I wasn't planning on going, either."

Malina opened one eye. "Why not?"

"You're not the only one feeling ill." He turned away from the window and headed to the door, stopping by her side. "I'll send for you a nurse. Feel better."

She said nothing as he left the room and headed towards the east wing of the palace.

Barely anyone stirred in the hallways as family and servants alike prepped for chapel. Morning prayers were always a special occasion and attendees would wear their best clothes and make sure they were clean before going. Most prayed at the churches in the city while some of the richer nobles kept chapels for more private worship. The royal family had their own preacher, heading down to the chapel at the far back of the palace and praying with close friends and their servants.

Perhaps when everyone's anger died down, he would go. Until then he would content himself to wait.

He opened the door to a room that was small, almost cold due to a never used hearth, but with the summer heat the coolness of a room with only a slit for a window was more welcoming than a lake. Edward walked in, closing the door behind him, lighting a few candles and placing them in lanterns so he would have light.

His study room was a place he rarely went to. Unlike his brother, he was never very fond of books and was too impatient to sit for hours and write. The room became a place of thought and escape instead of study, and when Antoinette was around he found he didn't need the room as much as he once did. Now that she was gone, however, he had a feeling he would need it more often.

He went to his desk, placing a hand on the oak table and gliding his hand across its dusty surface. He passed the bookshelf full of texts he never bothered to read, stopping in front of the couch that sat firmly against the wall.

He knelt down, removing the cushions from the seat and reaching into the bottom of the couch and lifting a cloth flap. A small wooden box sat inside and Edward lifted it out, putting the cushions back and sitting on the couch with the box in his lap. He exhaled as he opened it, revealing small mementos inside.

His eyes glanced at the items before him, and a few were picked up and fingered in the candlelight. First was a piece of wood, jagged and broken with chips of yellow paint. It was part of a lance he had broken when jousting as a boy-his first hit on the cloth and metal dummy, and it was direct. He remembered his father being so proud that day, telling everyone his youngest was finally good at something. It was the only compliment he ever heard from the man.

Next were two wooden figurines-small, one in the shape of a knight and the other in the shape of an archer. It was part of a battalion set he used to play with as a child with his cousin, Emmerich. He was always the knight, Emery was always the archer; although some days Emery would insist on being the priest because no good army should ever go into battle without someone to pray for them on the field.

Edward placed the pieces back into the box, frowning. There were times he still wished he had a brother, real or pretend, but those were happy days long gone and never to return again.

His eye caught sight of a piece of parchment folded neatly and showing a partially broken seal. He felt his heart race as he lifted it out of the box and opened the flaps to reveal a short letter.

Don't.

He hushed the conscience in his mind and began to read it, knowing full well it would bring him lower than what he already was.

I'm tired of your taunts.

Is it so hard to love your own brother?

One of these days you'll regret everything.

It's your fault. ALL OF IT.

He couldn't read any more, couldn't even glance at Stephen's signature on the bottom without feeling the bile rise in his throat and his heart burn in guilt. His hands were shaking, and folding the letter back became more of an act of clumsiness than care. Edward rubbed his temple, closing his eyes and cursing himself for opening up such an old wound.

He was about to shut the box and put it back, to hide it away and not be reminded of what a failure in life he had been, but as he took the top, readying to pull it down, a faint glimmer shined from out of the bottom. He sifted through the items, removing old letters, trinkets, and pieces of his life that would be better forgotten than remembered, and came to a lone portrait sitting on the bottom of the box.

It was small, oval, able to fit into Edward's palm with plenty of room left over, but the picture inside the frame was clear and so detailed that any other artist had been unable to reproduce such a likeness of the subject. It was painted nearly a year ago, the young lady looking poised and kind in a simple burgundy dress, her hair down and intertwined with ribbon and roses.

He let a finger slide across the picture as if in a caress, and he felt his breath leave him as he studied the subject, thinking of happier times. He could see the memory replay in his mind- the happy maiden trying to sit still for the painter but being distracted by her beloved off to the side as he made silly faces. She laughed so much the painter scolded them both for their lack of artistic appreciation, and when word reached his father about their "inappropriate behavior", the king himself had to stay in the room to make sure no recklessness happened as the painting was being finished.

Those were happier times, Edward thought, times when every other memory was forgotten and every day was good because someone loved him and he loved her back.

He placed the portrait back into the box, eyeing it one last time before placing everything else atop of it. It pained him to know it was the only picture he had of Antoinette, doubtless the only likeness of her face he'd ever see again.

But though it pained him with what he did, he never wanted to forget that face, never wanted to forget that the few years he had with her were the only times he was happy. It was something he would hold on to for the rest of his life; the only flower left in a garden full of memories.

After returning the box to its place, he sat in the study, going through whatever work he could find. He organized shelves, worked on letters of state...he even tried reading those old books he forgot he had. Some of them were interesting while others had better usage as decoration. Regardless, he wanted to keep busy until the church bells rang again, meaning everyone went home to enjoy a family meal.

When the bells rang some hours later, he waited until the bustles outside of the hallway lessened so he wouldn't have to deal with running into people. Within minutes the sounds died down, and when all was silent he made his way out of the room and down the main corridor, careful to avoid any family or servants in the dining hall.

Down the steps he went into the lower half of the palace where the chapel was placed, opening the doors to find the tiny sanctuary quiet and still. Stained glass depicting stories from the Scriptures adorned the walls and the whiff of incense could still be sensed from the candles in front. He made his way to a pew towards the back, getting ready to kneel on the padded board and begin recitation until a voice made him stop.

"You missed a pleasant service."

He turned to find Malina, dressed and adorned in what was probably her favorite red dress, standing near the window depicting the story of Samson and Delilah. "I thought you said you were ill."

"I lied." Malina smirked. "You should be used to that now, don't you think?"

Edward sighed, rubbing the back of his neck. So much for quiet time in the church. "What made you change your mind?"

"I thought I'd spend some time with your family and servants."

"And?"

"And what?" Malina asked, pouting her face in innocence. "Is it wrong to participate in the traditions of my husband's kingdom?"

Edward rolled his eyes. "You don't exactly seem like the church type."

"And you do?"

Edward pursed his lips in frustration, saying nothing.

"Really, Edward, what purpose would you even have here?" Malina asked, stepping forward and circling him. "Would God listen to a liar? How would He know you pray the truth? And what of a thief? Would God listen to one of those, someone who is far from thankful for what the Lord Almighty gave him? What about an adulterer? A fornicator? A man who just couldn't say no to a little pleasure?"

She faced him, her lips so close to his he could feel her heat. "And a murderer?" She gave a soft laugh, turning him to face the second stained glass picture on the wall. It was a scene from the book of Genesis, two brothers where one was killing the other. "An eye for an eye, a tooth for a tooth, a life for a life," Malina whispered in his ear. "Do you remember the story of Cain and Abel, where Abel was so perfect and loved while Cain became jealous? The story is all too familiar for you, isn't it?"

Edward looked at her, his brow lowering. "I'm not Cain."

"Of course you aren't." Malina laughed. "Just like I'm not your Jezebel."

She turned his cheek roughly, her eyes bright. "Do you honestly think God will listen to you after everything you've done? You've seen what your people think of you. Your family ignores you. Your servants talk behind your back. Your people curse your name in the streets. You have no one,

Edward." Her voice became quiet as she kissed him gently. "No one but me."

She stepped away as he remained still. "If the people you serve want nothing to do with you, why would God be different? You are godless, Edward, as you are friendless." She paused, offering him a smile that was more hurting than comfort. "Say your prayers, but do not expect them to be answered. You waste your flattery when it could be more appreciated by me."

She began heading out of the chapel, stopping at the door and giving him one last look. "Don't be long. I'm going to have a meal prepared and I expect you to join me."

Edward watched as Malina slithered out of the room, the echo of the door shutting filling the entire chapel. He stood there in the silence, his spirit feeling low, and he began to wonder why he even bothered with morning prayers in the first place.

He remembered being so scared of church after Stephen had died. It took him months to come back, his parents thinking it was grief that kept him away because the chapel was where Stephen's funeral was held. He didn't have the heart to tell anyone it was because he was afraid-afraid God would strike him dead as soon as he walked into the sanctuary because his brother's death was his fault.

Why am I here? he wondered to himself as he sighed, looking up at the ceiling. *If I knew God was listening, I'd talk. I'd say a lot of things...*

He had a book's worth of apologies to account for.

As he was stepping towards the door, though, a sound, high and sweet, came from one of the stained glass windows. Edward turned to see a little sparrow perched on the sill of a window with a picture of King David on it. It sang softly in the stillness of the church, and Edward watched as it hopped along the edge, as if wanting attention.

The bird must've come through an open window, Edward reasoned as he looked around to find it. The windows were closed, and he turned back to the bird, his eyes gazing up at the stained glass showing the great king.

He remembered hearing the story of David; the shepherd, the giant-slayer, one of the greatest kings who ever lived. A man after God's heart, he was called. A man who had such a relationship with the Almighty that he was promised a line that would never end.

He looked at the window closer, seeing smaller pictures around the portrait in glass. On top was a picture of David playing the harp amongst the sheep. Further down was him slaying Goliath with his sling. Even further was him being crowned, and on the bottom was a picture of the king with a woman.

Bathsheba, the woman he had an affair with, the woman whose husband he had killed to keep her pregnancy a secret, the woman who birthed him his heir.

It was David's greatest shame.

If God forgave him, don't you think He could forgive you?

Edward shook his head. He was no David. He was no mighty king. Why would God bother with him?

The sparrow gave a cry and flew across the chapel, landing on a sill in front of the largest window of all. Edward watched as the bird hopped along the edge, chirping sweetly and cocking its head. He looked up, noticing a portrait of Jesus Christ on the cross.

Guilt is not a sign of the condemned. It's a sign of the sorry, he thought.

Edward felt like he was the sorriest of them all.

He knelt to the ground, ignoring the padded kneelers by the pews reserved for the righteous. His head was bowed, his hands gathered to his chest like a child at prayer. Would God listen to him if he didn't recite the same prayers he'd always prayed? Would God hear him if he just simply talked, man to God?

He was tired of holding it all in. Even if God didn't listen, he wanted to speak anyways.

"I'm sorry..." The words were so simple, so childish, yet it was all he could say through quivering lip and trembling faith. "For Stephen, for Antoinette, for Emmerich, for...everything. If I could go back and change it all, I would. I would change everything..."

He paused, his voice catching. He cleared it, trying again. "I ask no mercy for myself. I don't expect it because I'm not worthy of Your grace, but I ask mercy and blessing for the people I've hurt. Bless them and give them better lives despite of what I've done."

One final request left his lips before he lifted his head. "Please don't let me hurt anyone else."

He looked up, expecting no sign from the Almighty that he was heard, but when his eyes went to the window, and then to the rest of the church, he noticed the sparrow was gone.

Instead, a wind went past his face and he felt the warmth of sunlight coming in through the windows touch his skin. Peace entered his heart, and for the first time in years, he felt like a burden had been lifted.

He felt loved, overwhelming and consuming his soul. Perhaps the Almighty really did hear him.

Then again, maybe He always did. Edward just needed to turn to Him.

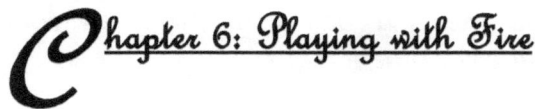

Chapter 6: Playing with Fire

Malina cursed the sweat that dripped from her brow.

She waved a hand at a servant, sending the young girl scuttling forward with a fan in her hand. "It's hot," Malina muttered as she lied on the couch, exhaling slowly. "Cool it down for me, *now*."

"Yes, Your Majesty," the young girl said as she began to fan the princess.

Malina looked at the other girls standing in the corner. Did they not see she was overly warm? Were she in Verloris, *all* the servants would have catered to her whim. "You!" She pointed to them. "Fan me, now! Can you not see I am in a delicate condition? I carry Edward's heir! Do not make me miscarry because of your lack of concern for your mistress!"

The other girls hurried along, bringing fans and waving them in front of Malina. The princess shut her eyes, relaxing with a smile as she lounged on the couch and enjoyed the cool breeze now coming forth.

That was more like it, she thought to herself. Cooler temperature...servants doing her bidding. She felt at home already.

She was starting to doze in such a peaceful state, unaware of the male servant coming into the room with food. He wheeled a cart in, taking the plate and teacup from atop and setting it on the table near the window. He took some tea and poured it into the cup, setting the kettle back onto the cart and folding his hands in front of him.

"The princess should eat to keep up her strength," the servant said, making Malina's eyes suddenly open and fall upon the man standing near the window.

She sat up in a hurry, her face sporting a smirk, and she gathered herself to stand off the couch, facing him.

"I trust you have brought a palatable meal?" she asked.

The servant nodded. "Don't I always?"

Malina smiled.

The servant gazed at the fanning girls for a moment and returned to Malina. "Take comfort in the heat, Your Majesty. You don't want to catch cold while you are with child. It's not good being sick and pregnant at the same time."

His eyes were piercing, speaking to her when words were not able to. Malina met his gaze, giving a lick of her lips.

"You're right," she said with a flutter of her hand as she turned to the girls. "Leave us. I don't wish to become ill!"

The girls, confused yet silent, bowed their heads and left the room. Malina hurried to the door, locking it, turning back to the familiar face of the servant. She was amazed at how someone like Vacius could blend in so quickly-a poor farmer, a shopkeeper, a nobleman, or in the current case, a servant.

Vacius watched as she smiled at him, stepping forward to the window and drawing the curtains shut. "It has been long since I've seen you, Vacius. Near three weeks, I believe." When the curtains were drawn, she faced him, putting a hand on his chest. "I've missed you."

Vacius remained still, barely stirring from her touch. His eyes followed her hand for a moment until he met her piercing gaze. "Forgive me for being late. I was busy with other matters."

"Too busy for me?" she purred.

His face remained stoic.

"I've had to deal with everything all alone, Vacius." Malina pouted as she let her hand graze across his chest and back, circling him. "It's been so difficult here without you."

"Are you unable to handle your task?"

Malina stopped to his right and glared. "Don't insult me. The only difficulty I've had is how dreadfully easy this has all been. I have everyone eating out of my hand, Darling. Do you not see how the servants cater to my every whim?"

"Servants who follow their monarch-how difficult indeed," Vacius replied back.

Malina said nothing as she rolled her eyes.

"What is it you want from me? Have I not been playing my part to your liking?"

Vacius smirked. "You could say that."

"What have I done? Or not done, according to you?"

"Edward is unpopular."

Malina scoffed as she took a sip of tea from her cup. "A trifle," she said between drinks. "His unpopularity will die down in time. Let an affair happen or have someone give birth. Gossip changes things-we only need to wait it out."

Vacius narrowed his eyes. "You are unpopular."

Malina lowered her cup and scoffed. "Is that a problem?"

"It may become one."

Malina laughed as she returned to her drink. "Popularity isn't needed to rule a country, Vacius. You and I both know that."

"And what makes you think I speak of ruling this land?" Vacius' voice lowered into a rumble, and he took the cup from Malina's hand. "You are a *princess*, Malina. Not a queen. You rule no one but yourself at the moment."

Malina's face hardened into a snarl as she watched him put the cup back on the table.

"Word has reached Hugellia and Braiden of your marriage to Edward. People are upset with how the alliance between Audlin and Edeland was so easily severed."

"And how is this a problem?"

"They have taken their concerns to King Arden."

"So they complain." Malina shrugged, crossing her arms. "What difference does it make?"

Vacius lowered his brow. "It decides whether you rule this land or not." He clenched his fists, pacing around Malina as he watched her sudden change of expression. She kept her ground, remaining straight and firm; she was intimidated by no man. "The people of Reigal are saying they no longer want Edward as their king. The other lands are threatening to sever their alliances with Audlin because they are afraid Edward is not a trustworthy heir. The king is questioning whether to give the crown to him. Our plans may become forfeit because of a simple decree! Don't let months of work go to waste!"

Vacius stopped, leaning forward, his face a breath from Malina's. "Stop wasting your time on playing queen, Malina, and concern yourself with actually becoming one."

There was a moment of silence between the two until it broke from Malina's laugh. She raised her hand to her lips to try and stifle it, but could no longer contain the noise and walked away from him.

"Vacius, Vacius, you darling little man..." she sang as she picked a few pieces of fruit from her plate. "Do you think I am unprepared?"

Vacius said nothing as she laughed some more.

"Worry not, my sweet," she cooed as she approached him. "I am watching the king closely. If he trips up, I'll make sure he falls down a flight of stairs."

"Just make sure he doesn't take you down the stairs with him," Vacius replied.

Malina chuckled. "As if an old man could pull me down." She fingered Vacius' shirt, giving him a suggestive glance. "Or keep me down, really."

Vacius met her glance with his own. "You act as if you don't have a weakness. I think you're overconfident."

"Overconfident?" Malina said, running her fingers through his hair. "Vacius, you know me well enough. Have I a weakness? Have I any fear?" He watched as she inched her lips closer to his, her breath tickling his tongue. "Or am I a woman who always gets what she wants?"

"If I recall, you needed *help* getting what you want."

Malina frowned as she backed away, her eyes piercing with a glare.

Vacius smiled. "What? Do you not like the truth?"

"I prefer lies, actually."

"And I prefer action, which you are doing little of."

Malina crossed her arms and huffed. "Always impatient, aren't you, Vacius? You have the appetite of a ravenous wolf! Getting a throne takes time. We can do little until the child arrives."

"But we can do something." Vacius approached her, taking her by the arm and facing him. "Do not let the king undermine you. He doesn't trust you, nor does he trust his son. He holds our future in his hands, so either challenge him or remove him. There is no sitting idle!"

He let his fingers graze up her arm to her shoulder. "Do not forget who it was who brought you here, Malina," Vacius said as he played with the collar of her dress. "I have done my part. If you fail to do yours, I will be forced to act and will have no mercy on you."

"My father's wrath would fall on you if you betrayed me," she said with lowered brow.

"Your father is not that stupid. He is accountable to the Velori as you are."

Malina suppressed the urge to strike him, to make him cower before her and beg for mercy only to receive more pain. But she knew to stay her hand. All the Verloris knew it only took one Velori to hold everyone on a leash.

But even a leashed animal could bite back and cripple their owner.

"Very well," Malina began with a smirk, "but know that if you bring me down, I shall have no trouble in bringing you down with me."

Vacius scoffed. Malina only widened her smile, baring her teeth.

"Shall I tell them how you've aided me in this plan?" Malina chuckled. "What would your leader, Malum, say if he learned Vacius, the greatest and mightiest of the twenty four, broke the oath of his brethren with a woman?"

Vacius shook his head. "You wouldn't dare to try me."

"Are you sure on that?"

He remained silent, looking away.

She turned him to face her, embracing Vacius and tickling his ear with her breath. "You have sacrificed much, Vacius, and do not think I haven't noticed. I only ask that you trust me here and now. I have planned hard for our ascendance and you must not get impatient for the throne. If we move too quickly, we might lose it."

Silence followed, and Malina watched as Vacius tensed. He leaned into her, so close she could feel the desire within him, and cupped her cheek with his hand. "Who says I am getting impatient for the throne?" he whispered as he eyed the features offered to him. He pulled her close as he kissed her neck, making his way to her ear. "I am tired of hiding and lying. I want my freedom *now*, with you."

She relished in the touch of his lips as he held her close. "I understand, my love, yet you cannot deny our intrigues in the dark have been intoxicating. Even the mere thought of it heats me with passion."

Vacius smirked as he paused from his kissing. "You know, little girls who play with fire eventually get burned."

"Oh Vacius." Malina giggled as she led him to the couch. She tugged at his tunic and he followed her lead. "Every affair has a little danger, doesn't it? That is what makes it such a pleasure."

"As long as the fire still burns."

The searing of his touch made her sweat. "Darling, you know I set things ablaze."

She forced him down on the couch and faced him. "Now that you've been all bark, Vacius," she panted, "let's see how well you bite."

He said nothing as he kissed her lips.

Chapter 7: Calla and Chocolate

It had been years since Emmerich van Ketten stepped into the forest lands. Foliage covered every patch of dirt on the ground and trees shaded away the sky. Only strands of sunlight escaped their cover, and as Emmerich rode ahead of Antoinette's carriage, he grunted in frustration as his horse tripped every other step.

No wonder my parents hate to travel through this country.

No matter, he thought as he sped ahead, making sure he remained hidden from the carriage behind him. He wanted to reach the palace first and make sure Antoinette had a warm welcome. Coming home was going to be hard for her-the questions, the disbelief, her mother's incessant nagging. He could only imagine the difficulty that awaited her, and if he could lessen it in any way, he would.

He reached the city of Staalberg early, wanting to make sure he had enough time to gather his things before heading to the palace. He was happy that the Edelandian capital was small-much smaller than Reigal and tiny compared to Kettensburg. He guessed the city only boasted ten thousand inhabitants, which meant there were fewer shops to have to comb through and fewer people he had to find.

He tied the reins of his horse to a post and stepped into the merchant district of Staalberg. The first stop was at a chocolatier's near the edge of town. *Gustav's* it was called, and Emmerich remembered his father frequenting the shop well when he spent time in Edeland.

"Why are we getting chocolates from here, Dad?" Emmerich remembered asking his father when he was a young boy. *"There's ten other shops down the street."*

"Gustav is an old friend," Aldaric replied. *"Plus he's a kind man who does honest business."*

Emmerich looked around at the shop as they entered. It was beat up and run down with wallpaper scratched and nearly falling off. The place was as poor as poor would get, and whoever this Gustav was had little money to do anything else but keep the place open.

When they walked in, Aldaric greeted a man at the front who was covered in sugar, powder, and chocolate. Gustav was large and burly with a contagious laugh, and every time he smiled, Emmerich glanced at how many teeth the man had lost since his last visit.

"Out shopping for the Mrs., eh, Aldaric?" Gustav asked as he dusted himself off. *Aldaric nodded, forcing a small smile but sighing as he rested his hands on the counter.*

"You don't have any chocolate covered strawberries, do you?"

Gustav's smile faded and his hands fell at his sides. "She's lost another one?"

Aldaric nodded, looking towards the counter. "I don't think we'll ever have any more. This is the third one since Emery was born."

Emmerich watched as Gustav eyed him with a sad expression before turning back to Aldaric. "I'm so sorry to hear that. How is she?"

"Doing better," Aldaric said. "It's still hard for her, though. She was six months along this time. Apparently we would have had a girl."

Gustav exhaled as he turned and headed down the counter to a small display. "Here," he said as he placed the strawberries into a box and then tied it with ribbon. "Take these and give her my sympathy."

Aldaric reached into his pocket and pulled out the money, placing them on the counter. "Thank you, Gustav," he began, but Gustav pushed the money back.

"No payment. This is from me," he said firmly, taking the coins and placing them in Aldaric's hands. "Take the money and save up for adoption. You understand better than most what good that can do."

"And you need to keep your business open," Aldaric replied, pushing the money back. "I will give her your sympathy, my friend. Thank you. I'll see you soon."

Gustav reluctantly took the money, waving good-bye to Aldaric and Emmerich as they left the store.

As they walked down the street towards their carriage, Emmerich turned to his father in question. "Why did Gustav say you understood adoption?"

"Because I was adopted as a child," Aldaric replied.

"By who?"

"King Erick. My father had died when I was a baby. The king adopted me as his own after he married my mother."

"Is that what you and Mom are going to do, then? Adopt a brother or sister for me?"

"The king has to approve all adoptions." Aldaric sighed. *"We'll see if he approves it."*

"Do you think he will?"

Aldaric shook his head.

Emmerich approached Gustav's counter with memory, noting the décor hadn't changed at all since he was a boy. The place was still run down and the wallpaper was still falling, but the smell of powdered sugar and cocoa removed any doubt that the man was the best chocolatier in the city.

Gustav was busy placing little chocolate nuggets into a display tray when he saw Emmerich at the counter. The man hadn't changed much-still big, still burly-but his hair was completely white and his face filled with age spots.

"I don't believe my eyes!" Gustav replied with a gasp and toothless smile, rushing forward. "Aldaric van Ketten, is it really you?"

"Close." Emmerich smirked. "It's Emery, actually."

"Little Emery?" Gustav scratched his head. "It can't be! You're only five!"

"Try seventeen."

"No. I refuse to believe time has gone that fast."

"It's true." Emmerich chuckled.

Gustav kept his grin wide, wiping his hands on his apron. "Is your father and mother here, too?"

"No, they're in Kettensburg. How have you been?"

"Good," Gustav replied. "And you? And the family?"

"We are as well as can be expected."

Gustav nodded. "Wonderful! So what can I do for you today, Emery?"

"Chocolate covered strawberries, if you have them."

Gustav frowned. "Oh no. Has your Mother…"

"She's fine. You needn't worry," Emmerich replied. "This is actually for a friend of mine."

Gustav got a box and began packing it with the strawberries. "It must be bad for you to get these."

"It's pretty bad, unfortunately." Emmerich sighed, running a finger across the counter and picking at the holes.

"No one has died, have they?" Gustav asked.

Emmerich shook his head, stifling a laugh. "Not quite. Though I daresay my lady friend's ex has a lot of people who want him dead at the moment."

"Oh…" Gustav raised his brow. "It's one of those cases, is it?"

"A bit," Emmerich said. "I just want to make sure my lady friend knows that not all men are evil, rude, obnoxious individuals."

"Nothing says 'nice guy' like chocolate." Gustav laughed.

"My thoughts exactly," Emmerich said, placing the money on the counter. "Thank you, Gustav."

"Keep it," Gustav said, pushing the money forward. "For old times!"

"You'll never keep your business open if you keep giving away your chocolate!" Emmerich snickered, pushing the money back.

"You're just like your father." Gustav shook his head, taking the money.

"I'm glad to hear it," Emmerich said, heading out the door. "I'll tell them you send your greetings."

"Please do! Good-bye, Emery."

"Farewell!"

Emmerich walked out the door, heading down the bustling streets of the city towards an open flower market. He looked around, searching for a seller who had calla flowers. They were a rare find in Edeland as the nearest bogs and lakes were a twenty minute ride away, but he knew they were Antoinette's favorite flower and he was going to find them if he had to ride to the lake himself.

He remembered the last time she was upset when he was around. He and Antoinette were both ten, the Edelandian court holding a summer celebration out by the lake with his parents attending after an invitation from her father, the king. While the parents discussed business and took a boat ride across the lake, the children received their lessons from a tutor out in the grass.

He remembered sitting next to Antoinette as they listened to the teacher explain her lesson. They were learning history, and as the teacher quizzed the students on various facts from what they had learned before, Emmerich remained quiet so as to give everyone else a chance to impress the teacher with their answers.

"Who was the first king of Edeland?" the teacher would ask.

The answers always came from the same person: the young son of a nobleman named Richard. "King Thaddeus the Great!"

"Very good, Richard."

Emmerich remembered watching Antoinette keep her head down. With a brilliant sister who knew every fact under the sun and two brothers who were considered "gifted" in all matters high and low by their parents, Antoinette found herself keeping quiet when it came to conversation. Unless she was spoken to, she would rarely speak herself.

"Who was the only ruling queen of Edeland?"

The teacher's question hung in the air as a breeze passed by and all the students were silent. The question was difficult- even Richard didn't know the answer. Emmerich had a guess in Queen Catherine of the Edellwood, the only child of the king who ruled for three years before dying in childbirth, but he kept quiet so as not to seem imposing.

"Catherine," he heard a whisper next to him say. He turned to see Antoinette, hands folded and twitching in her lap, looking up at the teacher. "It was Queen Catherine of the Edellwood."

He leaned in towards her, motioning his arm up. "Raise your hand," he mouthed.

She hesitated at first as she noticed Richard's gaze turn away from her. When he stopped looking, she slowly put her hand up.

As the teacher's sight went around the group, Emmerich noticed Richard's hand went up suddenly. He didn't know the answer earlier. Emery could tell by the way his features fell in confusion during the question, but he heard Antoinette's whisper. Emmerich lowered his brow.

A fly buzzed by Antoinette's face and she lowered her hand to swat it away. As the teacher's eyes came towards her and

Richard, the teacher saw Richard's hand in the air. She called on him.

"Queen Catherine!" He grinned, and the teacher clapped in surprise.

"Very good, Richard! That question was a difficult one!"

The other children cheered as Richard threw his nose up in glory, but Antoinette only lowered her head, looking back down at the grass.

When class was over, Antoinette took a stroll by the lake. Emmerich followed her, clenching his fists in frustration.

"I can't believe that know-it-all, Richard!" Emmerich huffed. "He stole your answer! You knew it was Queen Catherine and he stole it from you!"

"It doesn't matter," Antoinette muttered as she kept her eyes down.

"It does matter," Emery fumed. "You're smart and everyone else should know how smart you are!"

Antoinette frowned. "I'm not that smart."

"Of course you are. You're the smartest girl I know!"

"I'm the only girl you know."

His face soured as he looked at her, ignoring the smirk that came from her lips.

"Now you're just toying with me," he mumbled.

"You're an easy target."

"See? Only a smart girl would know that."

She shook her head, stifling a laugh as they stopped in front of the lake's edge, their parents' boat sailing in the distance. "I appreciate the support, Emery, but it's not that big of a deal."

"So it doesn't bother you that Richard stole your answer and made himself look like the genius he isn't?"

Antoinette picked at a piece of long grass. "It bothers me that he stole my answer, yes, but what can I do about it? Things like this happen."

"Well, it shouldn't," Emery replied. "I...I don't like it when people treat you bad. You don't deserve it."

"We get a lot of things we don't deserve," Antoinette said quietly. "But Richard isn't treating me bad. He's just making himself look arrogant."

Emmerich remained quiet as he grumbled to himself. He wanted nothing more than to have a talk with Richard and make him apologize to Antoinette for stealing her answer and making her feel insecure about her intelligence.

"Those are pretty," Antoinette said, pointing to a bunch of callas sticking out of the lakeside.

Emmerich looked ahead and noticed the green and white flowers gently swaying in the breeze. "Do you like those?"

"They're very pretty," Antoinette said. "I've never seen them before."

"They're callas," Emmerich explained. "We have them all over the lakes in Hugellia. My mother fancies them as well."

"She has good taste." Antoinette smiled as she looked at the flowers longingly.

It was then Emmerich knew what to do. He couldn't force Richard to become humble and he couldn't make Antoinette realize how smart she was, but he could certainly make her feel better.

"Do you want one?" he asked, heading towards the flowers.

"What?"

"A calla. Do you want one?"

Antoinette's eyes widened. "Emery, don't get all wet and muddy just because I want a flower!"

"But it'll make you feel better," he said as he stepped into the water, his feet feeling soaked and squishy. He ignored the urge to grimace and pressed on.

"I don't need it!" Antoinette followed to the edge of the water and watched him nervously, putting her hands to her head.

Emery carefully treaded through the swampy mess, ignoring the mosquito bites that were coming and being careful not to get tangled in the weeds that wanted to wrap around his knees. He made it to the first calla and pulled out his pocket knife, starting to cut the base of the flower.

He didn't notice the family of water snakes beside him. As he began to cut the flower, he felt a sharp sting on his leg.

"Ow!" he grunted, looking around. He saw nothing and shrugged, thinking it a large and hungry mosquito.

"What's wrong?" Antoinette called from the back.

"Nothing. Just mosquitoes."

"What's that gray thing sticking out of the water?"

Emmerich looked up, still bent as he finished cutting off the flower. "What gray thing?"

"That gray thing by your hand!"

"There's weeds here. It's probably that," he replied, until he felt another sting on his hand and two others on his arm. When his eyes went back to the water, he nearly screamed at the sight. Water snakes were swarming around him and a big one suddenly latched onto his left hand.

He had just finished cutting the flower before going into a panic and stumbling back, giving a yell.

"SNAKES!"

Antoinette gave a cry as Emmerich's foot slipped on a weed and he fell backwards into the water, getting soaked. He felt a few more bites on his hands and one on his ear before he scrambled up and out of the water, the flower still clutched in his hand. He ran forward, flinging himself on the ground as Antoinette rushed to his side and looked at his hands.

"You got bit…" she panted, her eyes filling with tears.

"Only a little." Emmerich cleared his throat, desperate to reclaim whatever dignity he had left. He held up the soaked and drooping calla, its leaves half broken off. "I got your flower, though."

Emmerich couldn't help but smirk at the memory. Though the snakes that bit him were far from poisonous, it scared Antoinette into thinking he was dying for a week. She never left his side and he had never felt happier.

He made his way through the market and found a young boy selling callas with his mother. As the boy held the flowers out for Emmerich's inspection, he gave a chuckle at seeing the boy's marked hands.

"I take it you ran into water snakes when getting these?" he asked the boy.

The boy nodded, rolling his eyes. "You have no idea."

Emmerich handed the boy some extra coins for his trouble as he took the flowers. If the boy only knew…

He hurried back to his horse and untied the reins. galloping as fast as he could to the palace and hiding his horse in the tree groves. He patted the horse's nose gently, feeding it a few sugar cubes from his pocket as he tied the reins back to a tree. "You'll get new hooves and a tub full of sugar if I have my way," Emmerich replied as the horse neighed in delight. "What a faithful friend you are."

He rubbed the horse's face one last time before rushing to the back of the palace. It had only been four years since he was last there at the Edelandian royal palace, and he figured the place hadn't changed much. Antoinette's room was on the top floor, about two stories up from the ground, on the right side. Emmerich looked around the house, careful to not let any guards see him as he didn't want to alarm anyone, let alone the queen who did not want him to be there. He watched and waited as the patrol moved past him, getting ready to climb the lattice that led to Antoinette's balcony.

When he reached the door, he took out a piece of paper and portable quill from his pocket, scribbling a quick note to stick under the door.

Meet me in the apple grove. I have a few surprises for you. See you soon.

-Emery.

He quickly folded it up and slid it under the door, climbing down the lattice before the patrol returned. Within minutes he was back at his horse, waiting in the grove and watching for the carriage to arrive.

Chapter 8: A Date in the Apple Orchard

When the carriage stopped in front of the palace, Antoinette didn't have time to collect her thoughts on returning home.

The carriage door remained shut as the queen held her arm out, signaling to the guards to give her a moment with her daughters. When they nodded, Susanna turned to her eldest, her face a serious glare.

"Most will not know of what's transpired in Reigal," Susanna began as Antoinette folded her hands to her lap and listened. "Yet do not estimate the power of gossip. It travels faster than the plague and doubtless does more damage. Whatever you do, do not admit that Edward has chosen another woman. It makes you look weak, demeaning, and undesirable. If they ask why you are no longer with Edward, say that he wasn't good enough for you and you wanted someone better."

"But that's not true," Antoinette said, her hands clasped tightly from nerves. "Edward left me, Mother. He did choose another woman. Am I supposed to pretend that never happened?"

"Your inability to keep your fiancé on a tight leash is no one's concern but your own," Susanna replied. Antoinette bit her tongue to keep herself from talking back. "Did you not see Edward's wife, how thin and beautiful she was? Perhaps your weight drove Edward away. Now learn from your mistakes and move on! We can fix this if only you'll listen to me."

"What kind of garbage is this?" Bernie butted in, her voice rising as she leaned forward in her seat. Antoinette smirked inwardly. Leave it to her sister to tell it like it was no matter what. "You're blaming Antoinette for Edward being a good-for-nothing rat?"

"Watch that tongue of yours, *child*," Susanna seethed. "And yes, it is Antoinette's fault. I see it that way because everyone else sees it that way, too." She turned to Antoinette in what looked like sympathy, but Antoinette could only breathe as she felt her mother's blame cut through her soul. "This is a difficult lesson to learn in life, Antoinette, but you're old enough now to understand. If you want to keep a man, you must do anything-even things you don't want-for him to stay. That is the nature of things."

"So you're saying she should've been Edward's servant?" Bernie threw herself back in her seat when Susanna shook her head.

"I'm not saying that at all," Susanna replied. "We're not servants to our husbands, but men are fickle. They never think with their minds, child. They only think with their desires. If you don't fulfill those desires, they'll find it with someone else."

Susanna put her hand on Antoinette's, making her daughter want to jerk her hand away and never touch it again. Antoinette remained frozen, however, and kept her hand still out of not wanting to upset anyone else like she had already done. "Why do you think I remain thin? If I wasn't, your father would leave."

"So you're saying all men are shallow?" Bernie asked, her arms crossed. "That they only want thin, beautiful women who are nothing but prizes to them?"

Susanna nodded. "Exactly," she said with a laugh. "Really, Bernette, I thought you would have learned this lesson already. Why else do you think you can't get a man?"

The look on Bernie's face was morbid, as if someone took her favorite book and began to rip the pages out and throw them into a fire. Bernie uncrossed her arms slowly, her mouth slightly agape, and she suddenly became quiet.

"Now remember, Darling." Susanna turned back to Antoinette, who still sat in silence, her breath coming in tiny spurts. "If anyone asks, it's you who left Edward. He wasn't good enough for you. He never was. He was too immature and fickle and ugly and you knew you could do better."

"Do better with whom?" Antoinette asked quietly. She searched her mind for anyone else who she could even *try* to love. Her mind was empty except one name-Emery.

But he had always been a friend. No more, no less.

"Do better, indeed..." Susanna muttered to herself, tapping her chin in thought. "We'll need to find you another man. We must make people think you've found someone else. Having one eligible daughter with no prospects is embarrassing enough. I daren't say I can handle two!"

She let go of Antoinette's hand and motioned for the guards to come to the door. They opened it, helping the queen down the step and onto the ground. As she brushed her dress off, she turned to her daughters before going back into the palace. "Worry not, my child. I shall have this little mess fixed in no time. Now come along."

The queen strode off towards the palace as Antoinette and Bernie remained in the carriage. They were both quiet, Antoinette doing her best to keep the tears from falling back down her face. She had cried so much since Edward's return and she wondered how many more tears would fall before her eyes would become dry. Her body remained still, her legs unable or unwilling to move, and she wanted nothing more than to stay in the carriage forever.

I can't go back home. I'm trapped, I'm trapped, I'm trapped...

"She's wrong, you know." The sound of Bernie's voice, rustic and quiet, interrupted Antoinette's thoughts. "I don't care what she says. None of this was your fault. I know it. Queen Maria and King Arden know it. Emmerich knows it. So don't you *ever* believe it was you."

Antoinette sighed at her sister's words. She wanted to believe it wasn't her fault. She was desperate for it. But the way Edward looked at her...the way he ran to Malina so quickly and so easily...whose fault was it but Antoinette's to make him throw away years of love and affection in a month's time?

"Whose fault was it if it wasn't mine?" Antoinette whispered.

"His, of course!" Bernie snapped.

"Why?"

"Because he's an idiot who doesn't know how to appreciate a good person!"

"If I was such a good person to him, he would've appreciated me anyways," Antoinette replied. "I had to drive him away somehow, Bernie. Mother is right. I wasn't good enough."

Antoinette rushed out of the carriage, ignoring the guards' offer to help her off or escort her to the palace. Bernie scrambled behind, her face red with fury. "Are you kidding me? You actually believe her?"

"You don't understand, Bernie," Antoinette seethed as she flung open the doors, desperate to keep her eyes away from the visiting nobles who now stared at her in disbelief. She turned away, keeping her eyes to the floor, as she rushed up the stairs towards her room. The stares, the questions undoubtedly entering everyone's minds…she wanted to run away from it all.

Why is the princess back?

Isn't she supposed to be getting married?

The queen looked disturbed when she came in.

Where is Prince Edward?

"Back so soon?" a visiting noblewoman asked as Antoinette stopped at the stairs. She turned as the lady gently touched her shoulder. "Shouldn't you be readying for the wedding?"

Antoinette paused, debating with herself on whether she should lie or tell the truth. "There isn't going to be a wedding anymore," she muttered quietly, watching as the woman's face went from confused to shocked.

"But…why is that, Princess Antoinette?"

Why indeed. Was she to be honest or lie like Mother wanted? She exhaled slowly, weighing her options. She hated to lie and was far from appreciative when others lied to her, so that only left the truth.

"He had an affair," Antoinette replied. "He met another woman while on his way to Hugellia and married her instead."

The woman's eyes widened in disbelief and she shook her head. "That makes no sense, Your Majesty. Why would he do such a thing? You were together for years. There must have been a reason for him to leave."

Antoinette's expression fell. A reason to leave? What reason did she give him to walk away? "There was no reason..." She was at a loss for words and she stammered as she spoke. "He...he just left...when he came back, he was with someone else. Does he need a reason for his actions?"

"There's always a reason why a man leaves, Your Majesty," the noblewoman replied, her brow growing up. "What exactly did he say to you?"

Antoinette frowned, Mother's words suddenly swirling back into her mind.

She ignored the noblewoman and turned and went up the stairs, wanting to escape the judgment that was already staring her down. If this was what conversation was going to be like, then she wanted to delay it. She didn't return home just so she could be blamed for Edward's mistake or be interrogated as to why everything went wrong. She just wanted to grieve in peace.

Antoinette slammed the door to her room, locking it, ignoring Bernie as she finally caught up, banging on the wood and begging to be let in. "Just leave!" Antoinette snapped, pressing her hands to her ears to try and drown out the sounds of everything around her. All she wanted was quiet-no blame, no help, no consolation, *no one.*

Of course, Bernie never quite understood boundaries or wishes to be left alone. She only continued to bang on the door. "I'm not leaving until you open it!"

Fine. Let her stay there all night if she has to, Antoinette thought. She lifted her head from the bed, rubbing her brow, wondering if she should call a guard and have Bernie removed just for the sake of getting a little privacy, until she saw a note lying by the glass door to the balcony.

Emery. She had almost forgotten he followed her home. She trudged out of bed and shuffled to the balcony door, picking up the note and reading the contents. A surprise? She crinkled her nose as to what it might be. The last thing she wanted was something happy and cheerful. Besides, from the way Mother talked, he would probably want something back. Men never did anything good just because they wanted to.

But Emery's different, isn't he?

She scoffed at the thought. Why would he be different? He was Edward's cousin. He had the potential to be just like him. After all, Emmerich admitted he fancied her. Always had, apparently. How did she not know this wasn't a ruse just to use the heart Edward dropped off?

And how do you know it's not?

She sighed, placing the note in her dresser drawer. She didn't feel like having company, even if it was friendly and on innocent terms. All she wanted was isolation, the chance to get away from everything and everyone because she didn't want to face the stares.

She didn't feel like seeing Emmerich van Ketten, but at the same time she didn't want him camping out in the apple orchard to be found by guards and arrested.

She made her way to the balcony door and opened it, heading outside. Normally she'd go the long way round, past her bedroom door and down the steps and into the courtyard, but climbing down the lattice kept her away from people. It kept her away from the stares and questions and judgments that were doubtless going to come her way.

She stepped over the rail and latched herself onto the lattice, carefully climbing down like she used to when she was a little girl sneaking out to go play when grounded. She flattened her skirt, wiping her hands on her sides, and headed to the orchard to see what Emmerich van Ketten had to say.

Emmerich sat quietly underneath an apple tree, scolding his horse for picking up the stray fruit that fell from above him. "That isn't yours, Waffles," he muttered as the horse gave a disappointed neigh, dropping the half-eaten apple from its mouth. "We can't have the queen charging you with thievery. She takes things very personally here, you know."

Waffles gave Emmerich's shoulder a gentle nudge as if to say, *Well, what if she finds you hiding out in her orchard?*

Emmerich shook his head, giving a laugh. "She'll go easier on me than she would on you. At least she's not willing to cook me for dinner."

The horse snorted, turning his head back to the apples in the tree.

Emery huffed in frustration. "You can't eat those either!"

Waffles neighed loudly, making Emmerich put his finger to his lips, trying to shush the creature. The last thing he needed was to be heard and caught because of his apple-loving horse.

"I promise I'll get you some apples from the market if you will just be patient."

The horse snorted again and Emmerich could've sworn he rolled his eyes at him.

"If I end up in the stocks for this, don't think I won't tell them to put you there as well!"

The horse ignored him as he bent down to eat another apple.

Chapter 8 – A Date in the Apple Orchard

Emmerich sighed, rubbing his brow. *Stupid, gluttonous horse...*

His thoughts were interrupted as he heard soft footsteps in the distance. He looked up, seeing Antoinette approaching, and he scrambled to his feet, gathering the calla and chocolate and making sure he was presentable when she arrived. He eyed the horse, hoping he would take a break from eating apples to say hello, but shrugged as any amount of poking or nudging only encouraged the horse to eat more.

Antoinette arrived, her composure still, and stood before him. "I got your note," she muttered.

Emmerich said nothing at first as he studied her features. There was no smile, no flicker of light in her eyes as she stood before him. The skin under her eyes was baggy and dark as if she was tired, and her shoulders were low like she was carrying an invisible burden. For a moment Emmerich thought she seemed wearier now than when she first learned of Edward's betrayal.

"Are you alright?" He lowered the calla and chocolate from his chest. "You look...sad."

Antoinette gave a sarcastic chuckle. "I guess I would be after all that's happened."

"No...I mean this is different," Emmerich replied. "Like it's not just Edward that's been bothering you."

"It's nothing," she said quickly. She glanced towards the ground as a breeze swept through the trees. "What did you want, Emery?"

He paused, unsure if he should press the matter, but seeing the look of impatience in her eyes, he decided to drop it for now. She would talk when she was ready. "I got you something," he said, extending his hands and offering her the calla and box of chocolate. "It's not much, but I know coming home has been hard for you. I just wanted you to have something that would make you smile."

Her eyes lifted and she took the gifts in her hand, turning them about as if inspecting them. "Thank you," she said, her voice soft yet monotone. "I appreciate it."

Her lack of enthusiasm made Emmerich's spirit sink. Was she unhappy with the gifts? Maybe she wanted something other than chocolate covered strawberries. Maybe she no longer fancied callas. Either way, he felt terrible. He thought he knew her well enough to know her likes and dislikes. Had she really changed that much in four years?

"If you want something different, I can..."

"No, it's fine," Antoinette interrupted.

Emmerich fiddled with the pockets in his cloak, not knowing what else to say to make her feel better. "I'm sorry," he began. "I was just trying to make you happy."

She looked up, a strange, almost scoffing look on her face. "Why?"

Emmerich's brow rose. "Should there be a reason?"

"There's a reason for everything, Emery."

Emmerich shook his head, unsure of what to make of Antoinette's wording. He didn't pretend to know much about women, but he knew enough to recognize Antoinette's hurt was going deeper than what he even observed. "Sometimes a reason isn't needed," he said, facing her. "I wanted to do something nice for you just because I could. Is that wrong?"

Antoinette's expression softened. "Well, no, it's just..." she stuttered. "I'm sorry, Emery. I'm just messing things up more."

Chapter 8 – A Date in the Apple Orchard

She looked away, her face red in embarrassment. It didn't take long for Emmerich to guess the reason for her strange behavior. *I'm just messing things up more?* Either she was blaming herself for what happened or others were starting to blame her.

Obviously, Mother van Echt had a talk with her daughter during the ride home.

"You know I'm repeating myself when I say this thing with Edward isn't your fault," Emmerich said firmly.

"I know."

"So why are you blaming yourself again?"

"I'm not."

Emmerich rolled his eyes. "It certainly sounds like you are."

"It's not just me." Antoinette sighed as she leaned against a tree. "People...they think what's happened is my fault. Mother thinks this, the nobles think this..."

"What about your sister?" Emmerich asked.

Antoinette shrugged. "No...she still blames Edward, but..."

"And you know I don't blame you."

Antoinette smirked. "Well of course you don't."

He stepped closer, flashing a smile that made her blush and look away. "And you know I never will. So who are you going to believe? The people who *think* they know you or the two people who know you best?"

She lowered her head, conceding defeat. "You're right," she mumbled, and Emmerich didn't know if she was upset at him for the revelation or upset with herself. It was likely the latter. "Why are you so good to me, Emery? I've barely seen you since I've been with Edward and yet out of everyone I know, you've made sure you're there for me. Even when we were kids..."

"You've always been good to me, Antoinette," Emmerich replied. "You were the only one who never looked down on me and I...I never forgot that. You're the most wonderful, special, godly woman I know. Don't you think you deserve someone to treat you right?"

She said nothing as she looked up, a faint smile gracing her lips. He matched her smile with his own.

She lifted the calla and chocolates, eyeing them with an approval that told Emery she really was happy with her gift. Relief washed over him as he saw the old Antoinette-the happy, peaceful girl he grew up with-come back. "I am thankful for these, Emery," she said. "You didn't have to get them, but I am thankful."

"What can I say?" he said, his voice soft. "You're worth it."

You always have been.

She smiled, taking his hand in hers and lifting it up. Her touch sent a tingle of warmth down his arm; it had been so long since his fingers met hers. He watched as she looked at his hand, turning it over and facing the palm up. "You didn't get any snakes bites getting this calla, I hope?"

He laughed. "You remember that?"

"You nearly gave me a heart attack." She snickered back. "I thought you were going to die because of me."

His fingers stroked her own, a reaction his mind scolded him as foolish. It was too soon; too selfish on his part to let his feelings come out so quickly. His heart seemed to laugh as he stuffed reason away for pleasure, though, as his caress remained. "To be fair, you wanted that flower."

She didn't object to his touch. Rather, her fingers twitched in delight. "A bog flower isn't worth your life, Emery," Antoinette said.

"Maybe not," he whispered, feeling the warmth of her face mix with his. "But you're worth it."

She smiled, and for a moment they stood there facing each other in silence, hands still locked in a caress.

A sudden desire to touch his lips to her own rippled through his gut and it took every ounce of willpower he had to keep himself still. Would she accept it? Would she deny it? Was she even ready at the thought of a relationship with someone other than her former fiancé? There were days he spent dreaming of what his first kiss with Antoinette would be like. Short, long, nervous, passionate. He thought of every scenario and scene it could be, but all thoughts stopped when he realized now could be the moment it actually happened.

He leaned forward, his heart beating faster and the world around him suddenly slowing. His eyes started to close, his lips just a breath away from hers when…

"Wait."

He stopped at the sound of Antoinette's voice, leaning back with eyes open. *Too soon*, he cursed himself. *Get a hold of yourself!*

Antoinette let go of his hand and left his gaze. Everything was going so right, so perfectly, and then he had to ruin it all. Antoinette ignored his attempt at hiding embarrassment as she began to squirm. "I'm sorry…I just…I can't…I…"

"Don't apologize," he stammered, rubbing the back of his neck, feeling the heat still burn where passion had been rising. "I'm...I'm sorry. It was me. I shouldn't have..." He paused, shaking his head. No. He wasn't going to apologize for having the desire to love her and take care of her when no one else would. "I'm sorry. I didn't mean to upset you. I didn't mean to imply I was only here to seek your hand. I came here for your comfort. Forgive me-my feelings bested me."

"It's alright," Antoinette replied, hiding her hands under crossed arms. Emmerich swore he noticed her starting to shake. Was it from nerves? Had he scared her? Or maybe she felt something too and she stopped it before it could happen. "Emery, I know how you feel about me. That's nothing to be ashamed of. I just...I don't know. I just broke up with my fiancé. Edward and I were together for years. I can't just forget that in a few weeks."

Emmerich felt his stomach feel sick at the thought she was still in love with Edward. Though it was far from surprising, he couldn't help but hope she would forget Edward as easily as he could.

Antoinette left the tree, putting a warm hand on his cheek, her thumb gently caressing his skin. His eyes met hers and her touch made him forget any frustration he felt from rejection. "You've always been a friend to me, Emery, and now...I don't know what I feel. Maybe you're still just a friend, maybe you're more, but I'm not about to jump into a relationship with you right now."

He nodded, understanding but certainly not wanting to.

"I don't want you to be a rebound, Emery," she said, pulling her hand away. "You're too dear to me for me to be that cruel. If we ever were in a relationship, I'd want it to be because it was something we *both* wanted, and for the right reasons. I can't pretend to love you just because I miss being loved by someone else."

Her words were coming so fast at him that he didn't know if he could process it all. Did she care for him? Did she care for Edward? He didn't know what to think, and for that he felt worse than knowing nothing at all. "I love you, Antoinette. You'd never have to worry about not being loved with me."

"I know." Antoinette smiled. "But I want you to be loved, too."

Emmerich's heart sank at her words. "I'm not as important as you, though."

"You *are* important, and I love you so much as a friend," Antoinette said, her voice trying to sound hopeful. "As something more? That's what I'm wanting to figure out."

A flicker of light lit itself in Emmerich's spirit. There was still hope they could get together.

"If you need time…" he began, but she put her finger to his lips, silencing him.

"Will you wait for me?" she asked.

His thoughts swirled at her touch, and as her finger left his lips, he nodded. "I've waited over ten years for you," he whispered, taking her hand in his and kissing it. "I'll wait a lifetime if you ask it."

"I don't think I'll need a lifetime, Emery," she said, still holding on to his hand. "I just need this time to grieve and think. I need this time to let go of Edward and find a new path, and I need this time to decide whether…us…is something that's going to happen or not."

Emmerich nodded, disappointed yet at the same time knowing it was the right decision. He didn't want to be

Edward's replacement; he wanted to be her choice and she needed time to find that. "Take however long you need," he said quietly, giving her hand a squeeze. "Say the word, and I'll be here."

"Okay," she said, smiling.

They stood there, facing each other in the silence of the apple grove. Emmerich had the urge to kiss her again, but as he fought with himself to stay still, he suddenly heard a noise come from Waffles the horse. At least...the back end of Waffles the horse.

Suddenly the scent of apples was replaced by a much fouler odor.

"*Waffles!*" Whatever thoughts of kissing had suddenly left and Emmerich couldn't help but shake his head and laugh. Surely God existed because of moments like these, where impure thoughts were interrupted by something that would doubtless keep his mind clean.

He turned sharply to Waffles as the horse neighed miserably, sick from all the fruit he ate. "I told you to not eat the apples!" Emmerich scolded the poor horse as more sounds came from him. Emmerich stepped away, trying to hide his nose.

"My sincerest apologies, Antoinette," Emmerich said as he went back to her. She snickered, trying to hide the laughter wanting to come as Emmerich huffed in amused frustration. "I'd be happy to pay for the apples my horse has gorged on. As for the...uhm...other stuff...do you know of anyone who needs good fertilizer?"

For the first time in over a week, Antoinette laughed.

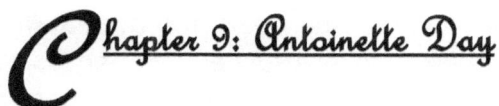

Chapter 9: Antoinette Day

August 21.

Antoinette opened her eyes. She knew this day would come, knew it would etch itself into her memory as one of the most important days of her life.

She sat up on her bed, taking in a deep breath, feeling her heart slowly beat against her chest. The room was empty save the speckles of dust that floated in the sunlight from her window, and she watched as they trickled to the ground.

Today's my wedding day.

She paused, swallowing hard. *Was...my wedding day.* Her eyes closed as she lowered her head. Today was supposed to be such a good day, the most memorable of her life, and now that it finally came she could only think of how much she wanted to get it over with and never think of it again. There was nothing good about August 21. Nothing good that could or ever would come out of it.

Maybe I should just go back to sleep.

She drew her knees close to her chest, resting her chin on them. Sleep was something that would only bring her dreams, and she wasn't sure she was ready to think of anything other than what could have been with Edward.

And that was too painful to think about just yet.

Before her mind could wander, she heard the door swing open and the sounds of quick footsteps rushed into her room. At first she thought it was the maids hurrying to wake her at Mother's request, but after a glance she saw that her sister, still in pajamas, had entered, flopping herself onto Antoinette's bed and making the entire mattress bob up and down.

"Good morning!" Bernie grinned.

Antoinette didn't offer so much as a smirk. "Hi."

"Awe, that's no way to greet the day." Bernie pouted. "Don't you know what today is?"

"Today's the day I was *supposed* to be getting married," Antoinette muttered bitterly. She gave a frustrated look to her sister, wondering why she would bring up such a painful topic.

"No, silly, that's not today," Bernie said. "Today's Antoinette Day!"

Antoinette's brow went up in confusion. "What?"

"Today's Antoinette Day."

"Says who?"

"Says me and Emmerich."

Antoinette blinked. Was this some sort of trick or joke? "What do you mean?"

"I mean we've planned a day for you," Bernie continued as she scooted on the bed to face her sister. "First things first! Breakfast in bed."

Bernie reached into a sack she was carrying and dumped the contents onto the bed, revealing wraps of candy and chocolate and some sort of pudding in a bag.

Antoinette's eyes widened. "Where did you get all of this, Bernie?"

"Mother has a secret stash. I just took a few items from it." Bernie winked as she picked up a chocolate bar. "Hungry?"

"Mother's going to skewer you for taking her candies."

"It was in the kitchen. If there's no guards, it's up for grabs!" She took a bite of a chocolate nugget and grinned. Antoinette hesitated, looking at the chocolate with a wary eye.

Bernie huffed. "Oh come on! Live life on the edge a little!"

"I'd rather live a long life, thanks."

"Ugh, fine," Bernie muttered as she gathered the chocolate to her sack. "Just remember you're not getting out of what Emmerich plans for you today!"

"What does he have planned?"

"Nothing much. Just the best day ever, that's all."

"Best day ever?"

"Well, as best as it could be, which you are ruining, I might add, by not eating your breakfast in bed."

Antoinette pursed her lips together in a frown, saying nothing.

"Look, skip the chocolate if you want, but at least eat some porridge and get dressed. You've got a meeting in three hours."

Antoinette's legs lowered and she crossed her arms. "A what?"

"A meeting," Bernie said as she stuffed her mouth with more chocolate. "I mean, I'd call it a date, but whatever."

Antoinette beaded her eyes. *"A what?"*

"Relax, nothing too romantic. Emmerich's just got something planned for you today."

"Which would be?"

"How should I know? I was just told to keep Mother distracted today."

Antoinette gasped. "You poor thing."

"I know." Bernie sighed as she popped another chocolate piece in her mouth. "Sometimes you just got to do what must be done. You can owe me later." She took a handful of chocolate nuggets and ate them in one gulp.

"Looks like you'll need the breakfast in bed more than me, then. Where am I supposed to meet him?"

"At the edge of the back yard," Bernie began, handing Antoinette a map. "There's a guard change at eleven so you shouldn't be noticed when you sneak out."

Antoinette rubbed her forehead, her eyes feeling heavy and wanting to close so she could go back to sleep and wallow in her misery. "And there's no way I can get out of this?"

"Not a chance."

Antoinette closed her eyes for a moment. "I don't have my own holiday, Bernie. I don't know why you're doing this 'Antoinette Day' and I certainly don't think it's of any value."

"Don't judge it just yet. You never know; today might be better than you think!" Bernie gathered a few wrappers from the bed and stood, stuffing whatever trash she had back into her sack. "Now be ready at eleven. I'm doing an awful lot to keep Mother distracted for this, so please don't let it go to waste."

Antoinette opened her eyes. "What exactly are you doing today, Bernie?"

Bernie smirked before walking out the door. "Oh, I'm sure you'll hear about it soon enough!"

The door closed, leaving Antoinette alone in the room and feeling more confused than depressed.

Perfect.

Emmerich smoothed out the linen of the picnic cloth against the grass, swatting a few ants away that tried to climb up to the basket full of food. The day had been meticulously planned to the point of perfection, and nothing was to stand in Emmerich's way to make Antoinette's day special, not even hungry ants.

"I think it's ready, Waffles," Emmerich said as he stood to his feet next to the horse, surveying the picnic area: smooth grass, swaying trees and flowers surrounding them, the sounds of birds singing in the distance. It was going to be a special lunch with just the two of them followed by a stroll in the forest and a lesson in archery in which Antoinette would learn to shoot an arrow, all the while aiming at a drawing of Edward's rear.

The horse neighed in delight, eyeing one of the four picnic baskets on the ground. He started to sniff it. "No!" Emmerich tugged the reins and pulled Waffles over to face him. "No, Waffles, you can't eat the food! This is for Antoinette and me because today I'm trying to make her feel better. You can't eat the food; you need to guard it!"

Waffles looked at him blankly as Emmerich gave a sigh.

"Look," Emmerich began as he patted Waffles' nose. "Today is the day Antoinette was supposed to marry Edward.

She's probably going to be upset about today and that's why we need to make it special for her. We need to make her laugh and have fun so she won't feel as bad, alright?"

Waffles snorted, giving a nod.

"Good." Emmerich grinned. "Now I've got a few jokes planned..."

Waffles lowered his head and neighed.

"Relax, they're hilarious!" Emmerich said as he stepped back like a showman. "Alright, here's the first one. A knight and a squire walk into a tavern..."

Waffles lifted his head and watched Emmerich with as much enthusiasm as a dog watching his owner sleep.

"So after the knight and squire eat their meal, suddenly a man runs into the tavern and says that there's a dragon attacking the town!"

The horse blinked, his eyes wandering to the picnic area.

"Well, then the knight turns to the squire and says, 'Quick! Find me a lance!' So the squire runs further into the tavern. After a minute the squire returns with the tavern cook." Emmerich gave a chuckle, making the horse blink again. "And then, this is the best part, the knight gets mad. 'Why did you bring me a cook? I asked you to find a lance!' And then the squire tells the knight, 'But I did! The cook's name is Lance!'"

Emmerich burst into laughter as the horse simply stared at him, saying nothing. After a few seconds of silence, Emmerich's laughter became a chuckle and soon faded altogether as he looked to the horse for approval. "So what do you think? I think she'll love it."

The horse snorted as it walked away and circled the picnic basket.

Emmerich crossed his arms in frustration. "Well I thought it was funny!"

The horse neighed as if to say, *you're the only one.*

Emmerich shook his head. Why did he even bother telling jokes to a horse who only cared about food?

"Fine. Be that way," Emmerich muttered as he checked the time. He looked up, the sun no longer visible amongst the rolling clouds, but he guessed it to be near the time when he was supposed to meet Antoinette at the forest's edge.

"I'm going out to get her, okay?" Emmerich faced Waffles, looking at him in the eye. "Remember, *guard the food.* Squish bugs and chase squirrels if you need to. I want this area to be perfect for her."

The horse snorted as if it understood.

"I'll be back in a few minutes," Emmerich called out as he trotted towards the edge of Antoinette's back yard, leaving the horse alone with the picnic.

Antoinette stood quietly amongst the bushes, keeping an eye out for any guards who might see her. She covered her arms, shivering in the cool breeze that suddenly came, and she wanted to shake her head. It figured the one cold day of the week had to fall on her wedding day.

Ex-wedding day, you mean.

She frowned as the thought hit her again, and more than anything she wished there was a machine that could force her to skip the day ahead and go to tomorrow.

Today is not a good day.

It didn't take long for Emmerich to appear through the trees, trotting up to her with his best attempt at a smile given the circumstances. Not too wide, not too small, but just enough grin to show that he was happy to see her yet feeling terrible today was a day she didn't want to see. She waited for him to approach her, and as he stood before her his face changed from sweet to awestruck.

"You look lovely."

"Thank you." Antoinette shrugged at the compliment. She may have looked lovely to him but she felt far from being it. When she glanced in the mirror last, her eyes looked heavy, her hair felt frizzy, and her body was more than a little bloated.

Apparently Emmerich didn't care as he walked forward, eyeing her from head to toe.

"How have you been today?" he began as he led her down the trail and into the forest towards whatever surprise he had waiting. "Did you sleep well?"

"I did," she replied. "As for today, it's been...well, it's just been going, I suppose." She paused, a quiver in her lip being felt. "I'm not sure I've been enjoying it that much."

He nodded, a solemn look coming over his face. "I know today meant a lot to you. I can only imagine how you feel after everything that happened."

Antoinette shrugged. "It is what it is," she said quietly, looking towards the ground. "I'd rather not dwell on it, and yet it's all I can think about."

"That's what happens when you grieve," Emmerich replied, looking at her. "There's no shame in being hurt."

"There may be no shame in it, but it feels terrible all the same."

"You'll feel better in time," Emmerich said warmly. "You're strong, Antoinette, and you're going to come out of this even stronger."

She gave him a smile, yet said nothing. She wished she could believe what he said, but strength was never something she felt she had. Emmerich was strong; he knew nothing else. Bernie was strong, too, in her own special way. But Antoinette felt like all strength had been spent. There wasn't any left inside her.

When Emmerich saw she was silent, he began to speak again. "I have some surprises planned for you today, if you don't mind."

"I don't mind," Antoinette said as she looked up. "Bernie said something about you two cooking up a plan to cheer me up."

Emmerich chuckled. "We did. Although the name 'Antoinette Day' was her idea."

"So I figured."

"Regardless of what we call today, it's your day." Emmerich turned to walk backwards so he could face her as he led her down the trail. "This is a day for you to laugh, cry, talk, listen, or do whatever else you want to do. Though I admit our aim was for you to enjoy today instead of dread it."

A small laugh escaped her lips as Antoinette shook her head. "You two are quite the schemers. Never will you let me mope around and become depressed, will you?"

"Never." Emmerich grinned.

"I appreciate this, Emery," Antoinette said as their pace slowed. "To have people who care means a lot."

"Your sister and I will always be there for you," he said, holding out his arm for her to take. She put her hand around it, letting him escort her. He smiled while she still frowned. "Now, shall I show you the first surprise?"

"Show away," she mumbled. As much as she tried, joy was the last thing on her mind.

She was thankful Emmerich understood. He toned down his cheerfulness and led her quietly down the trail towards a small grove with flowers and grass in the middle. She could hear Waffles the horse neigh in the distance and her best guess was that the surprise awaited for her was where the horse was.

I hope the surprise isn't apples, she chuckled to herself.

"So I heard a funny joke the other day," Emmerich said after clearing his throat.

Antoinette perked up. Emmerich was never a good joke teller, which made it all the funnier.

"Do tell," she said.

"So a knight and a squire walk into a tavern," he began, hiding a chuckle as they approached where Waffles was neighing. "They sit down and eat lunch until someone bursts into the tavern all in a panic."

They passed a row of trees and came upon where Emmerich's surprise was. When Antoinette saw it, her eyes widened in shock, and suddenly she burst into laughter.

"Wait, I haven't said the funny part yet," Emmerich stammered, confused, as he turned to see what Antoinette was looking at. "So the guy runs into the tavern and says that there's a *OH MY WORD-WAFFLES! WHAT HAPPENED TO THE FOOD?*"

Emmerich's eyes widened in horror as he surveyed the scene. Wadded picnic cloth was strewn about, scattered food was smashed into grass, pieces of four picnic baskets were trampled down with Waffles the horse trying to follow a squirrel that ran up a tree.

Antoinette didn't know whether to laugh at poor Emmerich's luck or laugh in spite of it.

"CONFOUND IT WAFFLES!" Emmerich rushed to the horse, desperate to pull him away from the tree. "I thought I told you to watch the food, not destroy it!"

The horse only neighed angrily as it kept on darting towards the squirrel.

"I don't care whose fault it was," Emmerich scolded. "This was supposed to be ready by the time we got here!"

The horse snorted as it left the tree and the squirrel that hid in it. Emmerich put his hands on his hips, surveying the scene, his eyes apologetically glancing to Antoinette. "I'm so sorry," he began. "I was only gone a few minutes. Apparently squirrels do more damage than I thought."

"It's alright," Antoinette said as she carefully stepped over a broken half piece of watermelon. "You meant well and it's the thought that counts. I'm sure we can find something else to do."

"Well, at least it's just the picnic that was ruined," Emmerich said with a sigh. "It could be worse, I suppose."

As soon as he finished speaking, however, a drop of water hit the top of his head.

Emmerich looked up at the clouds in the sky, his face morbid as another drop of water hit him on the face. "You've got to be kidding me..."

It only took a few seconds for the sprinkle to turn into a downpour.

"No, no, no, NO!" Emmerich began to circle around the area, looking at the clouds and getting drenched as he wrung his slippery hands through his hair. "WHY IS IT RAINING? IT'S NOT SUPPOSED TO RAIN!"

Antoinette couldn't help but snicker as she watched Emmerich's frustration turn to panic.

On he went, cursing his rotten luck when it came to weather, but Antoinette noticed that the squirrel Waffles had been chasing earlier suddenly ran down the tree trunk. Waffles caught sight of the critter and began to chase, not looking that Emmerich was too busy worrying over rain than his own safety. The horse began to charge, ignorant of everything else save the squirrel, and soon Emmerich was in his path.

Instinct made Antoinette run and push Emmerich out of the way before the horse reached him. They both tumbled to the ground, landing on muddy dirt and grass as Waffles left the area, still chasing the squirrel. Sore, achy, and more than a little muddy, the two friends both lied on the ground for a few seconds before saying a word.

"Are you okay?" Antoinette asked as she turned to look at Emmerich.

He met her look of surprise with his own and nodded. "Fine, thanks."

They were silent for a few more seconds before Emmerich sat up, turning to her apologetically. "I'm sorry...I'm so sorry," he stuttered amidst the rain. "This wasn't supposed to turn out like this. It was supposed to be perfect and..."

He suddenly stopped speaking as he heard what sounded like whimpering coming from Antoinette. He edged closer, putting his hand to her cheek, and Antoinette could tell the poor man thought the love of his life was now injured all because of him and his stupid horse.

But she wasn't whimpering or crying. She was laughing. "Only you..." she said as she laughed harder, holding on to the sleeves of his shirt. "I thought my luck was rotten, but yours has got to be the worst!"

He sat there, watching her with a confused and somewhat scared glance. "You're...you're not hurt, are you?"

"Of course not!" She laughed again. "Though I'm sure Mother will not have mercy on me when I show up all dirty and muddy."

Emmerich grinned nervously as he kept his hand near her cheek. "Sorry about that."

"Help me think of a good excuse, then," she said as she sat up, taking hold of his hand. "I'm not about to get in trouble for this, you know."

"I wouldn't want you to," Emmerich replied as he sat with her. "How about this? A wild horse was running rampant in the streets and you pushed an idiotic little boy out of the horse's path and saved his life."

Antoinette snickered. "You're far from a little boy, Emery."

"Well, it's close enough to the truth, isn't it?"

"She won't be impressed if it's a little boy, though," Antoinette said as she picked up a carrot that was sitting beside her on the ground, tossing it at Emmerich playfully. "Let's make it interesting. We'll pretend I saved a young nobleman visiting from out of town. Of course, the good man is single and rich and he was so thankful I saved his life that he took me out to dinner."

Emmerich grinned widely. "I guess we're going to have to find a new source of food."

"See? Our excuse is working marvelously."

"It's a story your mother would enjoy very much," Emmerich replied. "I think I'm enjoying it too."

Antoinette matched his look with her own smile, clasping the hand she was holding with both hands now, feeling the warmth of his skin against her fingers and palms. She let out a sigh as she looked at his hands, his fingers gently around her own. "I missed this."

"What? Us getting into trouble?"

Antoinette gave a chuckle as she remembered the times she and Emmerich were scolded by their parents for all the times they played and got muddy or stayed up past bedtime talking near the hearth. "Yes," she said, looking up at him, "but it's not just that. I missed having so much fun. I almost forgot what it was like to laugh."

She looked away towards the grass for a moment, giving another chuckle to herself. "You know what's funny, though? I never realized how good it feels to laugh in the rain."

"Well then." Emmerich smiled as he took her hands in his and stood, lifting her to her feet. "Let's make a day of it, shall we? To laugh in the rain?"

She didn't object as he ran with her to the first newly formed puddle and jumped into it, laughing the rest of the day away.

When Antoinette returned home later in the afternoon, Mother was found to be in a state of panic.

Mud had been tracked all through the floors and carpet. Linens had been shredded and ruined. Tea cups had shattered and plates had been cracked and every servant in the household had been called to clean up the disaster that was Staalberg Palace.

So when Antoinette arrived all dirty and spent, no one seemed to bat an eye as a muddy princess became the least of their worries.

"*What madness has gotten into you, child?*" Antoinette heard Mother yell. She peaked around the corner of the wall to see a filthy looking Bernie, just as muddy as her sister, and a livid Queen Susanna in her scolding pose.

"It was a science experiment."

"You should know better than to partake in such monstrosities!" Mother scolded. "Besides, what sort of learning comes from releasing a pig into the kitchen?"

"I wanted to track its acceleration and response to a fearful stimulus."

"*What is that supposed to mean?*"

Bernie grinned. "I wanted to see how fast it would run when chased."

"And you would do that *why*?"

Antoinette could barely hide the amusement that escaped her lips. Only her sister would loosen a pig into the house to distract their mother so she could get some free time.

A young maid approached the queen and curtseyed. "Pardon me, Your Majesty, but we found some more feathers in the dining room."

Susanna rubbed her weary brow. "What now?"

"I believe there were chickens on the counter tops."

"WHAT?"

Antoinette saw the queen give an ugly glare to Bernie. "And what were the chickens for? Testing to see how fast they would run, too?"

"No, I wouldn't do that to the chickens!" Bernie replied. "The poor dears just looked so cold out in the rain. I brought them in so their feathers wouldn't get wet. We don't want sick chickens getting pneumonia! How else would we get eggs for breakfast?"

Susanna gave a huff as she shook her head. "Impossible, unbearable child..."

"You'll thank me later when you find our chickens are nice and healthy."

"Just...go." Susanna waved her hand, shooing her daughter away. "Give me time to organize a cleaning for all of this. Just get washed up and we'll discuss your punishment when I'm finished!"

"Yes, ma'am," Bernie said, skipping off towards her room.

Antoinette was going to follow quietly behind, but soon heard a yell coming from where Mother had been. Antoinette turned and found herself being chased by the queen, moaning and wailing at the sight of her eldest daughter being so unkempt.

"Heavens!" Susanna cried as she looked at her daughter, grasping her shoulders. "The pig trampled all over you! You poor dear!"

Antoinette feigned embarrassment. "Forgive me, Mother. I was hoping to sneak and get another bath before you saw me."

"Of course, my dear, of course!" Susanna replied. "I shan't keep you. Just make sure you scrub really hard and get all the dirt off of you."

"I will."

"Oh, what a maddening day this has been!" Susanna sighed. "Wild animals running amuck in my home and my youngest daughter turning insane! Oh dear, oh dear! My poor heart can't take much more commotion..." Susanna patted Antoinette's cheek warmly. "That's why I'm so thankful for you, child. It seems you and I are the only sane ones around here! At least I know you wouldn't be so foolish."

Antoinette grinned nervously.

"Now off you go to the baths," Susanna replied as she shooed Antoinette away. "What a day! What a terrible, terrible day!"

Antoinette could barely contain the grin as she scrambled up the stairs. *What a day,* she repeated in her mind. *What a wonderful, wonderful day...*

Chapter 10: The Treaty

Autumn passed and the trees had covered the land in old foliage when the representative from Circh came. A young man, along with his wife and three children, had come to visit the royal family and give an update on the profit made during the autumn trading months. His name was Harald Rodgers, and from what Edward had heard, the man had come to boast of the greatest naval profit Audlin had seen in twenty years. It was good news for the economy and even better news for the king's treasury, making everyone in a better mood after the heartbreak that was the summer.

It was morning when the king called the House of Nobles to a meeting in order to discuss the autumn profits. Edward awoke early, making sure to attend. Since his return from Verloris, his father spoke little and barely included him in any matters of business. That left Edward to attend the matters himself, whether invited or not, though most of the time he found himself handling the domestic management of the palace. Though it was "women's work", as the servants secretly called it, Edward didn't complain. He was fortunate he was still allowed to live in the palace. Any duty he could take was one more chance to make amends for all his wrongs.

"That's a fancy tunic." Malina yawned as she watched Edward dress from the bed. He turned, a brow going up as he secured a belt around the dark blue fabric he wore. It wasn't every day Malina gave him a compliment, he pondered as he tightened the belt. Surely she wanted something.

"Thanks," he muttered, returning to dress. He sat on the bed and donned a pair of boots, not paying attention as his wife sat up on the bed.

He felt cold hands wrapping around his waist and her lips grace his neck. It sent a chill down his spine-not out of desire, but of disgust. He was not in the mood for her embrace; then again, he never was.

"Where are you going?" she whispered in his ear.

"The House of Nobles is meeting to discuss last season's profits," Edward began. "Harald Rodgers has come from Circh to give a presentation. Apparently we surpassed Hugellia in exports."

"Well that's wonderful, Darling," she cooed, giving him a gentle squeeze. "I bet your father is pleased."

"With Harald, I'm sure," Edward replied, eyeing Malina's hands as she caressed his chest. He turned, taking her hands in his to make her stop, and faced her. "Is everything alright with you? With the baby?"

"Of course," Malina said. "Why wouldn't it be?"

"You're being..." He paused. Nice? *Too* kind? Sweet to the point of it becoming creepy? He shook his head. "Never mind."

"What?" Her eyes followed him as he walked to the mirror. "Can a wife not dote on her husband from time to time?"

He straightened his tunic, adjusting the collar. "Forgive me if I don't find you the doting type."

"Oh Edward, I think I can surprise you."

"If you really doted on me, it would be a surprise."

Malina smirked. "Fine. Do not accept my advances. Would you at least like to feel the baby? He's moving."

He paused with the collar, sighing as he returned to his wife. She was further along now, her pregnancy visibly obvious. He sat back on the bed and faced her, putting his hand on her stomach. "How do you know it's a boy?" he asked as he felt for movement. He felt nothing.

"I saw a seer the other day," Malina replied as she guided his hand towards the right of her belly. "She told me I would have a son."

The thought of Edward bringing a child like himself into the world filled him with dread. He hoped for a daughter; a girl would be easier to care for, easier to please instead of disappoint. If it were a son, he worried more; not so much of what the boy was, but what he would become. Didn't sons mimic their fathers?

The sound of King Arden's condemnation echoed in his thoughts. *You're not ready to be a father. I feel sorry for the child who is born to you.*

The last thing Edward wanted was to ruin another life.

But when he felt the little *bump* underneath his hand, the little flicker of life growing inside the woman who sat before him, he felt his heart sink into his stomach. The reality of fatherhood suddenly bore down on his shoulders, and as he felt his child move beneath his hand, he started to worry what the future would bring.

He sat in silence, Malina's hand atop of his, and bowed his head. *I don't want to let you down,* he thought as he lowered himself and moved Malina's other hand from her stomach, replacing her touch with a kiss from his lips. He felt another *bump* from the baby as he caressed the area with his hand. *I promise I'll try to be a good father to you. I don't want you to pay for my mistake.*

But he heard King Arden's words in his mind. *You'll never be a good father.*

Fear gripped him as he thought of failing again.

"I have to go," he muttered as he stood from the bed, heading towards the door. Malina followed, wrapping her robe across her chest.

"Already?" she asked.

Edward nodded. "Yes."

"Then make me proud," she said from behind as he opened the door. "Show the king you are worthy as his son."

Edward scoffed as he pulled the door closed behind him. *I'll never be a worthy son,* he thought as he headed down the hall towards the throne room. *Just like I'll never be a worthy father.*

The House of Nobles is busier than usual, Edward noted as he joined them in the throne room. He eyed the front, noticing his father sitting on the throne, the seat next to him empty. Normally the crowned heir would be expected to be at the king's side during the meeting. Edward figured he shouldn't bother-the last time he tried to be at the king's side during a meeting, his father stormed off and dismissed everyone home.

Edward found a spot to the side, a small area towards the back so he could sneak out if things got carried away again. Most of the nobles paid him no heed as they took their seats in the room, all facing the king as he began his introductions.

Edward fidgeted with his sleeve as the king blathered on about the state of the economy. Trade was good, money was gained, and more iron was mined from the mountains in the south. Edward feigned listening, finding it difficult to pay attention and feeling an urge to shut his eyes and sleep in his seat. Economics never interested him; it was too dull, too boring, and too full of long speeches and debates with no one ever agreeing how to fix the problems that were left.

But when the king mentioned Harald Rodgers, Edward's ears pricked up and his eyes awakened. He watched as the king held his arm out, motioning for Harald to stand and begin his report on the Circh trade. Harald stood, Edward having a perfect view from across, and took a small stack of parchments in his hand, holding them to his chest as he spoke.

"Thank you, Your Majesty," Harald began. "I have in my hand here the records of our recent trade in Circh. In short, we have earned from our exports twenty thousand gold pieces worth of ore, five hundred pieces worth of silver, ten thousand pieces worth of marble, and four thousand pieces worth of timber."

There were nods of approval from around the room, a few of the men clapping. Harald grinned as he blushed, bowing his head in thanks. "This, of course, does not include our seafood export, which has remained steady at ten thousand," Harald continued, "but our mining exports have more than doubled and I am pleased to announce that we have gained more in trade than our honorable neighbors in Hugellia. If we continue as projected, we may even surpass Hugellian earnings for the year."

"I am glad to hear of this, Representative Rodgers." The king held his hand up in approval, and Edward noticed it was the first time he saw his father smile since his return from Verloris. "Your hard work in increasing trade has paid off. I, and the treasury, thank you for the success in Circh."

"I cannot take all the credit, Sire," Harald replied. He turned to Edward, making the prince want to lower and hide in his seat. Why was he looking at him? Was the prince about to be blamed for something else?

Harald smiled, making Edward raise a brow in confusion. "Our honorable Prince Edward is the man who made it possible. You should be proud, Your Majesty, of your son. With his marriage to the lady of Verloris, we have gained a valuable partner in trade with her people. It was he who signed the treaty with King Calimus and garnered trade with their ports. Without it, we would not have had half the earnings we now boast of."

The king looked perplexed. "How so?"

"The Verloris have provided half of our earnings within the last month since the treaty began."

If Edward was ignoring the meeting before, he was now at full attention. He straightened his posture as the entire room suddenly faced him, and he gulped at the attention, expecting every face to spit at him in fury. But when he met their eyes, no such fury came. It was more of shock, surprise, even...gratitude. Soon silence became nods of approval, and before long, a few of the men cheered.

It was the first time Edward felt appreciated. "The kingdom is in good hands with Prince Edward!" Harald proclaimed as the other nobles nodded. "We'll be the richest country around!"

The nobles agreed, but as Edward nodded in thanks, his mind began to ponder. He remembered no treaty with the Verloris regarding trade. He neither spoke of it with Malina's father nor discussed politics with anyone during his stay. There were gaps when he was drunk and couldn't remember, but no...no, he wouldn't have signed a treaty of trade during that time. Malina would've gloated about it and rubbed it in his face.

Edward turned to face the king, looking for answers, looking for some sort of approval. The king showed neither. He only beaded his eyes, his hand on his forehead, looking away as his eyes met his son's.

As Harald continued on with his report, Edward noticed the king whisper to his aide and request the stack of parchments. Within minutes the stack went from Harald's hands to the king's, and for the rest of the meeting the king said nothing as he read every export that came out of Circh.

Edward remained silent as he watched his father's face for a reaction. The king remained stoic, his brow lowered and his lips barely moving as he read. An hour passed and the king stayed still during the other presentations. When the meeting ended, however, the king rushed out of the room and the rest of the nobles slowly made their way out.

After the meeting, Edward was greeted by a few new supporters. "Well done!" he heard an older nobleman reply. "I wasn't happy with your decision at first, but now I see why you made it!"

Edward thanked him nervously, unsure of whether to be honest and say he knew nothing of the treaty or to remain quiet and accept the praise. He chose the latter. "Thank you," he said, shaking the man's hand. "I want to see our country do well."

Another noble from one of the western towns approached, nearly knocking Edward over with a slap on the back. "We should've traded with Verloris a long time ago," he replied. "Who knew they had so much money to spend?"

Edward nodded in faux agreement, knowing there had to be a reason for the "treaty's" success. The urge to find the truth hit him hard, and he left his seat in haste.

He searched the room for Harald, unable to find him amidst the crowd of nobles talking and bustling out into the foyer. Edward followed them out, glancing around the hallway to find the missing representative, but after minutes of searching, he couldn't find him.

Edward sighed, wondering if Harald and the king were meeting to discuss the mysterious Verloris treaty. If that were the case, he would doubtless hear from his father soon.

As the nobles left the foyer and returned to their carriages, Edward made his way down the hall. He planned on returning to his domestic duties, hoping to get the dinner with the Braiden diplomats set before the week's end. If he hadn't, he was sure to hear from his mother, not to mention the palace cook.

As he walked and rounded a corner, the sound of soft voices hit his ear. He looked ahead, seeing Malina talking with a young man near the dining room. Edward backed up, hiding behind the corner, peering past the wall and listening intently to who his wife was conversing with.

A man's voice was heard and Edward squinted to see who it was. The man shifted in his stance, giving a curt nod to the princess, and Edward nearly froze when he saw the man's face. It was Harald.

Edward strained to hear what the two said, but he was so far away that any words sounded like muffles. He cursed to himself, thinking Malina connected to the new treaty, and knew he had to get closer. He wasn't one to interrupt conversations, but when it was needed, he ran for the opportunity.

He hurried past the corner, his boots echoing in the hall and making both Harald and Malina turn to face him. They didn't look surprised to see Edward coming towards them, nor did they look displeased. Rather, they looked happy, especially Harald.

"Your Majesty!" Harald gave a bow as Edward arrived. "I was just telling the princess of our success. I think the king was pleased with the report."

Pleased indeed, Edward wanted to scoff. He knew the king better than most. The king was about as pleased as a deer being hunted for sport.

"I am so proud of my husband," Malina beamed, putting her hand on Edward's chest and embracing him. "I hope the people will stop doubting him. He's always had everyone's best interests at heart."

"I hope the prince's popularity rises from this," Harald replied. "Everyone worries over trade with Edeland, but they are foolish to worry so. Trade is still minimal, yes, but I do not foresee them cutting ties. We are their greatest suppliers; if they cut off trade, they will be wanting of many resources. They will come around in time."

"And Harald was telling me that your father has calmed things down with Hugellia," Malina cooed. "Trade has resumed and we are now stronger than ever."

Edward forced a smile. "That is good news."

"Indeed," Harald replied. "And I shall spread our success to the people of Circh. Thank you, Your Majesty, for the income you have brought into my city. You can expect our full support when you ascend to the throne."

Malina clapped in delight as Harald bowed to Edward once more. "I shall take my leave," he said, putting his hand to his heart. "I bid you a good day, and please-if you need anything, let me know."

"Thank you," Edward said with a nod, watching as Harald left down the hall.

When the representative was out of sight, Edward pulled Malina into the empty dining room. "We need to talk," he muttered, his voice hard. Malina followed him into the room with a chuckle as they stopped near the table.

"Tell me, *my wife*," Edward began, seething. "What devilry is this that our treasury has now gained so much coin? What is this treaty I hear of with the Verloris?"

"Oh, Darling, do you not know?" Malina pouted.

Edward beaded his eyes. "Apparently I should, since everyone says I signed it!"

"Well." Malina began to play with his collar. "It's only a silly piece of paper. It brings money from my country into yours via trade. We get rock and ore and you reap the profits."

He took her hands and stilled them, making her look up in a frown. "I know how trade works, Malina. It usually involves a two-way agreement. What are we taking from the Verloris for them to purchase our resources?"

"Nothing," Malina replied. "Just friendship. Nothing more."

Edward huffed as he let go of her hands, turning his back on her. "I know you, Malina. It has to be more than that."

"You are welcome to view the treaty yourself," Malina said. "Though I hear the king has it at the moment."

Edward rubbed his brow. He would certainly look at the treaty once his father was finished and ready to scold him for it. "Fine. I shall look at it," he said, facing his wife once again.

"What I wish to be informed of, however, is why my name is on it. I signed no trade agreement in Verloris, Malina. You busied me with yourself during my stay there."

"You caught me." She lifted her hands playfully as if in surrender, giving a soft purr of a laugh. "I admit it was me. I put your seal on it and signed your name and then gave it to the Verloris officials. Aren't you happy I helped?"

"Happy?" Edward burned as he faced her, his body tense and skin tinted red. *"Do I look pleased to you?* You have forged my name on a document that I know nothing about with repercussions that I can only imagine will be anything but good! How dare you go behind my back and do such a thing! Do you not know what this could do to my reputation, *my country?"*

Malina crossed her arms, remaining still as she smirked. "I know *exactly* what it will do, Edward. It will save it. Your name with the people was as good as mud until this treaty came along. Now you've showered your land with gold, and the people are turning back to you. You should thank me for pulling your sorry hide above the rubble you buried yourself in. I am making you a strong king and this country powerful!"

"I do not need your help," Edward said as he pointed his finger at her. "I've never needed it. I certainly *do not need any more of your lies!"*

"You need me, Edward," Malina said as she licked her lips and approached him. "Did I not say you were nothing without me?"

Edward lowered his brow. "You won't get away with this. I…I won't let you continue these lies!"

"And what are you going to do?" she asked as she cocked her head to the side. "Are you going to scold me? Correct me?" She smiled as she inched closer to his face. "Oh, I'd love to see you be naughty, Edward..." She moved to kiss him but he turned his head, making her brush his cheek. "Then again," she hissed, her eyes suddenly fiery, "I can be naughty myself."

She grabbed him by the collar and yanked him close. "You *will* go along with this treaty, Edward. You'll go along with anything I do in this palace. Can you not see I am aiding you? That I'm being *merciful*? I am building your kingdom and prepping you for the throne. Look what you have done on your own-nothing! All you have bothered yourself with is housewifery. *Hmph!* What a waste. But I will make you listen, Edward. I can build your kingdom up but I can also tear it to shreds."

She put her lips to his ear and whispered. "Do you think your father would have mercy on you if he learned you had killed your brother? I will let it be known. Your father will want you dead for your crimes!"

Murderer. Edward closed his eyes, conceding defeat. "No one..." He swallowed hard. He saw what happened when he married another woman the people did not expect. Anger. Riots. The loss of family and friends. He couldn't chance his biggest lie getting out. He knew he would never recover. He opened his eyes and continued, "...no one should know. I'll...I'll do what you say."

"That's a good boy." Malina grinned as she pulled away. "Now the king will ask to see you. You mustn't deny that the treaty was your doing. Take responsibility for it. Is that understood?"

He lowered his head. Being controlled like a dog...he almost thought being an animal was a better life than this.

"I understand," he murmured. "I will do what you say."

She gave a laugh. "Good."

Chapter 11: The King and His Son

When the message came that the king wanted to see Edward, it didn't come as a surprise. The treaty and the mystery surrounding it remained in the prince's mind as he rested during the night and continued on to his work the next morning. He left his job administering the kitchen and hurried up the steps to the parlor his parents used for matters of business, entering quietly as a guard allowed him through.

Edward kept his head bowed as he stepped in, finding his father seated at a table with a goblet of wine in his hand. His father rarely drank, particularly for the sake of the queen, but since Maria was not in the room, Edward thought the king must've needed some sort of nerve calmer. Edward went forward, stopping in front of the table, taking a deep breath before he spoke. "You wanted to see me?"

The king took a sip from his wine, setting the goblet back onto the table. The stack of papers from Harald Rodgers sat in front of him in a neat pile. "I did," Arden replied. "We...have some things to discuss."

Edward felt a tremor rise in his heart. His father seemed too composed, as if he was trying to seem kind yet deep down hiding a cold-hearted nature that wanted to lash out at anyone who came near him. Edward gulped, knowing his father's anger was at its peak when it was like this. "What did you want to discuss?"

Arden held the stack up. "Did you know about this treaty?"

The urge to tell the truth burned his lips, but Malina's threat remained. The truth about Stephen couldn't come out. "Yes."

"And why did you not share this with me?"

The lies were so easy to tell sometimes. Practice made perfect. "I figured you wouldn't listen."

"When it comes to matters of state, I would."

"I was only trying to help. Forgive me."

The king's face began to tint red, but no words came as he pressed his lips firmly in a frown. Edward kept his head down, dreading the wrath to come.

"You do not help by keeping secrets from me, Edward."

The prince looked up. "What did you expect? You never acknowledge me, you never include me in your duties. I've been taking on tasks for Mother because she's the only one who trusts me to do anything!"

The king looked away, rolling his eyes.

"And you wonder why I don't come to you with things," Edward huffed. "You always expect me to listen, but when I talk, you never listen to me!"

"I am your father, Edward," the king replied, his face becoming redder. "A child is supposed to listen to the wisdom his father gives! Stephen did!"

Edward had hoped to keep the discussion calm, but the mention of his brother's name fueled him with anger. He loved his brother. He mourned for him every day and night. But every mention of how *perfect* Stephen was, how *he* was the better son, made Edward want to scream in fury. "And what do you think the duty of a father is? To just order your child around like a servant? Or is that only how you thought I should be treated?"

"I treated you and Stephen the same!" Arden's voice rose as he stood to his feet. "Do not blame your brother for your disobedience and folly!"

"Then do not blame me for your failures as a father!"

The king clenched his fists in rage, storming in front of Edward and growling in his face. "YOU made your choice, Edward!" the king fumed. "It was YOU who chose folly and YOU who chose to disobey me. I am not to blame for your insolence and failure-YOU ARE. If you were just more like Stephen..."

"WILL YOU STOP TALKING ABOUT STEPHEN?" Edward's voice was so loud a few of the guards came into the room only to back away at the king's glare. Edward ignored them. "THAT'S ALL I EVER HEAR FROM YOU! I need to be more like Stephen...why am I not more like Stephen. Will you get it through your head that Stephen is DEAD? NONE of us can bring him back and you can't make me his replacement! *I AM NOT STEPHEN!*"

"WELL YOU SHOULD BE!"

Fury remained, the anger boiling so hot that sweat started to bead from both of the men's brows. But after Arden's last words, Edward stopped, his voice suddenly going hoarse and his face changing from rage to sorrow. The king's words came like a blow to the gut. "Is that all I am to you?" Edward asked, his voice cracking. "A son you didn't want changed into the son you wished you had?"

Arden panted as he tried to regain some composure. "That's not what I said."

"But it's true, isn't it?" Edward replied. "My life has been spent trying to please you. I've been so desperate to be the son you really wanted and I've tried so, so hard to be Stephen. But no matter what I do, I fail. Even when I succeed, it's a failure in your eyes."

Edward felt a lump in his throat. "Do you know why I even stopped in Verloris?" he asked. "I didn't want to stay. I didn't want to go near Cathal. I only went there because I thought it was what you or Stephen would've done. I wanted to make you proud, to prove to you that I could be diplomatic. I was a fool to think you'd ever be proud of me."

"How could I be proud of what you've done, Edward?" Arden glared. "You weren't diplomatic. You entered a kingdom forbidden by our lands and whored yourself with the king's daughter. You betrayed everyone you knew-your family, your friends, your men! How could I ever be proud of *that*? You impregnated a girl out of wedlock while you were engaged to another woman, and a good woman at that!"

"I know what I did was wrong," Edward said. "Don't you think I regret my actions?"

"If you regretted them, you would have tried to fix things with Antoinette, with all of us!" Arden spat.

"What would you have me do? Abandon my child and throw away my responsibilities? I had to marry Malina; it was the right thing to do!"

"Don't quote your mother to me," Arden seethed, and Edward was surprised to hear the king mention Maria's support. His mother never told him he was right for marrying Malina, but then again, she never questioned his decision. "I do not trust a Verloris and I am ashamed that you would trust one! You should've denied the child was yours and be done with it! Nothing would've changed then."

Edward gasped. "How can you say that?"

"Because I think like a king!" Arden replied. "I put the greater good of this nation above all else. It's what I've always done."

"Then no wonder you're a terrible father." Edward shook his head. "How could you deny your own grandchild?"

"That *thing* is not my grandchild!" Arden waved his hand in anger. "I refuse to acknowledge it!"

"*Your* grandchild and I are the only ones left to carry on your legacy, Father!" Edward shouted. "Who else is there to rule these lands when you're gone?"

"Someone wiser than either of you." Arden lowered his brow. "Someone that isn't willing to take the throne by force!"

Edward's eyes widened. "What do you mean?"

"It's the reason I called you in here." Arden took the stack of papers on the table and held them to his face. "This *treaty*," he muttered as he threw the papers back to the table. "I know why you go behind my back, Edward. You seek to supplant me."

Edward felt his heart wanting to stop. Had his father gone mad? "What?"

"You gather foreign trade in secret and win allies by throwing gold in our peoples' laps!" Arden said. "Why else would you keep this from me if not to use it for your own gain?"

The conversation was spiraling out of control. Did Malina know the treaty would turn his father against him? If she did, she was more wicked than he thought. "Father, I *beg* you to understand that I have never sought your demise! I have only tried to make you strong and proud, not mock you!"

"You have failed miserably if that is true," Arden said, returning to his chair. "Long have you been arrogant, Edward. You have been selfish, cruel, and cold-hearted. I was foolish to think you could ever take the place of your brother on the throne, for I see that you do not hold anyone's interests above your own." He sat back on the chair and gathered some papers from the table to him. "Will you admit this treaty was your way of gaining power?"

"I will admit to no such thing." Edward frowned.

"Then will you admit you are a boy and not a man? That you are a child who pretends to be a prince but is no better than a beggar performing in the streets?" Arden looked up, his eyes narrow, and Edward stood still, in shock.

"I will admit," Edward began, "to being foolish in thinking that I could ever please you." He paused as Arden's stoic face barely flinched. "And I admit I have been an imperfect son who has failed in everything I have touched. I'm sorry you lost the son who would have made you proud and I'm sorry I was not worthy enough to take his place."

He pulled his signet ring off his right hand and placed it on the table in front of the king. The ring was his sign to rule, proof that he was the king's chosen heir. It had once belonged to Stephen. "Choose whom you deem fit as your heir, for I have never been worthy."

There was a pause as Edward searched his father's face. A sign of remorse, a flicker of hope in his eye that somehow, someway the king would embrace him and say he forgave him and that all would be well. But no sign from the king came, no glimmer of compassion for the son who knew his father did not love him. The king took the signet ring in his hand and held it, looking up at Edward. "I will. Now be off with you."

Edward nodded in silence, backing up and leaving the room. As the guards shut the door he hurried down the hall, unsure of where to go. Was he still allowed in the palace? Should he leave and find another home? According to tradition, he was technically still the heir until the king put the name of his replacement in a decree. But Edward knew it wouldn't take Arden long to gather a name.

"Edward?" His thoughts were interrupted as he looked up and noticed his mother leaving the drawing room with a finished needlepoint cloth. "What's wrong?" she asked as he stopped. "You look as if you are ill!"

She tossed the needlepoint to the floor, not caring where it landed, rushing to her son and feeling his forehead. "You don't feel like you're running a fever," she muttered as Edward looked away. "But your skin is so clammy! Perhaps it is something you ate."

"I'm alright, Mom," he said quietly as he put his arm around her in a loose embrace.

"Mom?" Maria frowned as she touched her son's cheek. "You haven't called me Mom since you were a little boy, and an upset one at that. Has something happened?"

"It's nothing."

"Edward," Maria said sternly, "don't keep secrets from your mother."

"Father and I just had a fight. It's nothing to worry over." He wanted to let her go and leave, perhaps hide in his study and never come out again. But he kept his hand on her back, not wanting to let go. He'd just lost his father; he didn't want to lose his mother, too.

"What did your father say?" Maria's voice lowered in a growl, like a lioness protecting her cub.

He didn't want to tell her the truth, didn't want to admit that he was such a failure as a son that his own father was content with his disownment. All he wanted was to know she was still there, that she was still his mother, that she loved him just as much as he loved her. "You know I'm sorry, Mom, right?" he began. "For everything; for Malina, for hurting Antoinette, for hurting you…"

"Of course," Maria replied, her face falling to show her growing worry. "I know you're sorry, Edward."

"And you know I would never want to deceive you, right?"

"Yes…" Maria's brow rose in confusion. "Sweetheart, what's this all about? You're being cryptic. What did your father say to you?"

"I'm sorry I failed you," he said as he embraced her, holding her tight as he felt her arms go around him and embrace him back. He felt like a child again, his spirits lifting as he relished in the warmth of her touch. There was never a comparison to a mother's love and he never wanted to let it go.

"I love you, Mom. Don't forget that," he said quietly as he let her go.

She pulled away. "I love you too, Edward. Why won't you tell me what's wrong?"

Because it would hurt you. He kissed her cheek. "I'll see you later," he muttered as he walked away, not looking behind as his mother called his name.

He didn't notice Maria clench her fists in fury nor see her face harden. He did, however, hear her call one of the guards to demand to know where the king was at. Edward couldn't help but smirk at the thought. When his mother was angry, she was terrifying. His father would be in for a fight.

Before returning to the kitchen, Edward made his way to Malina's personal parlor. She was busy readying for tea, a few of the nobles being invited to the palace so she could get acquainted with them. Edward figured it was her way of lauding around her new position as the next queen.

"Edward!" she called as she approached her husband, greeting him warmly in front of the servants. Edward accepted her embrace, faking a smile for the servants' sake. "I hear the king wished to see you! Did he congratulate you on the treaty?"

He gave her a smile, making her think her musings true. He pulled her close, pretending to kiss her cheek, as he whispered in her ear. "I hope you're happy, *Darling*," he began. "The king thinks the treaty is my way of trying to take his power. Thanks to you, I've just lost the throne of Audlin."

Malina's smile turned to shock. Edward swore he saw a glint of fear in her eyes. "I don't understand," she muttered.

"Enjoy the palace while you can," Edward replied with a frown. "As soon as the king finds another heir, we won't be living here anymore."

Malina said nothing as her eyes lit up with rage.

Chapter 12: The Next Heir

"I can't believe you, Arden!" Maria huffed as she paced in the bedroom, the king wanting to stuff the pillows through his ears so he could sleep in peace. She wrung her hands together, suppressing a growl as she glared at him, and swore under her breath. "Edward is *your son*-your own flesh and blood! How could you even think of replacing him on the throne? Do you think him that incapable to rule in your place?"

"I think him very incapable," Arden replied as he turned to his side, only for his wife to follow his line of sight. He sighed as he sat up, frustrated he would not be going to bed early that night. "What would you have me do, Maria? He gave me his signet ring. The throne was given up by him on his own accord!"

"Because you pressured him to do it!"

"I did no such thing!" Arden defended, his hands waving to mimic his speech. "How am I being deceptive when I was only correcting his behavior?"

Maria narrowed her eyes. "You compared him to Stephen."

"And rightly so. If he were more like Stephen, we would have none of this mess with Verloris."

"You don't know that," Maria said. "Stephen had his faults just as Edward has his. None of us are perfect."

"But at least Stephen had sense!"

"Yes, Stephen had more sense," Maria replied. "But if you just guided Edward instead of chastising him all the time!"

"Do not make excuses for him, Maria!"

"I'm not," Maria said. "Can't you see Edward's sorry for what he's done? He's trying so hard to make amends. What other boy would content himself with housework alongside an apology?"

"I haven't heard an apology." Arden lowered his brow.

"You said he apologized earlier this morning when you talked."

"Then I haven't heard enough apologies."

"Really, Arden." Maria shook her head. "The difference you made between our children! No wonder they never got along."

"They got along just fine!"

"In front of you!" Maria exclaimed. "They only wanted to make you happy."

Arden rubbed his face with his palms as he exhaled slowly. He longed for sleep-no dreams, no waking, no disturbance-just so he could escape the chaos his wife wanted to bring in the night. "Maria," he began slowly, "I know I have not done everything with your approval, but this is something I won't change my mind on. This is a mistake that doesn't just concern Edward's life; it affects the country as well. If it were only Edward inheriting the throne, my worries would be few. But Malina as queen? I would rather die than see a Verloris wench sitting in your chair!"

Maria remained silent as she looked away.

"And how do we know this child of theirs will be like us?" Arden continued. "I married you, Maria, because I knew you would be a wonderful wife and mother, but Edward married Malina out of necessity. She is a terrible wife and she will no doubt be a terrible mother. That child is doomed from the start! And with a father like Edward...I don't want to imagine the foolishness that will ensue. Edward will never have a good child-mark my words!"

"You don't know that, Arden," Maria replied. "Edward may surprise you. Even then, there are good children who come from bad parents just like there are bad children who come from good parents."

Arden rolled his eyes. "I'm not going to change my mind, Maria," he replied. "Edward must understand his actions have consequences. He's no longer a boy and I shan't treat him like one. I will honor my vows as a father and do what I think must be done. Do you not agree that this is a fitting punishment?"

"It's harsh." Maria frowned as she faced her husband. "But it's also not my decision. If you wish to take the throne from him, then do it." She crossed her arms and faced the burning hearth across the room.

A moment of silence passed, and though Arden was grateful for the quiet, the coldness that came from his wife made him more uncomfortable than the noise. Her silence was deafening.

"You're angry with me," he muttered.

"Not angry with you," she said quietly, bowing her head. "Angry knowing you're right."

Her voice, hoarse as if holding back tears, made the king want to get out of bed and hold her, but he remained still. She would be in no mood for his embrace, not tonight and perhaps not for a while. Maria always held Edward dear to her heart, whether it was because he was the youngest or because they were more alike, he didn't know, but Arden wondered if Edward losing the throne hurt his wife more than it hurt his son.

"Can you promise me something?" Maria asked, suddenly turning and facing him. Her arms remained crossed as Arden nodded, waiting for her request. "You are about to lose your heir, but promise me you won't lose your son."

Arden bit his lip. "I'll try, but..."

"No," Maria interrupted. "You either will lose him or you won't."

Arden paused, thinking she asked a miracle of him. "Fine. I won't."

Her demeanor warmed after he met her gaze. "Thank you," she replied, turning back to the hearth.

Edward stared out the window of the drawing room, watching the carriages cross the streets in the distance of the city. Everything looked so peaceful, so happy, and he wondered if life outside of the palace would be as kind to him as it was to the people of Reigal. Though he imagined civilian life would suit him-a career in the military was almost guaranteed to keep him busy-his greatest worries lied with Malina. Delusions of grandeur and a promise of a throne were buried deep within her heart, and to have it taken away so suddenly would doubtless bring trouble upon him.

She'll just have to learn, he thought to himself as he sighed. Though imagining Malina as a common noblewoman who kept house was easier than putting it into practice.

It was a change they'd both have to accept.

"I spoke with your father." Edward turned to see Maria at the door, her hands clasped in front of her but her face sunk in despair. She stepped forward, stopping beside him in front of the window. "He wishes to give the throne to someone else. I'm sorry, Edward. I tried to keep it for you."

"A new heir is for the best, Mother," Edward replied quietly. "We should trust Father's wisdom. It won't be hard to find a better replacement."

Maria frowned. "You sound as if you approve of this."

"Of course I approve," Edward said. "I would not make a good king, Mother. I'm not destined for this. I never was. It's folly to think someone like me could rule a country and succeed at it."

There was a pause as Maria bowed her head. "I thought you could do it."

"You're the only one who thinks that."

"Antoinette thought you could, too."

Edward pursed his lips. "But she doesn't count anymore," he murmured. "She was foolish to ever believe in me."

Maria faced him, her eyes looking heavy. "I still believe in you."

"You waste your faith, then."

Maria faced the window once more, crossing her arms as she licked her lips. "I don't think my faith is wasted, Edward. You've made a mess of things in the past, but you are young and can still make things right. Hoping that you will learn from your mistakes is a faith I refuse to give up on."

"I'm trying to do things right," Edward whispered. He felt Maria take his hand and hold it like when he was a child in need of comfort. His fingers wrapped around her own, and he gave her a gentle squeeze. "It just seems like every time I try to fix things I fall even further. I blame others for my foolishness, but I know the truth. I am the fool who does the folly. I am the failure who's never done anything right."

"Just because you've failed in the past doesn't mean you'll fail in the future," Maria replied.

"I'm tired of hurting everyone," Edward said. "It's like it's all I'm good at."

"*I will not have this, Edward*," Maria said firmly as she pointed her finger to his chest. "I will *not* have you wallowing in regret and I will *not* have you live your life in self-pity. You've made mistakes and they are *done*. There is nothing you can do to change them! But you still have a choice to make things right. Now will you continue to be the fool and wallow in the past or will you be wise and take this opportunity to make your mother's faith a reality and be strong?"

"But...what if I fail again?" Edward asked.

"Since when did you let fear ever stop you from trying?" Maria's eyes narrowed.

She met his eyes for a second, glaring into him a defiance that lit a fire in his heart to prove her right. It was far from a blaze, but the little flicker of a match was a start, and he met her gaze with the most determined look he could muster.

"Prove them wrong, Edward," she whispered as she backed away. "And if you do fall, pick yourself up and try again. You still have a purpose."

"What purpose do I have now that Antoinette and the kingship are gone?"

"Well then," Maria began with a smirk. "That's up for you to find out."

She left him in the room, her words repeating in his mind.

"What did Maria say?"

Malina wasted no time as she sat down to lunch with Edward. Her food remained undisturbed and her tea was untouched. She only leaned forward, hungry for conversation, as she watched her husband with intense eyes. He shrugged as he took a sip of vegetable stew.

"My mother is unhappy with the king's wishes, but nothing's changed. Get used to the fact that we will no longer be royalty," he muttered with a full mouth. "Besides..." He swallowed. "It's not like we'll be paupers. I'm guaranteed a spot in the knighthood. I'm sure I'll be added to the royal guard and you'll remain in the circle of noblewomen. We'll have a nice house in the city and plenty to spare to provide for our family."

Her lips twisted as if bitterness resided in her mouth. "I do not want a house, Edward," she seethed. "I want a palace."

"My apologies, Malina," Edward replied. "But I cannot give you a palace."

Malina scoffed as she threw herself back into the chair, reminding Edward of a child being denied a toy. "Then you are useless to me!" he heard her mutter under her breath.

The words were cutting, and for a moment he felt a pain in his heart. This was to be expected-her reaction, her anger, her fear of loss. He reminded himself that in time she would get used to the fact they were no longer royalty. At least...he hoped she would.

"I tried to warn you of this," he said quietly as he took another bite of stew. "If you honestly think my father will overlook what we've done, then you do not know people as well as you think."

"And what have we done?" Malina asked. "Marry and conceive a child? Yes, I can see how that's threatening."

"It was all done in deception," Edward replied. "And after your stunt with the treaty, whatever credibility we had left was destroyed."

"The treaty helped us gain reputation and glory!"

"The treaty was a power play that the king noticed immediately."

Malina looked away. "Your father is a fool." She paused, her eyes turning back to him. "But you are an even bigger fool to allow the throne to slip from your fingers."

"I can't force my father to change his mind." Edward sighed. "Nor do I want to. I will accept whatever decree he gives."

"*Weakling!*" Malina spat as she stood from her seat, nearly knocking her bowl of stew onto the floor. "You would dare allow your father to take what is rightfully ours?"

"You and I both know the throne was never meant to be mine," Edward said, pausing from eating, his eyes remaining on the bowl. "Stephen was meant to have it. Not me...never me."

"Does that mean you should give it up?" Malina asked. "Is *your mother* the only one that does not quiver at every word from the king?"

"I can't question my father's decision."

"Then content yourself with losing the throne!" Malina took her napkin and threw it to the table. Edward didn't jump; he was used to her bouts of anger by now. "But do not think I shall be demoted so easily!"

Malina stormed from the room, slamming the door behind her and leaving Edward alone with his thoughts.

"You must remember, my daughters, that tonight is a very important event," Susanna began as she circled the room, Antoinette and Bernie sitting in front of the mirror with their heads turned, watching their mother. "The Feast of the Edellwood is one of the most highlighted and attended events in the country and we must be on our best behavior."

Antoinette nodded, giving a sigh. The last thing she felt like going to was a party, especially while in the town nearest to Audlin's border. The Edellwood was small, heavily forested, yet it was also the most beautiful area in Edeland with its trees and foliage and view of Audlin's mountains in the background. It was where the capital of Edeland once was before the country expanded and grew.

It was also a place where she would meet Edward when he came to visit. He was never fond of Staalberg or the fact that her mother would nose about their business while he was there. In the Edellwood, they had privacy and a place where palace gossips were few and far between. They had some of their most intimate conversations there amongst the trees.

It would be a terrible evening to have to remember all that she lost.

"There will also be many eligible bachelors there," Susanna continued as she stopped in front of Antoinette, making her look up. "Many noblemen will be there as well as their sons. I also should make it a point to add that a few members of the von Liegen family will be there for talks with your father."

"Splendid!" Bernie added as she clapped her hands. "I always wanted to go to a buffet!"

"And who says there shall be a buffet of food for you, my pig?" Susanna glared.

"And who says I was talking about food?" Bernie pouted. "I was talking about the men!"

"If any of them would give you a second look, child, I would think they were desperate," Susanna replied as Bernie lowered her brow. "Now fix yourselves up. I know we do not have as many resources here in the Edellwood as we do back home, but make do with what you have. I shall be back to check on you in a little while before we leave for the feast."

"Yes, Mother," Antoinette said, and she watched Susanna walk out the door.

The girls were left alone in their room to ready themselves. They quickly dressed in their planned attire and set forth to work on hair and makeup. As Bernie was busy putting on powder, Antoinette returned to the mirror to do her hair.

She typically wore it down, usually with a few small braids added in for decoration, but tonight would be an experiment. She would wear it up, her hair intertwined with matching ribbon, and bigger earrings to bring attention to her facial features. In the back of her mind, she wondered if she didn't show enough of her assets in front of Edward by wearing her hair down all the time. Malina wore her hair up, so why shouldn't she do the same?

Her hands went to work, pulling strands this way and that and tying them with olive colored ribbon to match her dress.

As she was working, however, her thoughts were interrupted by her sister off to the side.

"Ugh!" Bernie groaned as she tossed the powder box to the dresser. "I have another zit! Where is all this acne coming from?" She put her hands to her face and began to search for more of the red bumps suddenly plaguing her complexion only to find a few more.

"I don't know," Antoinette replied.

"Mother's not going to let me have any chocolate," Bernie muttered.

"She doesn't let you have any chocolate to begin with."

"Well this is stressful enough! I think I should have some for therapy."

"You look fine. It's really not that bad; I can't even see it."

"You don't have Mother's eagle eyes."

Antoinette chuckled as she continued with her hair. She was thankful she usually had a clear complexion, though lately she started to see a few oily spots on her face. She could only imagine what Mother would say if it were different.

"You know what I *am* looking forward to?" Bernie grinned as her brows went up and down. "All the fun I'm going to have with our male visitors."

"Mother's going to insist a match be made tonight." Antoinette sighed. "I know she's going to introduce me to a bunch of men to replace Edward."

"You mean a bunch of idiots to replace Edward," Bernie clarified.

"Probably." Antoinette smirked. "I just…I'm not ready to replace him yet."

"Especially since things are going so well with Emmerich."

Antoinette heard a snicker come from her sister's lips and she blushed. Things were going well with Emmerich, but then again, things had always gone well with him. There was never a question on whether they were compatible or not, for they always were. The question was did she see him as a friend or something more? She was still debating on the answer to that.

But even with him she was taking things slow. She had been with Edward for so long that it was unusual for her to imagine being with anyone else.

Now that he was with Malina, however, someone else was her only option.

"I wonder who she has in mind for me," Antoinette said.

"Probably someone rich, handsome, and a brain full of goose eggs."

Antoinette laughed. "I'm sure she's got some in mind for you."

"I'm sure she does." Bernie chuckled. "Which is why I'm looking forward to it. Nothing is more enjoyable than conversing with a goose egg brain and making him look like the idiot he is."

"But what if he likes you? You might not want to humiliate him so badly."

"I've been going to this thing for sixteen years, Sis," Bernie replied. "Since when would a guy give me the time of day?"

"You never know."

Bernie shrugged as she picked up some more makeup to cover the acne on her cheek. "I've been pretty accurate on my predictions so far."

"So what do you predict for us tonight?" Antoinette asked.

"You'll be surrounded by morons asking for your hand in marriage," Bernie began. "And I'll be right beside you, slapping their hands away."

Antoinette laughed as she continued with her hair.

Ten, four, seven, nine, three, Bernie thought to herself as she scanned the ballroom, taking a sip of the sweet fruity drink in her hand. A young man with a funny looking hat and pants that were too tight walked by and she nearly spit her drink out. *Negative one hundred...*

She swallowed hard, trying to get the image of the man's horrendous sense of fitting out of her mind. Some things just weren't meant to be seen.

She carefully lowered her cup away from her face as Antoinette approached to her side. "Well?" Antoinette began as she took a look about the room, eyeing the guests as they conversed and danced. "What do you think?"

Bernie shrugged. "I think we had an average of 6.6 until Lumpy Stockingbottoms walked by."

Antoinette stifled a snicker. "Lumpy who?"

"Trust me." Bernie shuddered, that horrible image coming back. "You *don't* want to know."

Antoinette giggled as she took a sip of her drink. "Sounds dreadful. But look at the bright side! We have a higher average this time. Well…at least I think it's a higher average. What scale are we using again?"

The scale they always used when scoping out future husbands, Bernie thought. "One means *get away you freak*. Five means *I like you as a last resort*. Ten means *marry me now so I can have your babies*."

"Ah," Antoinette replied as she nodded, taking a sip of drink. "Average is pretty good tonight compared to normal. With the exception of Lumpy, of course. Are there any tens?"

Bernie waved her brows up and down. "The waiter serving the appetizers."

"Really?"

"Dark hair, dark eyes, muscular build, and a smidge of stubble on his face." Bernie let out a sigh as she dreamily looked over to the appetizer table. "Did I mention he was wearing a perfectly fit tunic? Pinch me, Antoinette; I think I'm dreaming!"

Antoinette leaned to the side, her eyes gazing towards the appetizer table. Sure enough, there was the waiter. "Not bad," Antoinette replied casually. "Seems more like a seven to me, though."

"Seven?" Bernie looked to her sister, mortified. Was she blind? How could she not see that waiter was a gift from Heaven? She crossed her arms in a huff. "You need your eyes checked."

"Relax," Antoinette said. "I didn't say he was ugly. He's just not my type. Apparently he is yours, though."

"I don't have a type."

"Sure you do. All the guys you've ever whistled at look the same."

Bernie rose one of her brows. "Not all of them."

"The majority of them."

"Whatever," Bernie muttered, wanting to change the subject. "So how about you? Any tens out there that you could see?"

"Not really," Antoinette said with a sigh. "I guess I'm not looking, though. It's a little too soon for matchmaking. I'm still getting used to being single again."

Bernie gave Antoinette a confused glance. Surely she wasn't missing Edward after all this time. That pig baboon excuse of a man did her dirtier than all the other men she knew combined. "No offense, though, but I'd rather you be single now than be stuck with a jerk like Edward."

Antoinette took another sip of her drink quietly, looking out into the distance. "I know. It still feels too soon, though." She lowered her now empty cup and turned to her sister. "And I suppose...in a way...I wish Emery was here. He always could make me laugh."

"It'd be disastrous if he were here. The mayor brought in apple cake for dessert and you know how Waffles would handle that."

Antoinette smirked. "You have to admit it'd be funny, though."

Bernie smiled to herself. It'd be funny, indeed.

Antoinette's smile faded as her gaze went back to the distance. "I do miss him, Bernie, as strange as it sounds. I miss him a lot."

"Miss who, my child?" Bernie and Antoinette turned to find their Mother standing behind them, her arms crossed and face leaning forward and listening in.

Bernie looked to Antoinette and then back to Mother. It'd do no good to mention Antoinette's thinking of Emmerich, especially since Mother didn't know the two had been seeing each other. The best choice was to lie, though Antoinette would cringe at the thought. "She was talking about Edward," Bernie replied before Antoinette could say anything. "The breakup is still a little near to her, after all."

"Well," Susanna began as she turned to her eldest. "The sooner you get over that, Antoinette, the sooner you can move on with your life. A man looking for a wife certainly doesn't want her pawning over her lost love, and you'll never catch a man if you can't let go of the old one. So be off with that silly time you had with Edward and start looking for someone new! Come along with me, now, so I can introduce you."

"See ya," Bernie muttered as she watched Mother take Antoinette by the hand and pull her forward. She hated to see Antoinette go, but at the same time she wanted to make another stop at the appetizer table and say hello to the angelic waiter.

"Not so fast, child," Susanna said as she yanked Bernie's hand, pulling her close. "I see you eyeing the appetizer table. Don't think I shall let you stand a second more over there! You've already eaten twice your weight in cheese balls!"

"Cheese balls?" Bernie scowled as she looked back to the waiter in the distance. "Mother, I'm being perfectly serious when I say the cheese was the last thing on my mind!"

"Then what were you thinking of? The crackers? The tiny cuts of beef?"

"Actually, I was thinking about that beefy waiter over there. Have you seen him? He's like an angel that fell from Heaven!"

"An angel who fell from Heaven would not waste his time serving crackers to nobles."

"Come on, Mother!" Bernie pouted as she gave her best attempt at a puppy look. "You said I needed to be on the lookout for future prospects."

"Not amongst the waiting staff!"

"Please, Mother? *Please* can't I at least say hello?"

"Of course not, child," Susanna replied with a frown. "We don't associate with peasants. Now follow me with your sister. I'm going to introduce you to someone."

She pulled Bernie and Antoinette towards the other end of the room, Bernie grumbling underneath her breath as she was led further away from her angelic waiter. "I want you to be on your best behavior, girls. This young man has travelled an awful long way to get here and he's especially keen on meeting you, Antoinette."

Antoinette's eyes widened and she slowed in her pace. "Mother, I'm not sure I'm ready to court again just yet."

"Nonsense! If you don't marry now you won't marry later."

"But Mother…"

"Silence, child," Susanna said as she approached a young man standing beside some guards chatting. He was dressed perfectly like a peacock; not a wrinkle in his clothing and every hair was in place. Not a blemish lay upon his skin, and as he turned and greeted the women, he smiled widely, baring perfect teeth.

In short, Bernie hated him. No one was that perfect without having something major to hide, and she could see it on him.

"Ladies, may I introduce to you Prince Arnold von Liegen," Susanna said as she turned to the girls to curtsey. They complied, both with hesitation, as the young man standing before them looked at both of their faces with a keen eye.

"It is a pleasure to meet you both," he purred as his gaze turned to Bernie's sister. "And it is especially an honor to meet you, Lady Antoinette. Your mother spoke of your beauty but even her words do not convey the radiance of your eyes. Pray, tell me, how are you faring this fine evening?"

Bernie stifled a laugh as Antoinette turned to her with a quizzical brow and spoke. "This night has been rather average, though I've seen some highlights. How would you *rate* it, dear sister?"

She rose her brows to Bernie, making her snicker in response. If Antoinette wanted a rating on Prince Arnold, she could give it. "I may have *one* complaint, I'm sure."

"Then again," Antoinette cleared her throat, hiding a smirk, "I actually have *zero* complaints. It is a fine night indeed."

"You're right, dear sister!" Bernie exclaimed a little too dramatically, making Susanna give her a look. "I forgot about the appetizer table. It was certainly a perfect *ten*."

"I am pleased to hear you're enjoying your evening," Arnold said, oblivious to the sisters' word play. Bernie could only laugh at the lack of observation on his part. *Fool. A complete and utter fool.*

A moment of awkward silence passed until Susanna cleared her throat. "Prince Arnold was telling me of some of the business propositions he has proposed in Liegen. Please, sir, do tell us more of your dealings."

"It's nothing, really," Arnold replied with a wave of his hand. "We increased our ore mining production in the mountains and have been working on new trade partnerships with Braiden. I think we shall surpass our earnings by four percent by the end of the year."

"Splendid! Did you hear that, Antoinette?" Susanna said as her voice rose giddily. "A businessman and a diplomat!"

Antoinette seemed barely impressed. She offered him a friendly smile and nothing more. "Congratulations, Prince Arnold. Your country must be thrilled to have such a talent in the royal family."

"'Tis true. I've become a bit of a celebrity bringing glories and riches to the Liegen estate." Arnold grinned as he threw his nose in the air. Bernie could only imagine teal and blue feathers sticking out of him. He would make a great peacock.

"And to be so humble about it is even more astounding," Bernie muttered, feigning awe.

The prince gave her a look that could almost pass as a scowl until he turned his attention back to Antoinette. "I am certainly humbled by the experience, but I am even more humbled to be in the presence of such a lovely woman. Lady Antoinette, forgive my intrusion into your personal life, but I heard of the terrible news in Audlin. I am sorry to hear that your engagement to Prince Edward has ended, but I am happy that you are rid of a thorn in your side. You were wise to part from him when you saw he was no good for you."

Antoinette's eyes widened and Bernie could only wonder what sort of fanciful story their mother gave Arnold to explain why Antoinette's engagement ended. It didn't matter. Whatever the reasoning was, Antoinette was sure to set it straight.

"Thank you for your concern, Prince Arnold," Antoinette began kindly, though Bernie could sense a hint of frustration. "It truly was a difficult time for me, especially after I discovered Edward's unfaithfulness."

"I heard rumors of an affair with the princess of Verloris."

"I'm afraid the rumors are true," Antoinette continued, "but at the same time I know I shall recover from this great loss. I have had wonderful support in my family and I daresay I hope to love again."

Bernie gave Antoinette a nudge in surprise. Was her sister mad? Did she not know she was playing *right* into Mother and Arnold's plans?

Arnold's grin widened as he stepped closer to her, making Bernie clench her jaw in a snarl. "What a wonderful hope you have, Your Majesty. Yes, I do believe you shall find love again, even sooner than you hope!"

"I think I shall as well." Antoinette smiled, matching the look on Mother's face. "For you see, while I was in Audlin I learned the strangest thing. Do you know Edward's cousin, Emmericn van Ketten?"

The smile began to fade on Arnold's face as he nodded slowly. "Yes. I have heard of him."

Bernie's mouth felt like dropping in shock as she realized Antoinette was bringing up the one man Mother hated. She quickly looked to Mother and swore there was smoke coming from the woman's nostrils.

Bernie felt her heart racing in excitement. This was more entertaining than rating fellow guests any day!

"Well," Antoinette continued with a gleam, "he was there when Edward came back. Even after all that had happened, Emmerich refused to leave my side. I cried on his shoulder, I used up all his handkerchiefs…and he was so wonderful and supportive that I think I'd still be depressed if it wasn't for him. I knew he was a respectable man, surely, but I never realized what a wonderful gentleman he was to a lady such as I. And let us not forget how handsome he is…"

"Well!" Susanna interrupted as she quickly grabbed Antoinette's elbow and yanked her away from the prince. "My dear, *you must be tiring the poor prince with your silly tales!*" She turned back to Arnold, who now looked perturbed, as she offered him a humbling smile. "My prince, if I do recall you wished to meet my husband, the king. Let us not keep him waiting!"

"Of course, Your Majesty," Arnold replied with a clear of his throat. "I would be honored to meet your husband."

"Likewise, he would be honored to meet you," Susanna said with a smile as she gently escorted the prince away from her daughters. "Antoinette, Bernette, you are welcome to follow as long as you don't interrupt the conversation."

"Actually, I think we'll mingle a little more," Antoinette said. "I saw some appetizers that looked absolutely ravishing. If you'll excuse us both." The girls curtseyed, not even looking at the prince as they quickly exited and left the wrath of the queen.

"I call the cheese ball," Antoinette whispered with a laugh.

Bernie gave a mischievous wink. "I call the waiter!"

They joined arms as they laughed their way to the appetizer table.

Chapter 14: A Reason for Everything

The city of Hugellia was bustling with life. Emmerich had almost forgotten how noisy the city could be after being away from his home for so long. He counted nearly three months of absence, but after the events of Edward's elopement and the drama that followed, Emmerich found himself wishing he had been gone longer. Already he missed Antoinette and the time he spent with her in Edeland. Already he wished he could be back in her presence, if only to see her smile.

He rode up the street towards his home outside the palace, setting his horse to the stables and making sure Waffles was fed anything but apples. The poor horse was sick for weeks after all the apples he ate in the royal garden, leaving Emmerich an excuse not to travel and spend more time with Antoinette before coming back home.

He clamored up the steps of his house, a small two story reminiscent of a merchant's home near the center of town. The door was opened and he walked into the family room to find his mother helping his father with some documents of state. When they saw him arrive, they dropped the papers and ink and rushed to him, embracing him warmly.

"My sweet baby!" Anna cried, wrapping her arms around her son and making him blush. She never did understand he was no longer a child, but he loved her all the same and embraced her back. "You've been gone for ages! What took you so long to come home?"

"I had a bit of a detour," Emmerich mumbled from her shoulder as she still wouldn't let him go.

After a lack of air she finally relented, still holding to his arm as Aldaric embraced his son. "We heard of what happened with Edward. Is it true he came back with a Verloris princess?"

Emmerich's smile faded at the memory. "Unfortunately it is."

"Poor Antoinette!" Anna gasped. "How awful that this has happened to her! What would make Edward do such a thing?"

"I don't know," Emmerich replied. "He never did quite explain his reasoning."

"You talked to him?" Aldaric asked, his brow going up. "You were there when he arrived?"

"I was. The scene was…unpleasant."

"How awful," Anna said. "Was there fighting?"

Emmerich shrugged. He wasn't sure how his parents would feel knowing he punched Edward for what he did. "There was…a little bit, I suppose. I tried not to get in the middle of the family fights. I was more worried about Antoinette."

"You two always were so close," Anna said with a smile. "As much as I hate that you were away, I'm glad you were there for her."

"It's why I was so late coming back," Emmerich said. "I followed her back home and spent some time with her in Edeland. I just wanted to make sure she was alright."

"And how is she doing?" Aldaric asked in concern.

"Better," Emmerich replied. "I know everything that happened with Edward was hard on her, and I won't lie-I'm angry with him for what he's done and for making her cry. But at the same time, I think this is all for the best. She deserves someone better...someone who will treat her with respect and dignity."

Aldaric gave Anna a knowing glance but said nothing as they watched Emmerich wiggle away from their grasp and head towards the stairs to his room. "Not that I don't want to visit," he said as he hurried, "but there's a few letters I need to get out before dinner. I left Aunt Maria in a bit of a hurry, so I'm sure she's worried. I also told Antoinette I would write her when I arrived back home."

"Well get to it, then." Aldaric snickered.

"I promise we'll catch up when I'm finished!" he called from up the stairs, and hurried to his desk to pull out the ink and parchment.

He didn't notice Anna shaking her head, stifling a laugh as she stood at the end of the stairway, looking up. She turned to her husband and rolled her eyes. "Three months we don't see him and all I get is a 'hello' and 'I'll talk to you later'!"

Aldaric chuckled as he stood behind his wife, putting his arms around her waist. "Were we any different?" he asked as he kissed her cheek.

"I suppose not..." Anna sighed as she leaned into his embrace.

"It's only the beginning," Aldaric replied. "I have a feeling we'll be seeing less and less of him now that Antoinette's no longer engaged."

My dearest Antoinette,

"That's not right," Emmerich mumbled to himself as he wadded the piece of parchment and tossed it to the waste bin. It was the tenth letter he attempted to Antoinette within the last hour and already he was at a loss of words. He didn't want to seem too forward, yet he didn't want to seem too casual.

He put the quill to paper and started over. *Dear Antoinette...*

He shrugged. Every letter started with that. Besides, it was too casual, just like the letter before was too formal. Different introductions coursed through his mind as Emmerich thought of the best possible greeting to Antoinette. *To Antoinette? My friend?* Maybe he should just put her name and keep it at that.

His head leaned back in the chair and his eyes closed. If he were honest, he would write a completely new introduction. *To Antoinette, the woman who somehow manages to turn my eloquent mind into jelly and make me sound like a toddler learning his letters.*

The paper was quickly wadded in his hand and tossed to the waste bin atop the others.

The door to his bedroom opened and Emmerich turned to see who had entered. After walking in, Aldaric glanced at his son sitting at the desk, thinking he was studying for new courses at the university. After seeing the growing mountain of wadded parchment near the door, however, he began to snicker.

"Feeling at a loss for words?" Aldaric asked as he walked in, leaning against the wall by the desk.

Emmerich pursed his lips, not wanting to admit the truth. "I guess I'm just tired from the trip. My mind isn't very willing to cooperate at the moment."

"All this worry over a letter to your aunt?"

"No," Emmerich replied, pointing to a sealed envelope at the corner. "Hers is finished. I'm working on the second one."

"The one to Antoinette?"

Emmerich looked away, embarrassed. "Yes."

"I see," Aldaric said. "I'm a bit surprised to see you so careful in your wording, though. Usually your letters to her are quick."

Emmerich sighed. There would be no hiding his feelings from his father. Aldaric knew him better than anyone-the curse and the blessing of having a father for a best friend.

"Things are different now," Emmerich said after a pause. "She...she knows how I feel about her."

Aldaric's face showed no emotion as he simply nodded and listened. "Did you tell her?"

"She figured it out on her own. She asked, I was honest."

"Was this after Edward arrived?" Aldaric asked.

Emmerich shook his head. "We spoke of it just before he came back."

Aldaric shifted himself, becoming more comfortable in his position against the desk. "Do you think she feels the same about you?"

"That's what we talked about in Edeland," Emmerich replied. "There...there's something there, but after all that's happened with Edward, she's afraid she's only feeling that way because she's hurt. She said she doesn't want our relationship to be a rebound after what happened with Edward and she needs time to sort it all out."

"She's always been a smart girl," Aldaric said as he bowed his head, eyeing the floor. "It says a lot about how she already feels for you, Emery. She must care for you a lot to not rush into things. I applaud her for making sure you won't get hurt."

"That's what I tell myself," Emmerich said as he swirled the ink inside the bottle with his quill. "A part of me thinks she only sees me as a friend. That's how it has always been. But now that I have a chance, or at least *might* have a chance, I don't know what to do. I've never had anyone care for me like that and I'm not sure how to handle it."

"Relationships can be scary," Aldaric said, facing him. "Especially when it's your first one. Try not to let it make you nervous."

"I'm not nervous. I'm terrified."

"Which is only natural for anyone entering a potential relationship. You shouldn't let it frighten you, though."

"But how do I know I should pursue this?" Emmerich asked. "How do I know this isn't going to fail miserably? I've already lost her once, Dad; I don't want to lose her again."

Aldaric gave a quiet laugh, making Emmerich nearly huff in frustration. Aldaric always found difficult things so simple. "You'll be fine. If it's meant to be, it'll happen. You'll know whether it's the right choice or the wrong one."

He smiled as Emmerich watched in unbelief. "Before I married your mother," Aldaric began, "we were just friends. In fact, I was in a relationship with someone else."

"You courted someone other than Mom?"

"I did," Aldaric replied. "I courted her for years, actually. It was an agreeable match our parents had made and we went along with it. I was attracted to the woman, yes, but we never had a chance to become *friends* first. We had a good relationship. It was nothing too disagreeable. But when I met Anna things changed.

"Anna became my friend. We would talk for hours carrying on conversations over the silliest of things. She made me laugh, she made me think, she helped me grow in my faith, and she made me look at the world in a different light. I never wanted to depart from her because she was just so different from everyone else I'd ever known.

"I continued with the relationship my parents had arranged for me, but I began to spend time with Anna in secret. Your mother was very poor at the time, and I knew the king wouldn't approve me courting a pauper. But our friendship was everything to me. I couldn't give it up. Then, in the course of time, our friendship grew to something more. I started to fall in love with her.

"It was imperfect timing. I was engaged to the other woman. Not a choice of my own accord as the relationship was prearranged and our parents were pushing for a wedding. My fiancée was also hasting to marry, yet I was starting to have doubts. The relationship I had with my fiancée was not the same as what I had with Anna. It was special, but not close. It was based on mutual attraction and approval, but nothing more.

"It was then I realized I had to make a choice. I either went on with the marriage to my fiancée or end the engagement and confess my love to Anna."

"I take it you ended your engagement." Emmerich smirked.

"I did," Aldaric said. "Though I think I made some enemies that day. My fiancée was very hurt and to this day I feel terrible for going along with the arrangement for too long before breaking it off. But it was Anna I wanted to be with because she wasn't just a potential lover. She was my best friend."

"So then you and Mom got engaged."

"Not at first." Aldaric chuckled as he rolled his eyes. "I confessed my feelings to her and she didn't know what to think. She wasn't sure about how she felt about me and things were awkward for a while. But we remained friends, and after a few years, she began to see me as I saw her. Our relationship never changed. It just got better. We still talked to each other. We still enjoyed the same activities. The only difference was we added a few things to our relationship, like holding each other's hand when we felt lonely or kissing each other after a bad day."

Aldaric stood beside Emmerich and put a warm hand on his shoulder. "The point I'm trying to make, Son, is that sometimes the best relationships start out as friendships. Don't think that your relationship will change or fall apart just because you're deciding how you feel about each other. Don't worry about the future because it'll work itself out."

"How did you know Mom was the one?" Emmerich asked.

Aldaric paused, exhaling slowly. "I didn't know for sure at first. I always thought my fiancée was the one," he said quietly. "Some people know right away, I suppose, but with your mother...I didn't know she was the one until a few years into our friendship. We were talking one day out by the island, and I mentioned something about running errands for the king. She looked at me so sad that day, and she told me how she thought it bothered me that the king made a difference between me and his other children. I had never told that to anyone, even my own mother, that the difference bothered me. But she saw it. It was like she could peak into my soul and know everything about me without hearing a word from my lips. That was when I knew she was the one for me."

"Do you think Antoinette is the one for me?" Emmerich asked.

Aldaric shrugged. "I can't answer that for you, Emery. Only you and God know the answer to that question."

Emmerich leaned back in his chair. For years he pondered the question, thinking he knew the answer until she chose Edward years ago. But now, after the breakup, he began to wonder again. "I..." He paused, wondering if he should say anything. Though he shared his feelings with his father often, it was still an embarrassing subject. Knowing Aldaric, however, Emmerich would never get any peace until he confessed. His father always did care about what his son was going through-an annoying trait, Emmerich often thought, but one he loved the most about his father.

"I think she's the one, Dad," Emmerich said quietly as he looked up. "For years I tried so hard to forget her. I could let her go, let her be happy with someone else...but no matter how hard I tried, I couldn't forget her."

"You must care for her a lot then," Aldaric replied. "I knew you cared, but I didn't know it was that deep."

"I love her, Dad. Ever since we were kids, I've loved her."

Aldaric gave his son a smile and stood to his feet. "I don't doubt you care, Emery. Though I'm unhappy with what Edward has done, I can't help but think Antoinette would be happy with you."

Emmerich smiled back. "I appreciate that."

"Just take it slow, Son," Aldaric warned. "Go by her timing. She needs to get over Edward before she can fully be involved with you, if that's what she chooses."

"I know." Emmerich nodded. "That's what she told me, too."

"And if things don't work out or she doesn't see you as more than a friend, do not take it to heart."

Emmerich frowned. He hoped, prayed even, that it would never be the case. Regardless, he accepted it before. He could accept it again-at least, he thought he could. "I know."

"But," Aldaric said as he headed to the door, "if it does work out, well...then I have something for you." He rushed out of the room and Emmerich sat up in his chair, listening intently to the sound of rummaging down the hall. What his father was doing, he didn't know, but after hearing a few bangs and the sound of a pile of *something* falling, he got up and headed to the door. Before he could leave the room, Aldaric reappeared, holding a small box in his hand.

"What is that?" Emmerich asked as Aldaric opened the box.

Inside was a small gold ring, three stones of blue topaz arranged together and shining in the sunlight from the window. Aldaric held it up for Emmerich to see, marveling at the beauty. "This," Aldaric began, "was your grandmother's wedding ring."

Emmerich was puzzled. "I thought Mom is wearing grandmother's wedding ring."

"She's wearing the ring the king gave her during their engagement," Aldaric said. "It was the ring she gave to Anna before she died. But she gave me this ring to save for you. She wanted you to have it when you were ready to get married."

Aldaric handed Emmerich the ring to study it. It was the most beautiful ring he had ever seen, small and simple as it was compared to his mother's. "Did the king give this to her?" Emmerich asked.

"No," Aldaric replied. "It was the ring my father gave to her." He took the ring back and placed it into the box, closing it and handing it back to his son. "Whether it's Antoinette or another woman you marry, this ring is for her. Take it; I think it's ready to go to you now."

Emmerich clasped the box in his hand. He wondered if the king knew about the ring-any items from the king's brother had been sold or lost, and Emery had no memory of his grandfather's possessions ever being given to anyone in the family. "Does the king know you have this?" Emmerich asked.

Aldaric shook his head. "Your grandmother pretended she lost it. She knew the king would not wish her to have it, but she kept it hidden and gave it to me before she died."

"I don't know what to say," Emmerich said, looking back at the box, its weight feeling worth more than gold. "Thank you, Dad. This means the world to me..."

"Keep it safe," Aldaric said. "And if you do give it to Antoinette, let's hope she likes blue."

Emmerich smiled as he embraced his father tightly.

Chapter 15: A Man Named Arnold

When Antoinette got the request to see her parents in the throne room, she couldn't help but feel relieved. Much time had passed since her return from Audlin, but every day had been filled with some sort of dread. When she wasn't crying over Edward, she was being questioned about what went wrong by the servants or nobles. When she wasn't being questioned, she was stuck hearing recommendations for a good replacement. So far she had received glowing reviews from ten nobles and a very confident baker, though most assumed she had her eyes on a mystery man who was the reason she "left" her fiancé.

She couldn't help but think Mother had a hand in that one—the new rumor that somehow managed to flutter about.

But the request to come to the throne room was different. It was requested by both parents, her mother *and* her father, and doubtless it was related to something other than Edward or a potential match. The last time her parents called her into the throne room was to have her represent the royal family at the opening of a new hospital. A trivial task for her parents, but a welcome one for her to get out and meet people.

Antoinette walked down the hallway excited, eager to see what busy assignment her parents had mustered for her to get her mind off of Edward. As she looked to her sister beside her, though, she found herself feeling alone in the excitement.

"We're doomed," Bernie repeated as she wrung her hands.

"What makes you say that?" Antoinette asked.

"We've both been called to the throne room. Both!"

"And that dooms us because…?"

"Because we're both in trouble!" Bernie whined. "I knew that stupid horse would get us caught!"

"Horse?" Antoinette asked, her brow going up. "What horse?"

"That endless-supply-of-horse-poop-horse, Waffles!" Bernie huffed. "You can't tell me Mother doesn't know Emmerich followed you here. I mean, you sang his praises in the Edellwood and you know how upset she got at that. I'm sure she knows you spent time with him and that I kept it quiet for you! Lord help us, she'll stick us in the stables for weeks for lying…"

"Mother doesn't know Emery was here, Bernie. She still thinks I just spoke to him in Audlin." Antoinette tried to hide her laughter but failed. "Besides, we kept Waffles very hidden and you'd never know he got sick in the orchard."

"That's because I cleaned it up!"

"Emery took care of the…mess…" Antoinette replied. "All you did was hide Waffles."

"But who do you think cleaned up the horse?" Bernie muttered. "Did you honestly think all that poop just came out in the orchard? I've seen baby diapers cleaner than that horse's butt!"

"Bernie…"

"Oh don't Bernie me!" she said. "I guarantee that's how Mother found out. I smelled like horse poop with a hint of apple for days! You can't tell me she didn't notice that!"

"She never said anything, and it's been how long since this has happened?"

Bernie frowned, her arms straight and tense at her sides. "One of the servants must've found out; I know it! You can only hide things from Mother for so long before she learns of it."

Antoinette could only chuckle in response.

As they approached the doorway to the throne room, they stopped in front of the guards. "Mother and Father are expecting us," Antoinette said as the guard bowed. "May we go in?"

"Of course, Your Majesties," the guard replied. "And...if I may be so bold...I offer my congratulations."

Antoinette nodded in thanks but found it odd she would be congratulated for something she knew nothing about. She gave a polite nod to the guard as Bernie looked at him quizzically. Perhaps the news from her parents would be good after all.

When the doors opened, Antoinette noticed that the throne room was fuller than expected. The king and queen sat on the throne in front of a great hearth, and beside them stood Antoinette's brothers Caspar and Robert. Next to the queen stood another young man whom Antoinette had only seen once before, in the Edellwood at the feast. He was tall, well-built and muscular like Edward, yet his hair was lighter and his eyes darker, and he had a face that looked lean and hungry.

How could she forget Arnold von Liegen? He was just as creepy now as he was when she met him. Only why was he there?

"Oh, this is bad," Bernie muttered under her breath as they approached the throne. The room was so quiet the girls could hear themselves breathe. "We're really in trouble for everyone to be here. I think Mother's going to exile us. I mean, I knew she liked that orchard, but not that much..."

"I don't think this is about Emery or the orchard, Bernie," Antoinette replied as they stopped in front of the king and queen. Arnold's eyes remained fixed onto hers, making her want to look away.

"You sent for me?" Antoinette asked after she and Bernie bowed.

The king nodded. "I did. Your mother and I wished to speak to you about an important matter."

"Bernette," Queen Susanna interrupted, pointing to an empty spot near the king. "Stand beside your brothers."

Bernie did as she was told, giving Antoinette a concerned glance.

"Is everything alright? Have I done something wrong?" Antoinette asked.

"You've done nothing wrong," the king replied warmly.

"In fact, this is a happy announcement," Susanna interrupted again. The king gave a quiet sigh as he resigned to let his wife do the talking. "After recent events regarding your former engagement to Prince Edward, your father and I thought it best to take matters into our own hands and find a suitable husband for you."

Antoinette's eyes widened. "I don't understand."

"You are royalty, child," Susanna continued, "and with that comes privileges, but it also comes with a set of rules. You must marry within the royal circle-up or not at all, as the old saying goes. There are very few princes your age and with Prince Edward gone astray your father and I have had to make special arrangements to ensure you are taken care of when we're gone. You must have a husband, and since you have been unable to procure one yourself, we have decided to find one for you."

Antoinette looked over to the young man standing beside her mother. Arnold gave her a smile, a smirk that was deciding whether it wanted to be flirty or a little more. She hurriedly looked away, having a terrible feeling the man wasn't just there for pleasantries.

"Are you arranging a marriage for me?" Antoinette asked, her voice harsher than intended, as she felt her pulse speed up.

"We are," Susanna said. "And we are here to introduce you to your husband-to-be. You remember Arnold, prince of our neighbors to the south in Liegen?" She gave a curt nod to the prince as he gave a bow. "He is the youngest of seven sons from the Liegen family and will be serving as your father's financial advisor here in Staalberg while we send over extra timber and carpenters to help with their town renovations. We and his parents met and sealed the arrangement over the weekend and all that is left is for you two to walk down the aisle and be married. The wedding shall be in a month...perhaps less, perhaps more...depending on how quickly we can get the prince moved in."

Antoinette's eyes widened in horror as she turned to Bernie. Her sister looked livid, furious, like a rabid animal ready to strike. Before Antoinette could offer a rebuttal, Bernie was already stepping before the queen and offering her opinion. "You can't do this!" Bernie raged as the queen glared at her. "You can't marry off Antoinette after she just got back! Can't you let her get over Edward first and then get to know this Arnold guy before getting married?"

"My Lady, if I may answer your concerns…" Arnold began, but as soon as he opened his mouth Bernie scrambled to overpower him.

"Don't butt in just yet, pretty boy!" Bernie seethed. "If you don't have any objections to this, then you're obviously only thinking about one thing!"

"BERNETTE!" The queen stood, motioning for a guard. One of them hurried from the door. "Young lady, your outbursts are improper and an embarrassment to the court! How dare you treat your brother-in-law with such contempt!"

"*He is not my brother-in-law!*" Bernie yelled, her face red with fury. "Not unless Antoinette chose this!"

The guard approached the queen and Susanna pointed to her youngest. "Take the princess to her room and see that she stays there until I am finished with this business." The guard took Bernie by the arm, leading her away from the throne. Bernie struggled to stay, but after a glare from the king and a pleading look from Antoinette, she relented. The queen returned to a relaxing pose on the throne, shaking her head as Bernie was led away. "I shall speak with her later. Why I have been cursed with a wolf for a daughter is beyond me!"

"Don't agree to this Antoinette!" Bernie shouted before the door closed. "You know this isn't what you want! You know this doesn't just hurt you…"

Before she could hear her sister's words finish, the door was shut, leaving Antoinette alone with her family.

"My apologies, Prince Arnold," Susanna replied as the prince shrugged with a humble smile. "I did not think my daughter would behave so rudely in front of you."

"Do not blame yourself, Your Majesty," Arnold replied as his eyes turned back to Antoinette. His stare was piercing, making Antoinette feel exposed in his presence. "It is why I chose your eldest. I know a lady when I see one."

The queen smiled. "And you chose well."

Everyone turned to Antoinette as she stood there, shocked. They stared at her with expectant eyes, wanting an answer, but she found herself at a loss for words. It was almost like reliving the nightmare of Edward returning with another woman. It was unexpected, an unplanned change that threatened to turn her world upside down.

But instead of losing the man she wanted, she was being given to a man she didn't know.

"Why wasn't I told about this sooner?" Antoinette asked slowly, her voice careful and precise. "It would have pleased me to have been included in this discussion."

"Oh child, brides are rarely included in such things as these." Susanna laughed, making Antoinette take each chuckle like nails on glass. "You were privileged to have searched for love, but like many you know, such searches rarely produce results. As a royal, you also understand that power must be balanced and maintained. That is why most royals marry other royals. We can't have paupers sitting on thrones, now, can we?"

Antoinette beaded her eyes. At least paupers knew what love was and celebrated it.

"I still should have been consulted," Antoinette replied quietly.

"And you are right now," Susanna said. "Come, admit it, Antoinette-look at the prince! Is he not handsome? Is he not regal? Is he not capable of providing for you and your future children?"

Antoinette turned to the prince. Though not as handsome as Edward, he had pleasant features, especially in his hair and figure. But his eyes showed something dark, deceptive...she couldn't quite figure it out, but something about him bothered her.

But how could she tell that to her family?

"With all due respect, Prince Arnold," Antoinette said, "but I have just ended an unpleasant relationship with the prince of Audlin. If you would but grant me time to grieve and get over him, I should feel more comfortable pursuing our own friendship in due time."

"But that is what marriage is for," Arnold interrupted, making Antoinette's heart sink. He stepped forward, approaching her hesitantly, almost as if every move was planned. He took her hand in his and held it as he inched closer. "We are both products of successful marriages, Your Majesty. Do you not think we could continue the tradition?"

"I...I don't know," Antoinette muttered, looking away. His hand felt like ice that burned her hand, but he didn't let go. She wanted to run.

"You are beautiful," he said, lifting her hand to his lips and kissing it. "And I daresay I shall make it my life's work to bring you happiness. Tell me, angel of the forest, what must I do to please you?"

He kept her hand at his lips, the kiss lingering to the point of making her look to her mother to pull him away. Her mother only smiled, enjoying the scene, her father and brothers showing the same support.

Antoinette wished Bernie was there to kick the prince for her.

She pulled her hand away. "I'm not sure..."

The prince grinned as he turned to the queen. "Your daughter has exceeded my expectations, Your Majesties. I daresay I have never eyed a beauty such as her in my homeland or abroad!"

"She is the most beautiful girl in Edeland," Susanna boasted, her back straightening in pride. "She will make a lovely wife for you."

"I know she will," Arnold replied.

The queen clapped in delight. "Then it is settled! Now Antoinette, if you'd like to..."

"May I speak with you, Mother?" Antoinette asked, meeting her glance. "In private?"

The queen paused for a moment before giving a nod. "Very well. Excuse me, gentleman, while my daughter and I discuss the wedding plans."

Antoinette did not wait for her mother as she stormed off past the door and into the hallway, Susanna trailing behind. When the queen caught up to her daughter, she found herself looking into the eyes of an Antoinette she rarely saw: the angry one, a face flushed and heart beating so loudly she could hear it.

"*What is this?*" she demanded.

The queen shrugged. "A marriage contract. What else?"

"I don't wish to be married to a man I don't like!"

"Well we can't have you running around like your sister," the queen huffed. "One spinster is already an embarrassment. I'm not about to have two. Besides, we've already discussed this!"

"But Mother, please." Antoinette bit her quivering lip as she looked away.

"Oh what, my daughter? Are you going to cry? Are you going to weep because the fairy tale you thought you had didn't come true?" The queen lowered her brow and turned Antoinette to face her. "This is a part of life, child-a part of royal life. Do you think I don't understand your hurt over Edward? Do you think I don't comprehend your worry of change and marrying a man you don't know? I was in your shoes once. I tried to marry for love only to find myself in love with a man who was far from good enough for me. I was fortunate to have parents that helped me see my childishness and they arranged the marriage with your father. And look at how happy I am! A throne, life and wealth and beauty…not to mention four children!"

"I don't want a throne, I don't want the wealth…" Antoinette felt tears stream down her cheek.

"Then why were you with Edward?" Susanna asked.

"Because he's a good man and…"

"*Was* a good man," Susanna corrected, and Antoinette nodded as more tears fell. "And look at how he deceived you! How he broke your heart. He was a waste of wanted fantasy, but Arnold…oh, Prince Arnold! He is a splendid match for you. He can offer you wealth and power and will doubtless provide you with children."

"Can I at least get to know him better? I don't want to marry someone I don't know well."

"That is what the marriage is for, child-to get to know your spouse."

"But..." Antoinette paused. She didn't want to mention Emery, didn't want her mother to punish her for lying and keeping her continuing friendship with him a secret. But she didn't want to marry Arnold von Liegen. Perhaps, if she dared to hope, she could appeal to her mother's reason. "Mother, I've already promised Emery..."

"Emmerich?" Susanna's face hardened and her voice lowered to a snarl. "What of *him*, child?"

"He...he cares for me," Antoinette stuttered. "We talked after Edward and I broke up and I thought perhaps, maybe in time, we could get closer and become more than friends, and..."

"*No!*" Susanna seethed, her voice firm. "Absolutely not! That is out of the question! Did you not hear me when I said a royal must marry another royal?"

"But his grandmother was the queen."

"HE IS NOT A ROYAL!" Susanna grabbed Antoinette's wrist, clutching it and making her cringe in pain. "You are *not* to see that boy, Antoinette! If I see him here I shall take matters into my own hands and make sure he never steps foot here again!" She pushed Antoinette's wrist away and faced her daughter with piercing eyes. "There is no more discussion on this, Antoinette. *You will not...EVER...enter a relationship with Emmerich van Ketten. You WILL go through with this arranged marriage and you WILL make yourself presentable to Prince Arnold.* You have already embarrassed your family enough with your failure to please Edward. Do not drive another potential mate away with your childish demands of love and attention!"

She stepped away as Antoinette stood in silence, her body shaking from nerves. "We will begin making wedding arrangements right away. I expect you to be fully compliant and not breathe a word of disagreement. If you do, do not think I will go easy on you. Now clean yourself up and present yourself to Prince Arnold once more! You two are to dine together this evening. Now go!"

Susanna left to return to the throne room, but Antoinette only leaned against the wall, sinking to the floor in a sob. The thought of marrying a man she didn't care for, trapped like an animal being sent away to a new owner, made her feel sick to the very core. She desperately prayed for comfort, wishing that Emmerich was not in Hugellia but in the hallway with her so she could feel his protective embrace.

But a part of her mind drifted back to Edward. She wished more than ever that he stayed faithful, that he never married Malina and never did what he did. If things had just gone the way she planned, her life would be so much better.

She cried bitter tears before making her way to the washroom.

Chapter 16: The Last Decree

Time passed with no word from the king regarding an heir. For a moment Edward wondered if his father changed his mind and decided to leave the throne to his son anyway. It was a foolish thought, one Edward doubted had any credibility, but it was the only explanation for the king's silence on the matter.

There were many cousins to choose from to succeed Arden as king, and off the top of Edward's head he could think of five good candidates alone in Hugellia. Unfortunately for Arden, the Engels were a much smaller family. Aside from Edward, there were no other surviving members. There were, however, plenty of van Kettens, and Edward didn't doubt a successor would be chosen from among their ranks.

A van Ketten on the throne of Audlin would also strengthen the alliance between Audlin and Hugellia, something Edward knew needed healing after the rift he caused only months before.

As he walked down the hallway of the palace taking in the sights, he found himself heading towards his father's throne room. Why, he wasn't sure, but the words his mother spoke to him before in the drawing room had resonated with him. He did have a choice now, to make things right and fix all that he had done wrong. After helping his mother manage the palace, he figured it was time for change. No more apathy. No more self-pity. It was now all about penance.

He stopped in front of the throne room, turning to one of the guards. "May I request permission to speak to my father?"

The guard gave him a puzzled look at first, and Edward knew he questioned why the prince of Audlin was asking permission to enter a throne that was already his. At least…it once was his. Doubtless Arden had kept quiet of his musings regarding his heir, and Edward didn't know whether to be grateful or concerned. The guard nodded, opening the door for him, and Edward stepped forward into the darkness of the throne room.

The room was empty; as Edward walked, he heard his footsteps echo around him. The king, busy looking at a stack of parchment with a scribe, didn't turn his head until Edward had stopped in front of him.

Arden looked up from his work, his face puzzled at meeting Edward's gaze. "What do you want?" he asked gruffly.

Edward bowed his head in respect. "I wanted to speak to you."

"About?"

"About your heir."

Arden turned to his scribe, giving him a nod in dismissal. The scribe hastened out of the room, carrying the stack of parchments with him. Arden returned to his seat, lounging onto the throne and resting his chin on his palm. "If you think I'm going to change my mind, I…"

"I'm not asking to be your heir," Edward interrupted, his head still bowed low. "I've given up that position and do not expect it to return. I do, however, wish to provide a suggestion as to who may be my replacement."

Arden remained quiet, searching Edward's face intently for a sign of deceit. Edward peaked up from his bowed head, looking for a chance to continue, and the king nodded, giving a wave of his hand. "Very well. Let's hear it."

"You've told me before that you wished me to be more like Stephen," Edward began, the thought of their previous conversation threatening to haunt his mind as he spoke. He suppressed the memory, unwilling to be brought down by it just yet. "You and I both agree that Stephen would've made the better king, but since he was taken from us, that is no longer an option."

Arden's face hardened at the mention of Stephen's death. Edward cleared his throat. "Since I have failed in my duty to live up to your expectations and have failed to fill the void that Stephen has left, I would like to suggest a candidate for the throne that will, and already has, been able to do what I could not."

Arden leaned forward. The sight made Edward glad his father was listening for once.

"Then who do you suggest?" Arden asked.

Edward swallowed hard. He had done much wrong in his life and had hurt many people. For once, he wanted to change that, and that started with the first person he ever hurt. "I'd like to suggest Emmerich van Ketten."

Arden's eyes widened for a moment, a look of surprise on his face. "And why do you suggest Emmerich?"

"He is knowledgeable in matters of state and has learned much from his father regarding international relations," Edward began. "He is already familiar to many of the ruling families we are allied with and is both wise and compassionate. He would rule this kingdom with the best of intentions and would do anything for their benefit. He would be selfless, just, kind, and worthy of the throne you could offer him. Has it not been said that Emmerich and Stephen were much alike?"

"It has..." Arden muttered.

"Then you cannot go wrong with choosing Emmerich. He may be young, but he is capable. You could even begin training him now to replace you so he is ready to ascend when you are gone."

Arden nodded to himself, stroking his chin as if in thought. Edward watched his reaction, hoping for a sign of approval, but his father's face remained unreadable. Edward sighed. "I...hope you consider my proposal, Father. Emmerich has been plagued with much unfairness in his past and I think that this is the first step of undoing all of that."

"Are you sure of your suggestion?" Arden asked, facing him.

"I am more than sure," Edward replied.

"You will make your mother a happy woman knowing she will be able to see her nephew more."

"I know."

"And I'm sure it will please you to see your cousin more, too."

"I doubt he would wish to speak with me," Edward replied sadly. He didn't forget the last conversation he had with Emmerich. Cold, angry, painful. That's why the request had to come from the king and not him. "Emmerich and I exchanged words after Antoinette left. He was unhappy with my treatment of her and does not wish to speak to me again."

"And rightly so," Arden said quietly.

Edward nodded. "I agree."

A moment of silence followed until Arden broke it with a sigh. "I will take your suggestion into consideration. Emmerich seems a fine choice for a king."

"He is more deserving of it than anyone I know," Edward replied as he bowed. Arden remained still as Edward straightened back up. "Thank you, Father, for hearing me. I shall take my leave of you."

He turned and left in silence as Arden watched him walk out the door.

When Edward walked into the throne room, Arden fully expected a plea. A plea of "Please, Father, don't give away my throne!" or "I've changed, Father-I'm now a worthy son!" But when Edward arrived looking haggard and worn, asking his father to consider Emmerich as his replacement, the king could do nothing but contemplate who the young man really was that stood before him.

The young man didn't beg to keep his throne, but agreed to give it away...to *Emmerich.*

Not that the kind Hugellian was a bad choice. Arden had thought long and hard over who would be a good replacement, and out of all the kin he and Maria had, Emmerich was considered the best choice. Edward was right-Emmerich was like Stephen. But the fact that Edward suggested it was what put the king at a loss.

Arden knew what Edward and Emmerich really thought of each other. They were friends as children, yes, but after a while they grew apart. Arden even wondered if they became enemies. It was obvious Emmerich had always fancied

Antoinette, and when Edward announced his courtship with the young maiden, Emmerich had all but shut himself away from the family, never speaking to Edward unless having to.

As for the fight between them after Edward's return from Verloris, Arden was familiar with what happened in the throne room. Did anyone think him blind of the happenings in his palace? He had heard Edward was hit by an angry Emmerich who held nothing back, giving the man such a bash that the guards began to wonder if the prince was as tough as they previously thought.

And yet after the betrayal, after the fighting, after every amount of proof the cousins would feel nothing but disdain for each other, Edward offered a suggestion: give Emmerich the throne.

Arden sighed, leaning back in his chair as he eyed the light coming from the fire in the hearth. Piles of papers and books were scattered around his study, mostly going unheeded save the piece of parchment that sat before him on the table.

He read the words on the top of the paper, intricately written in the finest of calligraphy.

The last decree of Arden Amadeus Engel VI, King of Audlin and ruler of the peoples therein, concerning his successor to the throne...

His eyes followed the rest of the paper, reading protocol and wording passed down from generations since the first king ascended the throne six hundred years prior. The decree was finished save for two spots meant for Arden's hand-the name of his successor and his signature at the bottom of the page.

Both currently remained blank.

He leaned back, giving off a sigh as the dimly lit room threatened him with fatigue. He wanted nothing more than to rest and let the decree write itself, but he knew an answer was needed. Before Edward arrived, choosing an heir was simple. After he arrived, however...the king felt conflicted.

He didn't think it would be hard to write his foolish son off the line of succession. Edward deserved it; nothing he did earned him the right to wear a crown.

Except what he did that morning.

Arden sighed, picking up the quill. He had to put a name on the parchment, had to choose an heir before anything could go further. He put the quill to the paper and drew an "E", but as he was making the "m", he stopped.

He's your son, Arden, Maria's voice repeated in his head.

He knew that. It's what made his decision so difficult.

He lowered the quill, making the ink slowly drip off the side. His head rested on his palm and he closed his eyes, thinking of better days in the past.

He remembered the day Edward was born. Maria had been in labor for hours, a delivery so painful the nurses thought she wouldn't make it through the birth. The queen pushed through, though, and their son was born. But when he came out, he was blue, the air having trouble meeting his lungs.

The king stayed up all night praying for his newborn son. Somehow, someway the boy survived, and the next morning he was as normal as any other child.

But he never forgot how close he was to losing his son when he had just arrived.

He remembered when Edward was a child in the middle of a jousting match. He and Stephen had come to watch and sat quietly in the stands. Stephen fiddled with a book, barely paying attention, but Arden was proud watching his youngest fight with the skill of a warrior. He had unhorsed men twice his size and had yet to be knocked down on his own.

But after the third match something happened. As he charged forward, the horse suddenly panicked and bucked, throwing Edward to the ground. Dust flew into the air and Arden stood to his feet, fearing the boy had been trampled.

He paid no heed as he ran onto the field, Stephen trailing behind alongside some guards. Arden was the first to reach Edward, and as he picked the boy up, holding him in his arms, he noticed his son's eyes were closed and his face was bloody.

Edward was dead, he thought. His son had just been killed in front of his very eyes.

It wasn't until Edward had coughed and regained consciousness that the king realized his son had lived. The boy had been trampled, but walked away with only a few bruises and a gash above his eye.

He was amazed Edward wanted to continue the joust after such a trauma. Most boys would have run away or have felt too afraid to continue, but Edward ran towards the danger, not away from it.

Arden never worried over a child so much in his life.

He remembered the day Stephen had died. He and Maria were in the dining room eating lunch when the guards came, panicked and stricken with dread. "Your son, oh king…" The guard had trouble speaking as he stifled a cry. "He is dead."

Maria began to weep as Arden froze. He knew it was Edward. Knew that it would be the boy who never feared death would be the first to face it. Had his son not trained every day in the fields for battle? He thought himself destined for a life as a knight and Arden worried that destiny might come true. He never wanted a son to die in battle...didn't want to see his son be taken like his brothers had, leaving him as the last Engel in the family line.

But when the guard said it was Stephen, that a blade had went through his chest while he was at the fields for his sword training, Arden froze. Dread washed over him as his firstborn was suddenly taken away, but a hint of relief came over him that it wasn't Edward who died.

He never felt so guilty in his life. His worry showed his favor, and now the son he never worried over was gone.

Years later and he still wondered if Stephen truly knew how much he cared.

Father-what a terrible title he had been given. The man who could govern a nation could not govern two children: one who was loved and one who was loved less, one who became penance for the one who was ignored.

Edward was never meant to be atonement for his failure with Stephen, yet somehow that was how it ended up.

And now Edward had to make his own atonement for the mistakes he had made.

Arden grasped the quill and finished writing Emmerich's name in the decree. As much as it pained him to remove Edward from the throne, to take away everything that was held so dear to him, it had to be done for punishment's sake. Edward might never forgive him for what he'd done, but as a king, Arden knew the nation came before family.

He wiped his eyes as a knock was heard at the door. A man appeared, carrying a tray with tea and some biscuits on a plate. "Forgive me for interrupting, Your Majesty," the servant said with a bow. "Your evening tea is here as requested."

The king waved his hand, motioning for the servant to come in. The young man set the tray down on the table, bowing again before heading to the door. The king thanked him, watching him leave, as he took a biscuit in his hand and nibbled on it.

He set the food down, not feeling hungry after his self-debate. He took a sip of the tea, making a face at its bitterness, wishing for wine instead. The tea was downed regardless, the king hoping the chamomile would calm his mind. If that failed, there was wine hidden in the pantry he could get after Maria fell asleep.

After finishing the tea, he took a last look at the decree. Emmerich's name was now on it, the king's signature being the final piece before the decree became law. The quill in his hand, Arden pointed the tip towards the signature line. He stayed his hand, still unwilling to write his son away.

He sighed as he stuffed the quill back into the ink bottle, rubbing his forehead and stifling a yawn. He was so, so tired, and the night was still late. Whether it was fatigue or the lack of desire to take away Edward's royal title, he no longer had the desire to finish the decree at the moment. He needed rest…wanted it…couldn't the decree wait until morning?

He sat there in the silence of the study, his eyes remaining on the decree. It was now or never-either it would be finished tonight or never at all.

He made his decision.

Chapter 17: A Departure Too Soon

"Edward?" Marcus Peterson lowered his bow and arrow away from the hay target in front of him, eyeing the approaching prince with a quizzical glance. "What brings you to the archery range this early in the morning? I thought you'd be assisting the queen in readying breakfast."

Edward trudged beside his friend, taking an extra bow and arrow set from the ground. "The servants don't need me," he said as he tested the bow's string. "They manage to ready every meal without my input. Not that they would ever need it, to be honest. I'm not sure I could boil water if asked."

"A culinary disaster like every other man in this place, no doubt." Marcus chuckled.

Edward smirked. "I don't know how the women do it." He fingered the arrow in his hands for a moment before putting it to the string. "Mind if I join you in your practice?"

Marcus stepped to the side to let Edward take a shot at the hay target. "I don't mind at all. It'd be nice to have the company."

"Thank you." Edward shot the arrow and it hit the target, right on the mark.

Marcus whistled. "I see you don't need any practice."

"I may not need it, but I should do it anyways. I'll be using these skills a lot more often now."

Marcus lowered his brow. "Why is that? Is the king moving you to other duties?"

Edward restrung the bow. "You could say that."

"Well it'll be a pleasure to have you with us in the knighthood," Marcus said. "Though I'm afraid to know the reason behind this. Are the Braideners attacking our outposts again? Or is it the mountain lions becoming a nuisance in the southern villages?"

"Neither," Edward replied as he shot another arrow, the hay being hit just offside the target. "In fact, there are no wars at the moment, but the king will be moving me to other duties. I am to join the royal guard."

Marcus rubbed his forehead, making a face. "Why would you be a part of your own guard? We're supposed to protect you, not the other way around."

"You needn't be protecting me anymore."

Marcus' face paled as he realized what Edward was trying to say. His lips sunk and he found himself giving a slight gasp in surprise. "The king…" he muttered. "The king is removing you from the throne?"

Edward nodded as he strung a third arrow.

"But why?"

"Why wouldn't he?" Edward asked as he lowered the bow. "No one wants a fool for a king, Marcus. Not you, not him, not anyone."

Marcus tightened his lips into a frown. "You aren't a fool, Edward."

"But I have done foolish things. Is there a difference?"

"A fool who learns from his foolishness becomes wise," Marcus replied. "Isn't that a proverb we hear as children?"

"We may hear it, but since when does anyone take proverbs to heart?" Edward asked as he lifted the bow and shot it towards the target. It missed completely and landed in the grass. "Besides, it isn't like this is coming as a surprise. I'm in full support of my father's decision."

"But Edward…"

"No," Edward said as he turned to his friend. "Don't question me or him on this, Marcus. The throne needs to go to someone who deserves it, and I am far from worthy of the crown or the chair."

Marcus looked away in frustration. "Did the king say who will replace him?"

"I suggested my cousin Emmerich. Whether he listens to me is unknown, but I think he and my mother would be supportive of him."

"Emmerich?" Marcus asked. "The cousin from Hugellia?"

"Yes."

Marcus couldn't deny that Emmerich would be a fine choice. If the boy was half like his father, Aldaric, the kingdom would be in wise hands, indeed. "Does Emmerich know you suggested him?"

"No," Edward replied. "I'm saying nothing until the king announces it, with the exception of my conversation with you." He paused, giving a scoff. "Don't say anything just in case I'm wrong, though. My father may choose someone completely different, and I'd hate to give my cousin another reason to loathe me."

Marcus remained quiet as he crossed his arms. He figured there was a rift between the cousins, but found it best to not expand on it just yet. Edward had enough on his mind and didn't need reminding how many people despised him. "Are you sure you're alright with this?" Marcus asked after a pause. "Are you sure you're alright with the king handing the throne to someone else?"

"It doesn't matter what I think." Edward sighed. "It only matters what I do. I have to start making things right after all I've done. This is just one way to do that."

Marcus nodded, knowing he couldn't argue with that logic. "What of Malina? I can't see her taking this lightly."

"She's barely spoken to me since learning of this," Edward said. "She's upset, but this is something she'll have to get used to."

"I don't think that'll be easy for her."

Edward frowned. "I don't think it will either, and that's what I'm afraid of."

"Fret not, my friend," Marcus said as he clasped the prince's shoulder. "No matter what happens, I am here for you. I will make sure your transition into the guard is as easy as can be and I will assist you in any way I can that will help Malina cope with her new role."

Edward smiled, giving him a nod in thanks. "I appreciate that, Marcus. You don't know how…"

Before he could finish the sentence, a yell from the distance interrupted him. "*Your Majesty!*" the call from a young page boy running from the palace cried. Edward turned, stepping forward as he watched the boy in concern. He was frantic, his face red and beading with sweat yet his eyes bulging as if witnessing a monster come out from under his bed. The boy ran so fast he could barely stop, practically crashing into the prince as he arrived. Edward steadied the boy, bending down to his level so he could see him.

"What's wrong?" Edward asked, feeling the boy shake from underneath his grasp. "You look terrified! Has something happened?"

"The king!" the boy stuttered through tears. "The king! Something's wrong!"

Edward felt a lump come in his throat, a sick feeling developing in his stomach and churning worry in his gut. "Tell me what's happened. Where is the king now?"

"In his bedroom," the boy replied. He wiped his face with his sleeve and sniffled. "He can't speak or move. Some doubt he can even see! It's as if his body has decided not to work anymore."

Edward released the boy from his grasp and found himself shaking more than the page. It took him a moment to process what was happening. His father-he had seen him the night before, well and like himself as if nothing was amiss. What could have happened to make the king change so suddenly?

Edward found himself running towards the palace, the bow and arrow flying from his hands to the ground. His mind was racing as fast as his heart, and all he could think of was one thing.

His father was about to die, and if he did, that would make Edward king and Malina queen if there was no decree.

Please, God...don't let my father die.

The sound of wailing was what Edward noticed first when he approached his father's room. Maria stood by the bedside, still in her night gown and her hair unkempt, holding her husband's hand in vigil and praying out loud for a miracle. A few of the servants stood in the back of the room with their heads bowed, and a physician was in the corner going through his bag of medicines to see if there was anything that could be done for the king.

When Edward arrived, he wasn't sure what to expect. Maybe his father was ill, maybe he was simply weak and dehydrated from working too much. It wasn't like it didn't happen before. The king was once bedridden for two weeks because of exhaustion. But when Edward glanced upon his father's face as the man lay still upon the bed, he knew something was different. Something was wrong.

The king's face was pale and clammy as if life had been sucked from his skin. His eyes were glassy, unseeing, and his lips were blue from lack of air. He made muffled wheezing sounds as he breathed, but any noise that came from his voice was jumbled and incoherent like a baby learning how to talk. The king didn't move or stir, nor did he make attempt to, and when Edward came over to his side, the king barely noticed his presence.

"What happened?" Edward asked, his voice catching as he looked to his mother.

Maria's eyes were swollen and red where tears had been streaming since waking. "I turned to rouse him and he didn't stir. I shook him and his eyes opened, but all he could do was...this..." She pressed her quivering lips together and closed her eyes, desperate to remain in control of her emotions.

Edward put his hand on his mother's, giving it a gentle squeeze. "Was there any sign of something wrong? Anything out of the ordinary before he went to bed last night?"

"Nothing," Maria said. "He was a little tired, but there was nothing unusual. It wasn't until this morning when I awoke."

Edward turned to the doctor who stood in front of the king, listening to his heartbeat. "What do you think it is?" he asked.

The doctor shrugged. "I believe it to be a stroke," he began. "At least, many of the symptoms are there...but I've rarely seen a stroke paralyze both sides."

Edward watched as the doctor looked as confused as the rest of them, desperate to seem like the answer was obvious but knowing it was anyone's guess as to what happened to the king.

He turned back to his mother. "What was he doing last night? Anything strenuous, anything that may have caused stress?"

"He was in his study," Maria replied. "Working, I suppose. Perhaps going over paperwork."

She gave him a look as if there was something more, yet not wishing to speak it aloud. Edward knew that could only mean one thing: the decree.

He mouthed the answer to her and she nodded in agreement. So the king had been working on writing it into law as to who his successor would be. Doubtless it would be finished, as the king never left a work undone, and Edward found himself feeling sick. If his cousin was chosen, Emmerich would be called to lead a nation right away without training. What hurt Edward the most wasn't that Emmerich would be coming into the kingship unprepared, but that whatever had happened to the king happened because he was stressed about the decree.

At least that's what Edward told himself.

It was only a minute after Edward's arrival that Malina came, her belly swollen to the point of nearing birth. She looked to Maria and the king with sad eyes, but as she looked to Edward he could see the hint of a smile. Doubtless she would be happy that the king was dying and thinking herself inheriting a throne by nightfall. Little did she know the king finished the decree sooner than planned.

She asked what had happened and Edward repeated what Maria and the doctor had said. Malina stood beside him, her hands reaching for his and holding it with the warmth of a wife. Her touch felt cold to him, however. She was not mourning, nor would she ever mourn.

He watched in silence as his father slowly began to slip away.

It was around noon when the king's body began to shut down. Malina watched as Maria began to sob, pleading with her husband not to go and to stay with her just a little while longer.

The scene made her want to laugh. *As if he has the choice to stay.*

Malina turned to her husband and watched as Edward got up from the bed and stood in a corner, allowing Maria to be the first to say her good-byes. Edward had said little once Malina arrived and she followed him to the corner, curious as to what he was thinking watching the father who bothered him suddenly be taken away.

She figured he would be glad to be rid of the man who caused him so much grief in his past, but to her surprise, he looked troubled.

"You have been quiet, Edward," she whispered to him as they watched Maria caress her husband's face. "Methinks seeing your father getting what he deserves actually bothers you."

"He doesn't deserve this," Edward muttered as his eyes remained on his mother.

"You don't think so?" Malina asked. "He insults you, degrades you, humiliates you in front of the nation, and threatens to take away your throne. Do you not think he deserves such a fate?"

"Tell me, Malina. What do you think of your own father back in Verloris?"

Malina rolled her eyes. "He is a fool. He gives my sister a crown when he should've given it to me."

"And even though you think so lowly of him and know he has his faults, you still honor him?"

"As long as it suits me."

Edward turned to her, and for a moment she saw a deep hurt in his eyes. She couldn't help but think at what a weakling he was that he could show his emotions so easily. "My father and I may not have been on the best of terms, but as I see him like this I can't help but pity him. No one should have to leave this earth in such a state. No one."

"Except maybe someone who deserves it," Malina said as she leaned in to him. "Like yourself."

Edward said nothing as he lowered his brow, looking back to his parents.

Malina watched as Maria motioned for Edward and Malina to come say their good-byes. The couple approached the king, watching as his breathing was very raspy and shallow, his eyes staring off into the distance. Edward bent down and was the first to speak, taking Arden's hand in his and clasping it gently. The king did not move, though his eyes wandered, trying to find Edward's voice.

"I'm sorry," Edward said quietly as he leaned in towards his father. Malina watched as Edward's expression lowered, his face showing grief. She had to bite her lip hard to keep from laughing. "This is my fault, all the pain I've caused you and Mother." Edward paused, sniffling. "I didn't mean to be such a terrible son to you. Forgive me for being so foolish."

The king made a noise, almost like a groan, as his eyes found his son's voice. Edward met his gaze and watched as the king's expression changed from pain to hurt, and Edward held the king's hand to his lips and kissed it. "When you see Stephen..." He paused again, swallowing hard. "Tell him I'm sorry, too. I...I love you, Father."

The king made another groan, this time weaker. His breathing became shallower. His eyes were barely able to stay open. His time was almost spent.

"Let me say farewell," Malina said as she put her hand on Edward's shoulder. Edward looked up, puzzled, but nodded as she gave him her best attempt at a comforting smile. He stood and allowed her to lean in to the king, and she put her hand to his cheek gently.

"My dear king," she began as she came close to his ear, "it saddens me that I shan't have any more time with you." She eyed Edward warmly before turning back to the king. 'I promise to take care of your son," she said as she kissed his cheek. He made no noise as she moved towards his ear, whispering so only he could hear. "Just as I took care of you. Don't worry. You won't be separated long."

He made a groan but he was too weak to do anything else. Malina pouted, caressing his cheek as she stood, pretending to wipe away tears though none came. "Poor darling," she whimpered as she walked past Edward and Maria and made her way to the corner. "Such a shame this has all happened so suddenly!"

She listened as the sounds that came from the king were like struggles, as if he were fighting death for the chance to live just a little longer. It was a pathetic attempt, yet Malina held some respect for the dying king to be fighting with his last breaths. She turned from the corner and watched as he writhed before giving up, and as he breathed his last, his eyes met hers and she gave him a smile.

Within minutes the king was gone, leaving the cries of the queen the only sound in the room.

Chapter 18: The Next King of Audlin

It was late in the evening when Edward was sitting alone in his study, the warmth of candles and lanterns driving away the coldness of the room. He sat on his sofa, his chin resting on his palms and his mind lost in thought over the events of the day.

His father was dead. No longer breathing, no longer living, no longer seeing. Arden VI was gone and never coming back again.

Edward didn't know how to comprehend it all.

Just a day ago he had seen his father working. Everything was normal and the king showed no signs of illness or being weak. Night fell and the king had went to rest as usual only to wake a paralyzed man whose organs began to shut down one by one. Now that the king was gone, Edward had to realize he would no longer see his father until death came for himself.

It was a bittersweet thought for him. Bitter in the fact that deep down Edward truly did love his father and was desperate to please him, yet sweet knowing he would never again have to worry about shaming his father and seeing the look of disappointment on his face.

Now, Arden was with his favorite son. Now, the king could finally be at peace.

Now he knows the truth of what happened, Edward thought grimly. *I hope they both can forgive me.*

He sighed as he rubbed his eyes, wanting nothing more than sleep.

A knock at the door was heard. Edward sat up in anticipation, curious who would be up at so late an hour. "Who is it?" he asked, and he heard a muffled response.

"It's your mother, Dear."

Edward rushed to the door and opened it. Normally he would tell people to leave him alone for privacy, but after the day's events he was more than willing to make an exception for his mother.

She came into the room, now dressed in black yet still showing signs of weeping, and embraced her son. Edward held her close, rubbing her back as she clung to him. "Everyone's looking for you." Her voice was so weak and hoarse that it broke his heart. "You're needed in the throne room."

"Why?" he asked.

She pulled away from him and looked into his eyes. "They are going to crown the new king."

Edward felt confused. "How can they do that? Surely they could not have notified Emmerich in a few hours."

"Emmerich isn't being crowned," Maria replied. "It's you."

Edward's eyes widened. *What?*

Edward felt a sinking feeling in his stomach. He wasn't supposed to become king and was never meant for it. "I thought father finished the decree." Edward found himself stuttering, the shock overtaking his speech. "It was supposed…I mean, I thought…wasn't he making Emmerich king?"

"The decree was never finished," Maria said, bowing her head.

"But who is on the parchment? What name is there to succeed father on the throne?"

Maria looked up. "I have not seen it and therefore do not know. The king mentioned something about Emmerich, however."

"Then why isn't Emmerich becoming king?"

"The king never signed the decree."

Edward felt frustrated. The decree was so close to being finished; what madness overtook the king that he would leave his own law unfinished? "A signature shouldn't matter if Emmerich's name is on the decree," Edward said. "I still don't understand why the crown is going to me."

"Tradition states that if a decree is not finished, then it is not valid," Maria replied. "After Stephen's death, the crown went to you by default and that has not changed."

Edward flung himself back onto the sofa and lowered his head, burying it into the comfort of his hands. "Why did he not sign it?" Edward muttered. "Father never lets a law lay unfinished."

Maria followed him to the couch, sitting beside him. "Some laws are tougher to write than others."

"This one should've been easy, though."

Maria put her hand on Edward's back. "It wasn't for him." Her lip quivered and tears began to streak down her face.

"Before he woke up in his...state...we talked before going to bed last night."

Edward looked up. "About what?"

"You."

Edward frowned. It didn't please him to know his father's last coherent words were talking about his failure of a son.

Edward swallowed, his eyes darting back to the floor. "What did he say?"

"He talked about the decree," Maria began. "It was difficult for him to sign away your right to the throne. He was...wrestling with the decision. He wanted to show he didn't approve of your past behavior, yet at the same time he didn't want to make you think he no longer loved you."

Edward turned to his mother. This was...unexpected.

"Arden was so distraught over the matter," Maria continued. "He said he didn't even want to deal with it and wanted it all forgotten but knew something had to be done. So he let it go."

"Let it go?" Edward asked.

"He said he refused to sign the decree and burned what he had already written," Maria continued, giving her son a gentle hug. "He wasn't happy with what you did, but more than that, he wanted to give you a second chance because he believed in you."

Edward felt his lip quiver. "He said that?"

Maria nodded, forcing her smile up through her tears. "Yes."

"But...I thought...I mean, he never cared, he..."

Maria put her hand to Edward's cheek. "Your father loved you. He always has. Just because he didn't know how to show it all the time didn't mean his feelings changed."

Edward exhaled slowly as he sat up. "So…he wanted me to be king after him?"

"That's right."

"And I'm king now?"

"After the bishop crowns you, but yes…you are king now."

Edward felt proud yet terrified at the same time. His palms became sweaty and his heart started to flutter. His stomach flipped in sickness. "I'm not sure if I can do this, Mother."

"Your father believed in you," Maria said as she pushed a few strands of hair off his face. "And so do I."

She stood to her feet, offering her hand. "Not everyone gets a second chance at life, Edward. You have made mistakes in the past, but you must now learn from them. Prove to everyone that you are a good son by honoring your father's wishes. Prove to everyone that you can be a good king."

Her hand remained still as it was held out to him. "Will you not trust your mother in supporting her son?"

Edward paused before taking her hand and standing to his feet. "Do you really think I can do this?"

Maria gave his hand a squeeze. "I know you can."

He pulled her into an unexpected embrace, hugging her tight and kissing her cheek. "Thank you," he said quietly as he held her in the darkness. "I…I'm still unsure if I can do this, but I'm going to try. I want to make you and Father proud."

"And you will," she said, her voice catching.

He followed her down to the throne room, still holding onto her hand like he did when still a child. He was scared. He was terrified. He was so sure he could not fulfill his duties as a king.

But if his father believed in him, giving up a decree he knew to be wise, then maybe he could start believing in himself.

Maria had never cried so hard in her life.

Her tears came out as sobs, and she clutched her husband's pillow from their bed. She pressed the fabric to her face as it caught her tears, and every time she breathed in she could still smell the cologne he wore every day. The floor was where she rested, the hearth her only company, and she sat amidst a pile of sheets, crying the night away.

Her husband wasn't supposed to die like this.

She could still see the terror in his eyes when she woke up beside him and he realized he couldn't answer her when she called. The vision haunted her, filling her waking hours with nightmares that refused to leave, and she prayed desperately to forget the events of the morning. It all happened so suddenly...so fast. She didn't see it coming until it was too late.

I'm so sorry...I'm so sorry...

Sorry she was unable to be strong as every tear that was held back during Edward's coronation now flooded freely when she was alone. Sorry she wasn't more prepared for her husband's departure and couldn't handle life without her other half.

Sorry that the last words they spoke to each other were from a fight and they never did get a chance to make up.

But there was something she wasn't sorry for, something that she knew he'd be angry with; but there were some things that were more important than the wishes of a dying man.

She pulled the decree from her sleeve, carefully folded so as to remain hidden. She undid the edges and opened it up, reading the last words her husband ever wrote.

I, Arden VI, King of Audlin, declare that Emmerich Matthias van Ketten of Hugellia, son of Aldaric and Anna van Ketten, will become king in my place at the event of my death or departure.

She paused from her reading, remembering the last night with her husband.

"Where were you?" she asked as she rested on the bed, lowering the book in her hand. Arden had walked in looking tired and worn. He shrugged as he removed his tunic and changed into his nightclothes.

"Working," he muttered.

"Working on what?" Maria asked.

"Work."

She didn't like that answer. Never mind that she heard about Edward asking her husband to put Emmerich on the throne instead of him. Never mind that Arden had been avoiding her as if she was a plague since he and his son talked.

"Is it done?" she asked.

He looked up as he put on a nightshirt. "What?"

Did he really take her as a fool? Then he was one. "The decree."

He gave a sigh as he looked away from her piercing gaze. "Yes. It's finished."

"And what does it say?"

"The throne will go to Emmerich."

There was a pause as her face hardened. "Arden, how could you?"

He shook his head. "I'm not in the mood, Maria."

She threw the book onto the bed and lurched forward towards him. "But he's your son, Arden! He's done wrong, but can you not have mercy?"

"There is no mercy with a grown man," Arden replied. "This is his punishment. If he could not handle his responsibilities as a prince, then he cannot handle them as king!"

"Stop looking at him as a royal charge!" Maria's voice rose. "You do nothing but punish and scold him, yet when have you told him you loved him? When have you told him he made you proud?"

Arden scoffed. "I've told him plenty of times!"

"Name one time."

Arden threw his hands up in frustration. His face began to turn red and he sweated, but Maria ignored it. *Let his blood pressure make him look like a burning tomato for all she cared. Let him get a headache so he could have a miserable night's sleep.*

"Edward thinks you do not love him, Arden," Maria said as she put her hand to her forehead. "Sometimes I wonder if it's *true. Do you not think he has been punished enough with the wife he is now forced to deal with? Must you take away his purpose, too?"*

"He will never learn otherwise."

"Not unless you teach him! Have you ever even listened to him? He wants to do what is right but feels..."

Arden gave her a glare that made her fill with rage. "You make me ill with your nagging, woman! Can you not see I find no pleasure in ending my own line and giving it to another? Yet do you not know I must think for my country and give them a king they deserve?"

He calmed as he saw her look at him with teary eyes, and he shook his head as he got into the bed. "I am done discussing this," he muttered as he pulled the covers over himself. "Tomorrow morning I will take the decree from my office and announce it to the House of Nobles and there will be no change. It is my wish for Emmerich to have the throne, sorry as Edward may be. It is Emmerich who is worthy of the throne and it is Emmerich who is worthy of my legacy. Edward is worthy of none, yet it is my hope that by losing everything he will finally gain the wisdom he needs to live out the rest of his life in peace. Now leave me be, for I am feeling ill. All I want to do is sleep."

Those were the last words, and the memory only filled her with bitterness.

Minutes after the king was pronounced dead, she ran to his study and searched for the decree. She had not planned on going against her husband, nor had she planned on defying his wishes, but she was not one to waste an opportunity only fate could give. Though the deception pained her, she refused to let Edward lose his inheritance, his purpose. She took the decree before Arden's work could be gathered and processed.

Now, as she held the decree in her hand, she studied it one last time.

The king's signature was signed neatly at the bottom, the wax of his seal firmly pressed into the parchment. It was the king's final decree that Emmerich van Ketten would have the throne of Audlin. What she held in her hand was law. Yet though she loved her nephew deeply and knew him to be the better man, she loved her son more. And she would not let her son be denied the throne when she could ensure it.

She took the decree in her hands and threw it into the fire, the parchment and all its words slowly burning away into ashes.

Only she and the king knew of the decree's finality. Only she knew the king's last words refusing to let Edward have the throne. But as her husband went to the grave, so she would take his secret with her in time.

"Forgive me, my sweet Arden," she whispered as tears rolled down her cheek. "But this is one wish I will not honor for you."

She watched as the parchment slowly burned away into the night.

"Is it done?" Vacius asked as he faced Malina in the darkness.

The jewels of her new crown glittered in the moonlight. "I am a queen now. I told you I have it all under control."

Vacius grumbled as he faced the sky. "Your 'control' may endanger us if you aren't careful. Are you sure no one has suspected you?"

"Me? Have I done anything wrong? All I am is a simple mother-to-be caring for her unborn child." Malina smiled as she picked up her cup of tea and took a sip. "You act as if I'm a silly girl."

"Everything must fall into place. We cannot afford another close call like this," Vacius replied. "Are you sure the king did not have a decree?"

"There is none. Edward was crowned this evening alongside with me. He is now king."

Vacius narrowed his eyes. "And how long will Edward be king?"

"Relax." Malina gave a laugh. "All in due time, my dear Vacius. You must not rush these things. People will begin to suspect something if the son dies too close to the father."

"Edward will limit your power. He does not trust you."

"And yet who controls him? Me. Worry not, oh Velori. Everything is going as planned. For now, let us celebrate at yet another *coincidental* victory." Malina snickered as she lifted another tea cup and offered it to Vacius. "Chamomile? I promise it's the good kind."

Vacius took the cup and poured the tea onto the ground.

Chapter 19: The Friend or the Stranger

Bernie barely slept through the night.

The events that happened since arriving back in Staalberg had been like waves on the water, up and down to the point of making her sick. One minute things were looking better and the next minute Mother nuzzled into everyone's business and started taking control of Antoinette's life.

Bernie huffed in frustration as she stared at the ceiling. Leave it to Mother to pounce on a rebound while the daughter had sense.

The arranged marriage had to be stopped. Never mind that Mother had already started making plans and telling everyone in the town about it. Antoinette didn't want to marry Prince I'm-Greater-Than-Greatness-Itself, and Bernie didn't want her to marry him, either.

She had to come up with a plan-a plan to stop the wedding and keep Antoinette with her for just a little while longer.

She forced herself from the bed, squinting as the sunlight from the window hit her face. It was difficult to move at first as she slid her legs and touched the floor with her feet. She glanced at her pillow, strands of brown hair covering the case, and she forced herself to look away. Her hair was falling out so fast she stopped counting the strings she found on her bed and clothes. It was better not to know how much she lost, so she stood and put a night cap on, dressing quickly to go to her sister's room.

When she arrived, she found Antoinette sitting at a desk and overlooking a letter. Sleep had apparently evaded her, too. Her furniture was still being delivered back from Reigal and the room was bare, but otherwise things were starting to look like they had before the engagement. When Bernie walked in, Antoinette turned, putting the letter down.

She frowned at seeing Bernie's appearance. "You look terrible."

Bernie shrugged. "I'm fine."

"Are you feeling alright?"

"As well as usual."

"You look tired."

She felt tired. Felt more tired than she had in a long time. "I'm fine. How are you doing, though? With the...engagement and all?"

Antoinette looked back to the letters. "I've been better."

Bernie stepped forward, pulling up a chair and sitting to face her. She turned to the letters, giving a nod. "Wedding plans? Or are these love letters from 'Arnold I-Am-The-Greatest-Man-Alive'?"

"Neither," Antoinette said as she placed the letter gently on the desk, smoothing it. "It's from Emery."

Bernie frowned. If Antoinette was upset about the arranged marriage, doubtless Emmerich would be furious. "What's he saying? Have you told him about the marriage?"

"I just got this letter from him yesterday. He was letting me know how things were in Hugellia. He wanted to know how I was doing," she said, her fingers brushing over the words. "I haven't sent a reply yet. I'm...I'm not sure what to say without it sounding...morbid."

"What do you want to say?"

"I'm sorry." Antoinette sighed. "What else is there? 'I'm sorry for breaking your heart', 'I'm sorry my mother got in the way', 'I'm sorry you hoped for nothing'?" She leaned back in her chair and rubbed her brow. "'I'm sorry we didn't get a chance to try'?" She paused as she gave a scoff. "It figures, doesn't it? I was at my lowest point and I thought maybe, *just maybe*, things would get better. And then just as I was starting to have hope again, it gets dashed by this horrid marriage!"

Bernette stayed silent as she watched her sister in pity.

"I don't know what to do," Antoinette continued. "I don't want to go through this marriage. I just...I can't. Mother may be content with the idea of me marrying a fool and so may every other royal, but I don't want to be like everyone else. I want to live my life the way I want to live it. If Arnold was a good man, I'd have no issue, but he's not! I've heard so many rumors."

"I have, too. Apparently he's had more lovers than I've had books, and that's saying something. I say you should just tell him off and leave him at the altar."

Antoinette frowned. "If only it were that simple. I can't just get up and leave."

"Why can't you?"

"Because of expectations," Antoinette replied. "I'm the eldest, Bernie. I have to set the example of what it means to be the respective child in this family. But more than that, I have a responsibility to the crown. I may not wear it like our brother will one day, but I'm still bound to it. If the king and queen say I need to marry Arnold, who am I to go against that and disobey?"

Bernie looked away, knowing the truth in Antoinette's words. It was one of the curses of being a princess. Life wasn't something you planned. It was something that was planned for you.

"I didn't want this," Antoinette said as she put her head to her hands, sniffling. "Why couldn't Edward have just kept things the way they were? I wouldn't have to worry about an arranged marriage. I wouldn't have to worry about leaving you."

Bernie watched as tears fell from Antoinette's cheeks and onto Emmerich's letter beneath her chin. Guilt crept upon her, thinking back to when she forged the note to Emmerich to break Antoinette's engagement with Edward just so she could have more time with her sister. She wished she never sent that letter. "I'm sorry," she muttered as she laid her head on Antoinette's shoulder, wrapping her arms around her. "I'm sorry this happened to you. I'm sorry."

"It's not your fault," Antoinette said, lifting her head and giving her a hug back.

The words held greater meaning than what her sister realized. Bernie felt like it was her fault to a certain extent. Grant it, she didn't know Edward would walk out on his fiancée, but she wanted the engagement to end so she could have her sister back. Now that it came to pass, she was about to lose her sister all over again, this time to a man she didn't like. "It isn't my fault, but yet…it is." Bernie held her sister tight, never wanting to let go. "I have a confession, Antoinette."

"What is it?"

"Do you remember the note that Emmerich got that brought him to Reigal?" she asked. Bernie paused, biting her lip. She didn't want to confess, but her sister had to know the truth. "It was me. I sent the note because I thought it would delay the wedding. I didn't want you to get hurt, but I didn't want to lose you yet, either. I'm sorry...I didn't know it would be this bad, I..."

Bernie paused, refusing to cry. She was proud in the fact she could hide her emotions...sometimes...and she wasn't about to show them now. But her lip quivered and her eyes became watery, regardless. She couldn't help but show a little of what she was feeling. "I'm sorry, Antoinette. If I could go back and stop myself from sending that letter, I would."

Antoinette was quiet for a moment, but then patted her sister's hand gently. "I wondered if it was you. Emmerich wasn't convinced, but...I wondered if it was you."

"I'm so sorry, Antoinette."

"I know," Antoinette replied, turning and hugging her sister again. "I know you didn't mean anything by it. In a way, I'm sort of glad you sent it. I'm glad Emery was there when Edward came back. If he wasn't there, things would have been a lot more difficult."

"I promise I'll help you fix this," Bernie said, pulling away. "I'm not about to let you go to that jerk. If I have to lock Arnold in a closet, I will."

"You'll only be delaying the inevitable." Antoinette sighed. "I'm stuck, Bernie. Unless I find someone else to marry, I'm stuck."

And that's when it hit her. An idea came into Bernie's mind and she couldn't help but share it. "What about Emmerich?"

"Emery?" Antoinette asked. "Bernie, I couldn't do that to him! He would think himself a rebound off of Edward if I approached him with marriage."

Bernie rolled her eyes. "It's not like he'd object! Besides, who'd you rather marry? Your best friend you've known since childhood or some creepy guy you just met?"

"I'd rather marry Emery, but I could never throw such a commitment on him so soon!"

"Then don't marry him; just pretend!"

"I can't keep a lie like that going. You know King Erick and Father are friends. If there isn't a marriage, the king will send me right back!"

"Antoinette, you can't keep making excuses," Bernie said. "I know this isn't what you've planned, but these are your options. Either marry Arnold or ask Emmerich. Unless you want to see if you can become a servant and support yourself."

"Mother won't let that happen."

"Then you have to marry."

"She won't approve of Emmerich. It'll only cause trouble for him, and I doubt he wants to deal with that."

"You're getting married in two weeks unless you do something!" Bernie exclaimed. "Emmerich will stand by you, Antoinette, but none of it matters unless you make a choice. Are you going to live your own life, or are you going to let Mother live it for you?"

The door knocked and immediately both girls became quiet as they sat in their seats, their backs straight and hands folded. The door opened and in walked their mother, her face looking frustrated.

"Ladies, I'm afraid we must pause from our planning of the wedding," Susanna began as she stepped into the room. "We've just gotten word from Queen Maria in Reigal. King Arden has had a stroke and died."

"Died?" Antoinette's eyes widened as she stood to her feet. "When did this happen?"

"Four days ago," Susanna replied. Her face frowned further. "We are to attend the funeral."

Antoinette eyed Bernie, her expression sorrowful. Though Bernie was sad to hear of the king's death, she couldn't help but feel a strange sort of luck went along with it. Many would be attending King Arden's funeral. Royals, nobles, dignitaries from other lands.

And that included Emmerich van Ketten.

The timing was unfortunate, but also couldn't be better, as the plan developing in Bernie's mind was about to begin. If Antoinette couldn't save herself from her upcoming wedding, perhaps the Hugellian could.

Chapter 20: The Funeral

Edward never liked funerals.

He remembered how much it rained during Stephen's, how the summer seemed to turn to spring and the clouds wept as much as the people did as they said good-bye to their young prince. He remembered being stifled in the hot air, wanting to run and hide as if that would somehow make the procession finish faster. Everyone wept, the feeling of despair and guilt and fear smothering him so much it made him want to scream.

Though today would be reminiscent of Stephen's good-bye, he couldn't help but feel it would be different, too. Instead of rain, there was snow. Instead of heat, there was cold. Instead of guilt, there was peace.

The power of forgiveness overwhelmed his sorrow, and though he didn't want to say good-bye to his father, dreading every moment of the service, he was content this funeral would be unlike the last one he had to endure. His father's death wasn't his fault. He and the king parted on good terms, like a true father and son instead of enemies. That knowledge alone brought him more peace than what he had felt with his family in a long, long time.

The casket was laid out at the front of the church, draped in the cream and peach colored flag of Audlin. Edward stood, facing it as funeral goers trickled into the sanctuary, with his arm around his mother.

"How are you holding up?" Edward asked, giving her a gentle squeeze.

"I'm fine," Maria said quietly, her handkerchief being held tightly in her hand. "And you?"

"Fine for now."

"I think Arden would like how nice the church looks," Maria said as she put her hand on the casket. "You did well in planning the funeral."

"Thank you," Edward replied. "I wanted it to be special; not just for us, but for him, too."

"He would love it."

Edward smiled. "I hope so. I hope he knows I just wanted to make him proud."

"He knows that," Maria said. "And you will make him proud, Edward."

He kissed the top of his mother's head, holding her close as he watched her caress the flag atop the casket. "I'm glad we parted on good terms. Knowing that he cared enough to let me keep the throne...I don't know. It's not so much becoming king that's given me joy, but the fact that he forgave me and loved me enough to continue his legacy. I didn't feel worthy to be his son before. Now I do."

He felt his mother's arms wrap around his waist. The sound of a whimper sneaking from her lips caused Edward to turn to her in concern, pulling out his own handkerchief to give her in case the one she had wasn't enough. She only hugged him tighter as her whimpers turned to a cry, and he hugged her back, rubbing her arm.

"It's ok, Mother. It's alright," he comforted. "I miss him, too."

She said nothing as she remained in his arms until the funeral started.

Antoinette didn't think she'd see Edward so soon after their break up. Grant it, it had been six months since she had left Reigal, but seeing Edward suddenly brought feelings of nostalgia and memory. The last time she was at a funeral in Reigal was for Stephen, and she remembered it clearly.

Edward was quiet, his face red from the summer heat as they stood out in the rain, watching the casket be lowered into the ground. His fingers were tight around hers and she held him close, wondering if he'd ever smile again. She never saw him so distraught, so upset, after his brother died. He spoke little and ate even less. In a way, she feared Edward would not last since his brother was gone.

She vowed that day she would be strong for him; that if he had nothing else to live for, he could live for her.

She wanted to scoff at the irony of that vow. Here she was, sitting in the back with her parents and siblings, while Edward remained at the front with another woman at his side. Would Malina give him reason to carry on after such loss? She didn't think so, but Edward had proven to her before that those who were closest to him knew him the least. Her eyes remained on him, however, and even though she only saw the back of his head and shoulders, she wondered if he wanted to look back and see if she was there.

Her eyes drifted from him as she realized what a silly thought that was. When she turned to the side, however, she saw a different face, one who was now looking back and giving her a smile that warmed the cold away from her spirit. Emmerich sat quietly as the priest did the eulogy, sitting beside his parents and a few other relatives from Hugellia. But his eyes weren't at the front. He almost looked as if it didn't faze him that Edward was in mourning. He only came for her, an opportunity to see the girl he waited for and spend a moment in her gaze.

At first she smiled back at him, thinking back to the moments they shared together that always brought her joy. Walks in the forest, talking late into the night by the fire when they were supposed to be upstairs asleep, laughing until their bellies ached and trying to catch butterflies that sprung from the grass...

...holding the hand of someone who cared when all you could feel was loneliness...

Her smile faded as she felt nails dig into her hand. "Eyes up front," came the hissing sounds of her mother, making Antoinette break her gaze to Emmerich and turn back to the casket ahead. She felt her heart sink at the thought of Mother keeping such a tight grip on her. Antoinette doubted she'd be able to speak to anyone without Mother behind her back, stringing her like a puppet and feeding her the right words to say. She was fortunate Prince Arnold wasn't there, stuck in Liegen after a snow storm and unable to make it to the funeral.

Antoinette put her free hand on Bernie's as she gave her a quick glance. She suspected Mother would have her tethered and unable to tell Emmerich of the engagement, but that didn't mean they couldn't try and get the word to him. She hated to break the news at an event like a funeral, but if there was anyone who needed to hear about it, it was him. Emmerich didn't need to be deceived in thinking they actually had a chance to be together.

She took one final look at him before the eulogy was declared to end. As the congregation kneeled for the last prayer, she turned away and lowered her head to folded hands, catching a quick glimpse of Edward as he followed suit in front. Edward was in the past, and though she didn't want to leave the memories behind so quickly, she had to start thinking of the future, even though it was bleak.

She prayed for guidance as the congregation kneeled.

The last thing Maria wanted to do was greet people after saying farewell to her husband.

She felt like she had been standing for hours. Had it not been for Edward supporting her the entire morning, she would have left and feigned illness just to get away from everyone. Even Malina, her swollen belly looking as if it was going to pop, had left to rest, but Maria remained. She was no longer the queen, but she was the queen mother, and she refused to let her own heavy heart keep her from the duty she had to the people.

Most of the nobles and dignitaries were pleasant. They offered their condolences and gave hugs and handshakes as a means of saying they were sorry for her loss. They kept quiet about Edward and his affair with Malina, even though the new king received more than a few glares. But when Aldaric, Anna, and Emmerich arrived, Maria couldn't help but get teary-eyed at their display of affection.

Aldaric embraced her warmly, offering his own home to house his sister should she ever find the need for company. Anna cried with her, but when Emmerich embraced her she felt the guilt rise in her heart. Here was the nephew who had always been good to her, yet he didn't know how much she had robbed him.

He kissed her cheek, but she couldn't look him in the eye when she thanked him. She doubted she could ever do so again.

Aldaric and Anna went on to embrace Edward, but Emmerich only stood in silence. After a gentle nudge from his father, Emmerich stuck his hand out and shook Edward's, but the grip was far from firm. The cousins barely looked at each other, barely acknowledged the other's existence. Maria couldn't help but wonder if somehow, someway Emmerich found out.

She pushed the thought from her mind as more guests came her way.

When Susanna and her family approached, she felt at a loss as to what to do. There never was a protocol on how to handle an ex-fiancée, and when it came to pleasing Queen Susanna, there never was a protocol that was fool proof enough to please her. Maria tried her best to be amiable, though. Politeness to others was a trait she always was proud of and dared to share often.

"We're so sorry for your loss," Susanna said, a hint of flattery in her voice. Maria gave her an attempted smile, hoping it would suffice.

"We appreciate the condolence," Maria replied. "Good men are always taken away too soon, but our loss is made easier knowing we have friends who will stand by us."

"Never fear, dearest Maria!" Susanna said, taking her hand in hers. "Loyalty is a trait highly prized by our people. It is a virtue we pride ourselves in, especially since it is so rarely seen these days."

Susanna gave a quick glance to Edward as he stood next to his mother in silence. Maria cleared her throat, unsure of whether to smile politely and ignore the comment or say something in response. She decided the former as she noticed her son swallow hard, his eyes going from Susanna to Antoinette.

Antoinette only looked away as Susanna continued to speak. "You must forgive me that the entire family isn't here right now. You know how it is trying to get everyone in the same area at the same time."

Maria looked around, noticing the king, Antoinette, and the two sons. Bernette was missing, though she could have sworn she saw the young princess in the audience earlier. "It's alright, Susanna. I understand if Bernette couldn't make it. I trust you'll give her my greeting, though, when you return."

"Bernette?" The queen gave a sound that sounded too much like a laugh. "She is here, though I believe she mentioned having to run to the privy. She was feeling ill after the carriage ride." She shrugged her shoulders after looking around, doubtless not caring her daughter wasn't with her. "I was talking of Antoinette's fiancé. They are to be married very soon."

Maria was taken aback, her eyes widening in shock as she turned to Edward to see his reaction. He stood still, his expression falling into a deeper sadness, yet he nodded as if giving agreement to the matter. "I trust you have picked a suitable man to marry?" he asked as he looked to Antoinette. Before she could answer, Susanna gave a twirl of her hand and smiled.

"He is *perfect* for her. Noble, smart, handsome; everything she needs in a man." Susanna grinned. "So *loyal*, too."

"I'm sure he is," Edward muttered, his eyes narrowing.

"We would invite you to the wedding, but the couple wanted something small," Susanna continued, ignoring Maria's frown and Edward's reddening face. "I doubt even all of the family will be invited. Still...we'll send you all the gossip regarding the wedding once it happens."

"Well…" Maria gave a huff, stifling the urge to take Susanna by the hair and pull her to the ground. "I suppose congratulations are in order…"

But before anything else could be said, Antoinette shook her head, giving Maria an apologetic look before walking away from her mother.

"Insolent child!" Susanna muttered underneath her breath. "Come back here!" She gathered her skirt, ignoring Maria and Edward, scurrying after her daughter. Maria watched as the princess and queen headed into the crowd, and it wasn't too long until Edward left after them, doubtless wanting to speak with Antoinette about the engagement. Soon only Maria, King John, and the two boys were left.

She could only watch as the king rubbed his brow in frustration.

Emmerich was standing with his family, talking, when Bernie found him. They had just finished speaking with Maria and Edward and were now waiting for the crowds to disperse so the casket could be taken to the cemetery for burial. It wouldn't take long for her to talk to him, she figured, but if she didn't speak to him now, she knew there would be few chances left. She could only use the "I have to go to the bathroom or I'm going to throw up everywhere" excuse so many times in one day.

She made her way through the crowd, bumping and gliding through the church pews hastily. When she approached the van Kettens, she was greeted with warmth and smiles, but she only gave a nod as she went straight to Emmerich.

Her hand met his arm and she gave a gentle pull as she spoke quietly to him. "We need to talk."

He noticed the worry in her voice, giving a look of concern as he met her gaze. He nodded, turning back to his family and excusing himself, following her out of the church and into the snowy grass outside the door.

It didn't take Emmerich long to figure something was amiss. "You look troubled," he began as they stood in the snow, a gentle wind blowing flurries onto their heads.

"I am troubled," Bernie said as she crossed her arms to keep warm. "You need to come to Staalberg."

"What's wrong?"

"Mother arranged a marriage for Antoinette. She told us nothing until she finalized the engagement."

"Your Mother *did what?*"

Bernie paused as she saw the fury in Emmerich's eyes, feeling a chill as he undoubtedly started heating up. "Mother arranged a marriage between Antoinette and some guy named Arnold of Liegen. The wedding's in a little over a week."

"Arnold?" Emmerich's eyes beaded. "He's from the ruling family in Liegen, right?"

"Yeah. Apparently he's their youngest son."

"I know of him," Emmerich huffed as he began to pace, the snow and grass crunching underneath his boots. "I met his family once on a trip to Liegen. He is foolish, inappropriate, and far from noble. He is the worst man for her!"

"Well if it makes you feel any better, Antoinette and I both think he's a pig."

"He is more a snake than a pig," Emmerich replied. "Doubtless he charmed your mother with his wealth and speech. Do not believe a word he says, though. His entire family is deceptive. They tried to alter I don't know how many trade agreements between their nation and mine."

"Mother says he'll be moving to Edeland to act as Father's financial advisor," Bernie said. "And for that, I couldn't care less. Let him ruin it all. I just don't want him touching my sister!"

"He's not even worthy to look at her," Emmerich seethed. He stopped and stood in front of Bernie, putting his hand on her shoulder. "Fear not, Lady Bernette. I shall come to Staalberg and put an end to this marriage. I will speak to your parents."

"They won't listen to you, Emmerich." Bernie sighed in frustration. "You saw how Mother acts with you, and Father is such a coward he will only agree with her no matter what he thinks."

"So what are you proposing?" Emmerich asked.

Bernie shrugged. "Actually, that's what I was hoping you would do."

Emmerich's eyes widened and his brows went up in surprise, but he nodded, putting his hand to his chin in thought. "You wish your sister and I to elope?"

"I think it's the best option right now," Bernie replied. "I mean...I'm not trying to pressure you or anything, but Antoinette's not willing to save herself from this. She's not happy about being rushed into marrying this guy, but you know how she is. She can't say 'no' to Mother even though she wants to."

He was taken aback by her response and couldn't hide the concern that came upon his brow. "I don't like that she's being forced into this against her will."

"She wanted to tell you in person but Mother is watching," Bernie continued. "I know this is uncouth of me, but I've tried to think of so many other ways for her to get out. If you have any better ideas…"

"I'll do it. She can't marry Arnold if she's already married to me, right?"

Bernie blinked once, twice, as she looked at Emmerich. His face was calmer, almost warm in the cold winter air, but he had a look of such stout determination in his eyes that she almost felt a pang of jealousy seeing a man love her sister so devoutly instead of her. "So you'll come to Staalberg and you two can elope?"

Emmerich nodded. "As long as she agrees to it."

Bernie gave a laugh in relief as she ran forward, embracing him. He embraced her back, his arms wrapping around her tight. "Thank you!" she said, her voice muffled against his coat. "You have no idea how glad I am over this. I…I just want to make sure she's taken care of. She deserves someone that'll treat her good for once."

Emmerich pulled away, looking at her. "And what of you? I'd hate to leave you there facing your mother's wrath."

Bernie looked away. She thought about her own fate, but selfishness did her no good. Every time she thought about herself, others got hurt-like Antoinette. "I'll be fine. Your priority is taking care of my sister."

"And I will," Emmerich replied. "But if Arnold von Liegen is denied a bride in Antoinette, I do not wish to see your mother force you into your sister's place."

Bernie pursed her lips. She hadn't thought of that…not that it really mattered, anyways. "He won't want me," Bernie said.

"Besides, who cares what happens to me. Antoinette's more important!"

Emmerich frowned as he looked at her, making Bernie want to grab him by the shoulders and shake some sense into him. "Don't give me that look!" Bernie muttered. "I can handle myself."

"That may be true," Emmerich replied. "But Antoinette isn't the only one who deserves to be treated well."

Bernie didn't know whether to slap him or hug him again. She was perturbed he had to be the "save every damsel in distress" type of guy, yet at the same time she thought it very sweet. No other man even bothered with what happened to her. His concern was…refreshing.

"You could come with us," Emmerich said after a pause. "I'll take care of you both."

"Isn't polygamy illegal in Hugellia?" Bernie smirked.

Emmerich cleared his throat, his face blushing. "That's…uhm…not quite what I was suggesting…"

Bernie shoved his shoulder gently as she laughed. "You're going to be so much fun to torture, *brother-in-law*."

He shook his head, laughing along with her as the snow continued to fall.

Antoinette was near the choir seats when her mother finally caught up with her. She was fuming, her face flushing with heat as her blood boiled, and she stood with arms crossed, waiting for the lecture to begin. She didn't care; let Mother call her rude, weak, and childish. Let her belittle and nag.

Had it not been for the crowd of people around her, Antoinette knew she would've been yelled at. Mother was even angrier than Antoinette, her brows lowered so much her eyes looked like squinting dots. "I can't *believe* you, Antoinette!" Susanna hissed, taking Antoinette's arm and squeezing it. "The rudeness you displayed by walking away like that! You'd make the queen and Edward think you are unhappy with your engagement!"

"I *am* unhappy with my engagement!" Antoinette seethed. "And I'm even more unhappy that you'd bring it up at a time like this! This is a funeral, Mother, for a good man that you had known for the longest time, and you have the audacity to turn it into a gossip fest!"

"I was only spreading the good news, child!" Susanna replied. "And did you see the look on Edward's face! It turned so red, I thought he'd throw a tantrum right then and there!"

Antoinette frowned. "He wasn't angry, Mother. He was hurt."

Susanna scoffed. "Good."

"How can you say that?" Antoinette asked. "He's already lost his father. Do you take joy in the fact that you are increasing his sorrow by celebrating my engagement?"

Susanna rolled her eyes. "You seem to forget this poor, hurt soul of a man is the same man who left you for another woman! Are you feeling sorry for him now?"

Antoinette looked away. "Well...no...I..."

"You are living in a dream, Antoinette, and you need to wake up!" Susanna replied. "The man never loved you before and he doesn't love you now! But Arnold, he will."

"But the look in Edward's eyes..."

"You are seeing only what you want to see," Susanna said bluntly. She pulled at her daughter's arm to lead her away. "Now come, child. We must gather your sister. She must be causing trouble to be in the privy for so long!"

As she led Antoinette away, however, she stopped when she saw Edward approaching. There was a moment of awkward silence at first, and the three stared at each other, not knowing what to do or say. Edward cleared his throat, wringing his hands, as he turned to the queen.

"I need to speak with your daughter."

Susanna's eyes narrowed. "Why?"

"Because I want to tell her something," Edward replied. "Please, if I can just have a moment with her alone. It will only take five minutes."

"No," Susanna said, throwing her nose up in the air. "And if you wish to say anything, then you can say it in front of me. I shan't leave my daughter alone with you."

Antoinette watched as Edward looked at her sadly, giving a slow nod. "Very well. I..."

"Mother," Antoinette interrupted, turning to the queen. "Give us five minutes."

Susanna shook her head. "But..."

Antoinette lowered her brows. "I said give us five minutes. Please."

Antoinette's eyes remained on her mother, glaring her down until the queen buckled under her pressure. She let go of her arm, letting out a huff, pointing her finger at Antoinette as she walked away. "Five minutes. Not a minute more!"

"Thank you."

Antoinette's gaze went to Edward's face and she waited for him to speak. She was unsure of whether she wanted to hear from him or not, but the look he gave during their initial conversation spoke volumes to her heart. It was as if she got a glimpse of the Edward she knew before he married Malina.

"It's...it's good to see you again," Edward stammered, his eyes lowering to the ground as if embarrassed. Antoinette remained firm in her stance, refusing to give him any pity though her heart sunk at seeing his face.

"I wish it were under better circumstances," Antoinette replied.

"Yes. I do too."

"Is your wife still here?"

Edward looked up, rubbing the back of his neck. "She stayed for the funeral but went back to rest. The baby should be born soon. She didn't want all the excitement of the funeral to upset her and cause a premature delivery."

Antoinette wanted to scoff. "I'm sure she didn't."

"I...uhm...I just wanted to tell you congratulations," Edward said quickly, his eyes meeting hers. "On your engagement. I think I know who the lucky man is."

Antoinette's brow went up. "And that would be?"

"Emery."

Antoinette pressed her lips shut, looking away. She wondered how Edward could guess that she and Emmerich were involved, but said nothing. She didn't want to make him jealous. Or maybe she just didn't want to hear him try to talk her out of it.

"I'm happy for you," Edward continued, seeing her indifference. "He's a good man. He'll be good to you; much better than what I've been, anyways."

Antoinette looked back, frowning. "Edward, please, let's not talk of this now. It's your father's funeral."

"I'm not trying to open up old wounds," Edward said. "I just wanted you to know that if you're happy, I'm happy. I want you to be taken care of."

Antoinette was taken aback, surprised at his support. She was unsure how to take his sudden change of heart. The old Edward, the Edward she had once fallen in love with, was suddenly coming back. "You could've done that, Edward. We were supposed to take care of each other."

"I know. But you and Emery can take care of each other now."

If only that were true. "It could have been us, though."

"It's better this way, Antoinette," Edward said quietly, his expression matching hers. "You deserve the best and Emery...he's the best."

"Yes, he is."

He said nothing, taking her words quietly to heart and squirming where he stood, as if wanting to leave. He quickly took her hand in his and kissed it, holding it in silence. "I guess I should bid you farewell, then," he said. "Congratulations again. I...I wish you both the best."

She kept her eyes on the ground, unable to meet his gaze. She had missed his touch for so long, and yet at the same time the spark that was once between them was fading. Not because her love for him had waned and there was no longer any affection. It was still there, lingering, not wanting to part;

but as she felt the squeeze of his touch tighten on her fingers, she realized the love that was once between them had to be let go.

He was with Malina and always would be, and she would be bound to Arnold in the coming weeks.

"Thank you," she said as she pulled her hand away from him, his touch trying to tighten as if wanting to hold on. "Farewell, Edward. I am truly sorry for your loss."

He nodded, standing before her in silence and meeting her own teary gaze with his own. She looked at his face, realizing he understood this was her moment of forcing herself to let go. He said nothing, pressing his lips together in an urge to force a small smile before walking away, leaving her alone in the choir loft.

Chapter 21: A Play for Power

"What a lovely funeral!" Malina exclaimed with a laugh as she lounged on the sofa, watching Edward as he walked in. He frowned at her sudden expression of joy as her eyes followed him to the hearth where he warmed himself. "I hear the people are commending your honoring of the *former* king as an act worthy of a noble son."

"Your gossip must be inflated with flattery," Edward replied as he rubbed his hands together. "People rarely complain about a funeral."

Malina smirked. "I think people are starting to like you."

"And I think you are being overly optimistic."

"You weren't booed or chased away," Malina said. "That is a starch improvement from a few months ago."

Edward scoffed. "It's a funeral. Even our rude citizens aren't that tacky."

"Oh, ever the darling downer." Malina shook her head. "Edward, you must relish in the blessings fate has given you. The people respect you, your child is about to be born, and you have a crown above your head."

Edward frowned as he stared into the fire. "All of that means nothing. I have lost more than I have gained."

Malina's smile faded as she licked her lips. "I hear you talked to the Edelandian girl after the eulogy."

"I did," he muttered.

"And what did she say?"

Edward paused as he pressed his lips together, the admission of what was to come out feeling like vomit in his mouth. "She is getting married."

Malina let out a snort of laughter, making him frown further. "Well," she said with a giggle. "That was fast. And who is the lucky groom?"

"My cousin, Emmerich."

"The man with her when we first arrived here?" Malina laughed harder, putting her hand on her aching belly. "Oh, you poor, pathetic thing. I've never seen a woman be over a man so quickly! Except myself, that is."

He turned to face her, giving a hurt look. "It's better this way. Emmerich will be good to her."

"Of course he will," Malina cooed. "Good women always do better with good men."

Edward nodded as he returned his gaze to the hearth. As much as he knew Malina enjoyed talking down to him, he wanted to change the subject. He was in no mood for being reminded of his mistakes. "By the way," he said after a pause, "you were missed during the luncheon after the service."

Malina shrugged. "I was tired."

"I'm sure you were," Edward said in sarcasm. "You look exhausted."

Malina lowered her brow. "You try sticking a tiny human being in your belly and see how well you fare. Besides, I was busy."

"With what?" Edward asked.

"With my queenly duties." Malina grinned. "I have already sent letters to dignitaries in Verloris for us to dine with them. We shall set for expanding our naval trade through Circh starting in the spring once the snow melts. I was also thinking we should contact the people of Liegen where we could start trading the ore here in Reigal to…"

"What gave you the audacity to arrange such meetings already?" Edward snapped as he gave her a hard glare. Malina's face tensed with anger as she met his stare with her own. "You have had the crown for mere days and already you throw your whims here and there without a second thought! What about my duties as king?"

Malina scoffed. "If you expect me to be some kitchen manager like your mother, think again, Edward."

"I don't expect you to be a kitchen maid," Edward replied. "But I do expect you to share your musings before you go off and make them a reality!"

"Without my help you would be nothing, Edward. Remember that," Malina said sternly. "The riches brought in through the Circh trade were done by *me*. Verloris generosity was given by *me*. Our child, your heir, was given by *me*." She stood to her feet and approached him, stopping in front of his face. "*Everything* you have, I have given you. Don't think I can't take it away just as easily."

"You always threat," Edward said as he backed away. "And I am tired of hearing them. My father gave me this throne believing I could honor him and his legacy and I refuse to let myself be intimidated by you because of your childish taunts. You do not scare me, Malina. Not anymore."

Malina began to giggle slowly as she followed Edward to face him. She ran her finger down his cheek and to his chest, fingering his shirt with a playful look in her eye. "You silly, silly boy, you." She laughed as he stood there, his eyes beaded with a growing anger. "Always so foolish and so rash, aren't we? Do you really think I'm someone to trifle with?"

Edward's anger suddenly halted and he stared at her, wondering why she took his rebellion with such ease. It wasn't a good sign, but he wasn't about to give up. His father and mother believed in him. It was time he started believing in himself. "You must be mistaken if you think I'm easily put down."

"Darling, a master knows her own dog, and you're as weak as a pup."

She wrapped her arms around his neck and at first he wriggled free from her embrace. As he started to leave, she took him by the collar and pulled him back, giving another laugh. "What do you expect me to do as queen?" she asked.

Edward gulped, feeling his pulse rise as she stared at him with a smile that sent a chill of fear down his spine. "I expect you to work with me, not against me. I expect you to be more open and not secretive. I expect us to trust each other like a husband and wife should."

"That's not what I expect," she said. "I expect you to do everything I say. But lately you've been a naughty boy, Edward. You know you shouldn't question me or go against what I want."

"And you'll do what if I don't?" Edward asked. "Tell everyone about Stephen?"

"I can do that, certainly."

Edward frowned as he shook his head. He didn't want his secret out in the open, but he would play her bluff. She couldn't control him his entire life, could she? "Fine. Do it. Good luck trying to find people who will believe you. I'll deny everything."

Malina smirked as she put her hands on her hips. "You think my only weapons are words? You know me little indeed, then."

She approached him again, running her fingers through his hair and putting her lips to his ear. "Do you know what a girl does to get what she wants? *Anything.*

"Sometimes I do it myself, sometimes others do it for me," Malina said with a smile as she circled him. "Do you honestly think you are the only man I've charmed? I wanted power in Verloris so I worked my way to the top. I don't just control kings, Edward. I control warriors; I control the Velori. You'd be *shocked* how easily influenced all men are when it comes to a bed and a wanting woman."

Her hands rubbed his shoulders softly, and he squirmed under her touch. "I *dare* you to cross me, Edward. I'd like to show you what I can get away with."

Edward narrowed his eyes as he met her gaze. "You won't get away with everything."

"Oh silly, silly boy," she cooed. "Don't you know I already have?"

"You're going where?" Anna van Ketten asked as she watched her son add another pack to his horse.

"Staalberg," Emmerich replied as he tightened the strap near the saddle. Waffles gave a neigh of disapproval, clearly unhappy with all the weight he had to carry, but became quiet after he saw Emmerich pack a few jarred apples into the back pouch. Emmerich watched as Anna gave a pout, and he quickly embraced her, kissing her cheek. "I promise I won't be gone long. Maybe a month or so, and then I'll be back."

"A month is an awfully long time," Anna replied.

Aldaric gave a grunt after adding the last pack to the horse. "And why are you going to Staalberg? What about your studies? You're in the middle of your year at the university. I'd prefer if you didn't miss any more time than you had to."

"I don't want to miss any time either, Dad, but I have to go," Emmerich replied.

"But why now?" Aldaric said. "It's the middle of winter! There's storms, blizzards. I'd rather you not risk hypothermia traveling all alone."

"I won't be alone," Emmerich said. "I'll be following the king and queen's caravan."

Aldaric crossed his arms, one brow going up. "And Queen Susanna is fine with that?"

Emmerich pursed his lips. "I'm unsure. She doesn't really know."

"You're sneaking in?" Anna cried.

"Lady Antoinette and Lady Bernette both know I'm coming."

"That's all?" Anna frowned.

Emmerich ignored his mother's disapproval as he got atop Waffles and took the reins. "I have to go. It can't wait; I'm sorry."

Aldaric grabbed the reins before Emmerich could trot off, gently pulling him back towards himself and Anna. "Son, if you want to visit Antoinette, then you can do so in the spring when the weather clears. Why the rush?"

Emmerich sighed as he lowered his head, steadying Waffles. "I have to stop a wedding."

"Wedding?" Anna asked. "Who's getting married?"

"Antoinette, in about a week," Emmerich replied as he faced his parents. "Susanna arranged a marriage to one of the Liegen princes. Antoinette and Bernette are furious, and Antoinette does not wish to go through with it. I'm going because Bernette has asked for my help."

"Talking to the queen will not work," Aldaric said. "She's not one to listen to reason."

"I know."

"So what do you hope to accomplish?"

"I'm getting Antoinette out," Emmerich said quietly. "We're going to elope."

Emmerich expected Aldaric and Anna to offer protest or support, but their show of surprise and silence made him uneasy. Anna only stared at him with wide eyes, as if she didn't believe what he had just spoken. Aldaric, though less surprised, only looked at him with pity, shaking his head and rubbing his brow.

Emmerich gave a huff. "I take it you don't approve?"

"You're...you're not going to move there, are you?" Anna asked, mortified.

Emmerich shook his head. "No, we'll probably live in Hugellia."

Anna smiled at his answer, but Aldaric remained firm. "An elopement is risky, Emery. You'll not only taint your reputation but hers as well, not to mention John and Susanna will be furious with knowing what you've done. Do you realize this could harm relations between Edeland and Hugellia? You saw what happened after Edward eloped. Do you really want to create that for us?"

"What other choice do I have? Her mother is selling her off to another man, and a terrible one at that!"

Aldaric shrugged. "I don't like it either, Emery, but this is a part of life. She is a royal and doesn't have much of a say in who she marries. If your genders were switched, it might have been different, but unless her fiancé cancels the engagement, she's stuck with him."

"But you were in an arranged engagement and you broke it off!"

"My situation was different, Emery," Aldaric said. "My fiancée wasn't a royal."

"If she was, though," Emmerich said, "would it have stopped you from marrying Mom?"

Anna looked to Aldaric with a hopeful glance, making him look away. He paused for a moment as if in thought, but then conceded defeat as he turned back to his son. "It wouldn't. I would've still married Anna."

His wife gave him a peck on the cheek and smiled.

But Emmerich gave a scoff. "Then how are you any different from me? Antoinette and I want to get married, so why can't we?"

"It's still different, Emery," Aldaric replied. "Anna and I married because we loved each other and wanted to spend the rest of our lives together. The question you need to ask is Antoinette marrying you because she wants to, or because she has no other alternative?"

Emmerich lowered his brow, remaining silent as he looked away.

Aldaric put his hand on his son's arm, giving it a gentle squeeze. "Whatever you do, whether it be marrying Antoinette or simply helping her, I'll support you. Just do me a favor when you speak with her; explain to her what I just explained to you. Don't go into all of this blind. You don't want to live with regrets."

Emmerich's features softened, and he clasped his father's hand. "I'll talk with her."

Aldaric dropped the reins and stepped back with Anna. "Good luck, then. And be careful."

Emmerich nodded before galloping off towards the east. As his figure faded into the distance, Anna began to sniffle as Aldaric held her close. "My poor baby is all grown up!" she said as she wiped her eyes with her husband's handkerchief. "And he better live in Hugellia! I refuse to be away from my grandchildren when he has them!"

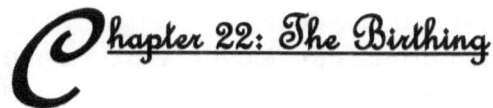

Chapter 22: The Birthing

It was in the middle of the night when Edward was roused from his sleep.

He felt a hard *thud* on the side of his head, waking him up with a jolt. As he got up he heard Malina give a groan, and before he could fully wake himself, he felt her take him by the shoulder and shove him off the bed.

"GET UP, YOU SLUG! I'M GOING INTO LABOR!"

Whether it was her words or impacting the floor, Edward found himself scrambling to light a lantern and find the midwife.

"How long have you been in labor?" he asked as he fumbled for a match.

"How am I supposed to know? I woke up in pain!" Malina clutched her belly and began to pant as she sat on the bed.

"You're not even at nine months yet! Why are you going into labor now?"

"It's not like things haven't been stressful lately, Edward!"

He quickly lit the lantern and set it upon the stand, his hands shaking. "I'm going to get the midwife, then. Hold on."

"Will you just shut up and go?" Malina spat. "Hurry!"

Edward complied, rushing out the door and calling a guard to fetch the midwife. Within minutes the elderly woman came along with three other ladies carrying bowls of water and cloths, and as they scuttled into the room they began preparing their surroundings for the birth.

As the woman set up the room, Edward hurried to Malina's side. "Do you need anything?" he asked, though he secretly hoped she didn't.

"Darling, are you worried?" Malina groaned as she forced a smirk, another spasm of pain hitting her abdomen. "Trust me, I hope for the safe delivery of our child more than you."

"Everything will go well," he encouraged.

"Of course it will," Malina replied. "Now be a man and stop whimpering! You look as if you're going to vomit. And men wonder why we kick them out during the birth. Just go!"

"But I can stay at least until..."

"Go, Edward!"

"She's right, Your Majesty." The midwife took Edward by the arm and led him out of the room. "We will call you if needed, but for now, we must make her and the baby comfortable and prepare for delivery."

"How long will that take?" Edward asked.

"Minutes, hours, maybe the entire day," the midwife replied. "But for now, fret not. Your child is in safe hands with us."

"You will let me know when it is born?"

The midwife nodded and smiled warmly. "Of course, Your Majesty. You will be the first to know."

"Thank you."

Edward was led into the darkness of the hallway and the door was shut.

It wasn't long before Edward fell asleep again and found himself dreaming.

The air was cold, like winter that refused to give way to spring.

Edward found himself panting, gasping for air. Heavy leather burdened his breathing and his arms were throbbing with ache. All he wanted to do was collapse and embrace the earth, to rest after being weary for so long.

But the cackle that plagued his ears kept him alert. A warrior, clad in armor from head to toe laughed at him, circling him like a vulture waiting for its prey to drop so it could feast. A sword was pointed towards Edward's chest, but he did not flinch. A fire burned inside of him, one of an undying urge to protect that which had fallen.

His eyes danced to the figure lying on the ground, moaning, as he struggled to get up. He saw the boy-no, maybe not a boy, but not quite a young man-look up to him, his face wracked with pain as he wheezed, the plate in his chest dented in. Edward turned back to the attacking warrior, restrained only by the wisdom of a knight.

"I won't let you hurt him."

The words bounced off uninterested ears as the warrior scoffed. "You knew this day was coming for you. A day of atonement. A day of penance. A day when the liar, thief, adulterer, and murderer was finally brought to justice."

Edward gripped the sword in his hand, holding it out. "I'm not those things anymore."

"Are you sure?" the warrior asked with a smirk that was all too familiar. *"You have lied to an entire nation. You seek to steal the crown. You have betrayed your wife. And now, you seek to destroy me. Does that not make you a murderer?"*

"I won't let you hurt my son."

The fury that came upon the warrior's face was so strong even Edward flinched. "You fool!" the warrior seethed as he lifted his sword and started to charge towards him. "I AM YOUR SON!"

As the killing stroke came, Edward shot up from the couch, his dream finally over but his reality feeling shaky and ready to crumble. His whole body shook and beaded with sweat, and as he clutched the blanket over him he gasped for breath, thinking his heart about to pound out of his chest.

A feeling of dread washed over him, and immediately the dream began to replay in his mind. He saw the fallen boy, writhing in pain, and he remembered his face. Dark hair, light eyes, strong features. All were familiar to Edward as he looked back at what seemed to be a younger reflection of himself. In the dream he remembered loving the boy so much that it hurt; he *was* his son, but he was being attacked by another who looked so much like him.

He sat up on the couch as he buried his face into shaking hands. What did the dream mean, or was it supposed to mean anything at all? Maybe it was a reflection of his worried subconscious, expressing his fears of becoming a father and reminding him of how unready he was to raise a child.

He shook his head, knowing well dreams so vividly remembered were rarely a coincidence. A few weeks before Stephen died, his mother dreamt that her son had jumped into a lake to swim and ended up drowning. His father told her to ignore it, that Stephen didn't like to swim anyways and if he did go, there would be supervision. Little did they realize that their son would die just weeks later, and for months Maria swore that her dream was meant to serve as a warning to prepare her for her son's death.

And so that left the meaning. Doubtless he was going to have a son, perhaps two if the dream could be interpreted literally. Could Malina be pregnant with twins? One who was good, one who was evil? The entire notion sounded like it came from a recycled horror story, one too strange to come true. Or perhaps the son who was attacked was his real son, and the attacker represented something? Would the child that Malina had really be good, while some other evil Edward was connected to would seek to attack him?

Malina was already competing for power with her husband. Doubtless she would do it with her son, as well.

The door knocked and Edward looked up, noticing the candles were still lit and that it had to be early morning. He rose to his feet, telling the knocker to come in, and out popped the head of the midwife, her face weary but happy.

"Your Majesty?" the woman asked. She looked at his uncouth appearance and apologized. "Forgive me for waking you. I didn't realize you were sleeping."

"I was awake earlier but must've dozed off," Edward replied, trying to regain his composure as he forced a smile. "Is everything alright?"

"Yes. Your wife has had the baby and both are well."

Edward swallowed hard. "What did she have?"

"A son, Your Majesty."

Edward felt his heart sink. Malina was right, his dream was right. His stomach felt sick at the thought of the future. "One child? Or has Malina born multiple children?"

The midwife looked confused, but answered him. "Only one."

At least the theory of a good and evil set of twins was false. But then who would the attacker be?

"Would you like to see him?"

Edward ignored the thoughts running through his mind and went to the door. "Yes, please take me to him."

"Of course. Follow me."

Edward hurried down the hallway to the room where Malina had given birth. The hallways were still empty save a few servants bustling about. "Much of the household is still asleep. I thought it best to keep the birth quiet to allow you some time with the child before any festivities," the midwife said.

Edward nodded in thanks. "Feel free to tell my mother as she would want to be woken for this. Otherwise, let us wait until the sun rises. I doubt the city wants to wake early over a baby being born."

"It's the future king, Sire." The midwife smiled. "That is cause for celebration."

Edward pressed his lips together, trying to smile but coming up short. A day he hoped would be a celebration suddenly felt like such a mourning.

He stopped at the door and opened it, revealing a room that was still being cleaned by servants. He saw Malina lying on the bed, resting comfortably after her ordeal, and he heard the gentle whimper of a baby being swaddled by one of the wet nurses.

Edward stepped in slowly, the sounds of his son pulling at his soul as he stepped closer. The nurse smiled as she held the newly bundled baby in her arms, gently rocking him, and presented him to the king.

"Your son, Your Majesty," the nurse replied, and she placed the child in his arms, showing him how to hold the baby.

The little boy felt so light and small, and Edward was stricken at how much he cared for a being he had just met. Flashes of the dream still crossed his mind, but the feeling of the baby and the way he grasped his father's finger to hold it close made Edward realize there wasn't anything he wouldn't do for his son. So many people had touched his heart, but few had truly held it, and in that moment he realized he would love his son for all eternity.

He met the child's gaze as he opened his eyes, giving out a yawn. The boy's eyes were of a dark blue, much like his father's when he was young, and his hair was shiny and dark. Many features, such as his eyes and nose, resembled his mother, but his jaw line and mouth were like Edward's, as were his unfortunately small ears.

All in all, he was beautiful.

"I take it you are pleased?" Malina said wearily as she opened her eyes, looking at him from the bed.

Edward's eyes remained on the baby as he kissed the child's fist. "Very."

"I am pleased as well."

Edward smiled as he turned to his wife. "Shall we name him?"

"I already have," Malina replied. "He is to be named after my father, Calimus."

Edward frowned. He had hoped to name the child after his own departed father, Arden. "I know we haven't discussed names, but surely you would consider Audlinian tradition. Calimus is not a typical name here, and after my father's death…"

"His name is Calimus," Malina repeated as she gave him a glare. The servants paused from their work and looked up to Edward, watching for his reaction. He said nothing at first, wondering if she was baiting him to play with power, but as they glared at each other, Malina smirked and said, "Or how about we name him Stephen? I know how much you *loved and admired* your brother."

It was her way of reining him in, back under control. He couldn't afford her slip of the tongue, as much as he had goaded her in the past. He had to play along now that he had a child. If Malina was symbolic of the attacker, he had to protect his son starting now. And if it meant his wife controlling him, so be it, as long as his son was safe.

"How about Calimus Stephen Engel?" Edward suggested, to which Malina smiled with approval. "That way we both get what we want."

"I can agree with that," Malina replied.

"Very well, then," Edward replied as he held Calimus close to his chest. He turned to his son, watched as blue eyes stared back at him, a hand still grasping his finger, and he kissed his forehead. "Calimus Stephen Engel," he whispered to himself. "My son."

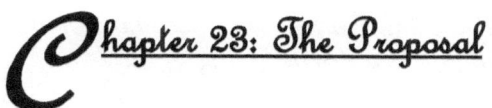

Antoinette watched from the parlor window as the snow gently fell from the sky. Snow was a rarity in Edeland, the land too far south and warmer than the mountains in Audlin or the tundra that was the north near Hugellia. Though the weather was colder, which she didn't enjoy, the scenery was beautiful, and every snowflake that fell onto the ground became a new memory of one of the most beautiful winters she had seen.

But the snow wasn't the reason she was watching the window, waiting for the sun to go down so the man she was supposed to meet could sneak into the palace without being watched. Her sister had arranged for Emmerich van Ketten to follow them to Staalberg and speak with her in the palace after nightfall.

She remembered the conversation she had with Bernie during the trip back from Reigal, when they were alone in their lodging at night while everyone else slept.

"Did you explain to him about the marriage?" she had asked as her sister removed her hat. *She paused as she noticed Bernie look at her head in the mirror with a frown, but said nothing as Bernie began to speak.*

"I told him everything he needed to know: who Mother wants you to marry, why you wanted to tell him about the marriage, why you were sorry things wouldn't work out the way you wanted them to..."

For some reason she felt like Bernie was holding her true words back. "What did he say?" Antoinette asked.

"He wasn't happy you're getting married," Bernie replied. "He's not holding it against you or anything. All he said was he wanted to talk to you before you went through with it."

"Did he say what about?"

"Not sure," Bernie continued. "Whatever it is, I'm sure it'll be entertaining, at any rate."

Her thoughts were interrupted as she heard a tap on the window. The sun had finally set and darkness overcame the area, and as she squinted she could see Emmerich's cloaked form outside the window, looking this way and that to make sure he wasn't being watched.

Antoinette chuckled to herself knowing she was sneaking a man into the house. Mother would certainly disapprove, and though normally Antoinette would agree that it was an uncouth way of seeing a person, desperate times really were calling.

She quickly opened the window and he climbed in, small clutches of snow falling from him as he stepped in. As Antoinette helped him steady himself, her hands became cold, and she quickly shut the window and pulled him towards the hearth.

"You're freezing."

Emmerich grinned as he tried his best not to shiver. "It's...not...that...bad..."

"How long have you been out there?"

"Since...Reigal..."

Antoinette's eyes widened as she threw his hood off and felt his face. He was frozen, his skin red and undoubtedly numb. "Emery! What?" She gave a frustrated grunt as she hurried to pull a few blankets from a closet, throwing his wet and snowy cloak to the side and wrapping the blankets around him.

"You could've gotten sick!" she muttered to herself. "Or hypothermia! I...I'm so sorry, Emery. I should've thought better..."

"Relax." He gently touched her arm, and she exhaled, keeping the blankets close across his chest. "We have winters colder than this in Hugellia. It's not like I'm not used to the weather."

Her hands stayed on him, and she looked up to meet his gaze. "Are you sure?"

"If I had hypothermia, I wouldn't be standing here right now." He grinned.

She smiled back, noticing his hand hadn't left her arm.

"How are you?" he asked. "Was the trip from Reigal pleasant for you?"

"A little cold, but otherwise it went well," Antoinette replied. She led him to the couch in front of the hearth and sat him on it, rewrapping the blankets around him as she sat close beside. "I take it you got my message via Bernie?"

Emmerich nodded. "She explained it to me. So your mother wishes you to marry Arnold of Liegen?"

"Four days from now," Antoinette said with a sigh. "He should be arriving from Liegen the day after tomorrow."

"That doesn't give you much time, then."

"I could've had more time had it not been for Mother," she said. "I'm sorry, Emery. I didn't want this to happen and I wished we could have had a chance. I really wanted to see if we could work as...you know...more than friends."

He gave her arm a gentle caress. "You needn't apologize. This was far from being your choice."

She nodded slowly, giving a polite grin, but it quickly faded as she looked towards the ground. "I don't want to marry Arnold, Emmerich. I don't know him, I don't like him, I don't trust him. Every time I look at him, I get this chill that makes me feel uncomfortable. There's something about him that just...isn't right."

"You don't have to have that, though."

"What choice do I have?" Antoinette replied, facing him. "I'm a royal. It's not like I have much control over what I can or cannot do."

"Have you talked to your mother about your feelings?" Emmerich asked. "Do you think she would call it off?"

"I talked to her first. You know how she is; she never listens to reason."

"Then refuse to marry him."

"I've spoken my peace, Emery," Antoinette muttered. "Mother ignored me every time."

Silence passed between them as Emmerich looked away, taking in a deep breath. "What if you married someone else?" he asked quietly before turning back to her. "If you're already married, the contract is breached, right?"

"I think that could work," Antoinette replied, and she felt her heart flutter. Emmerich watched her reaction warmly, his hand steady as it rested on her arm. She found that she still kept the blankets wrapped around his chest, and she was so, so close to him. Close enough to feel how much warmth really did come from him; close enough to realize she wanted to escape the cold by moving just a bit closer.

Was he hinting towards marriage with her? In a way, she was hoping he was. And yet at the same time she felt guilty. Wasn't she trying to escape a marriage with Arnold? How could she force Emmerich into a marriage just so she could escape her own?

"I'm sorry, Emery," Antoinette said quietly as she lowered her head. "I didn't mean to complain about my troubles to you. I'm sure you planned on better things to do here instead of listening to me."

"Antoinette, why do you think I'm here in the first place?" Emmerich asked. "I don't *have* to be here. I *want* to be."

"But..."

"If you think marrying someone else will get you out of the marriage with Arnold, then why not explore that option?"

Antoinette shook her head, rolling her eyes in sarcasm. "Is it really an option?"

"Of course it is," Emmerich said softly, turning her gaze to him. "With me."

Antoinette felt the part of her chin where he touched her start to tingle. Her heart began to beat faster as she suddenly realized he didn't just come to Staalberg to comfort her or say a final good-bye. He was there to propose.

The words were difficult to speak at first as she forced them out through nervous and giddy lips. "You...you'd want to marry me?"

He smiled at her, making her mirror his features. But as she moved closer to him, he suddenly moved away, standing up and letting the blankets fall off his shoulders. She found herself clutching to him, not wanting to let go, and she gave him a wondrous look as she asked, "What are you doing?"

He smiled as his hand moved from her arm to her cheek. "Giving you my choice and letting you decide our next step."

After he spoke, she watched him drop to one knee in front of her, taking both of her hands into his.

"Antoinette?" he asked.

She swallowed hard. "Yes?"

"I need to ask you a question."

"Okay."

He smirked. "Are you feeling a little rebellious?"

She snickered. Now he was sounding like Bernie. "Perhaps."

"Because the question I'm about to ask you will undoubtedly cause friction with some of the people we know. Your parents will be furious. My grandfather and uncles will be furious. Arnold will be more livid than all of them. It's safe to say that we could potentially make a lot of people unhappy with what I'm asking you to do, but I'm willing to forsake everyone else's opinions."

He let go of her hand for a moment and reached into his pocket, pulling out a blue ring. Antoinette's mouth dropped as she saw it, thinking he was more prepared than she gave him credit for, and he held the ring in front of her. "This was the ring my grandfather-my *real* grandfather-gave to my grandmother for their wedding. My father gave it to me so I could one day give it to the most important woman in my life. I guess you know now that I consider that person to be you.

"You know that I love you, Antoinette. You know that I have loved you since we were children and that love has remained in my heart even after all of these years. You are the woman I have spent my life waiting for…praying for. And if you would have me, I promise I will be the man who will love you always. I promise I will provide for you, take care of you, respect you, and encourage you. You deserve the very best, and though I am far from perfect, I promise to be the very best I can be, and it is my heart's desire to see you smile every day for the rest of your life.

"We didn't plan for it to be this way, and we wanted to take our time to know each other deeper, but I'm willing to throw reason to the wind as long as it saves you from hurt. My heart, my mind, my body, my life, I give to you. I want to be both your friend and your lover from this day forth until the end of eternity. Will you marry me?"

At first she only stared at him with mouth agape, and he watched and waited, his hopeful face suddenly looking nervous as she simply sat there in shock.

Her first thought was Edward's proposal was a joke compared to what he just said. She doubted even the best poets could have told her any better. Her second thought was he was right, there would be a lot of angry people if they found she eloped, especially since she was a royal and he was not.

But all other thoughts were forgotten as she realized how wonderful he was. She saw glimpses of Emmerich's qualities as a child, but now that she was older, and after seeing how loyal he was to her after Edward's departure, she found herself wondering why she hadn't seen him as more than a friend earlier. His looks hadn't changed. His personality was the same. His wants and needs remained. What was it about him that suddenly made her connect with him more than before?

No; perhaps it wasn't him, but her that had changed. Perhaps she realized the real man she should have been in love with wasn't the most handsome, strong warrior that Edward was. It was the man who made her laugh when her day was bad or who believed in her when she didn't believe in herself. It was her best friend, the man who knew her most-strengths and weaknesses combined-and loved her. It was the man she shared her heart with, someone who understood her just as much as she understood him.

She stretched out her hand, watching as he took the ring and put it on her finger. It was a perfect fit. He watched as she moved forward and into his arms, her hands cupping his jaw.

He said nothing as she gently pressed her forehead against his, holding still as she felt his arms wrap around her and pull her close. "You are..." she whispered to him, their breath mingling and their world suddenly stopping around them. "...the most amazing, kindest, gentlest man..." She paused as their eyes gazed into each other's, his face yearning for every grain of approval she could give. "I have been so blind to not have seen it before. I was such a fool to waste my heart on someone who broke it when I should've given it to the one who would've kept it whole."

Emmerich's hands rose, his finger grazing her jaw line. "Then let me mend the heart that was broken."

"I think you already have." Antoinette smiled. "Yes, Emery. I will marry you."

"Really?" She had never seen Emmerich smile so wide.

"Yeah."

"Well," he said as he moved his lips closer to hers, nearly touching. "I have a confession to make, Miss van Echt. Your heart wasn't the only one that was mended. You just mended mine as well."

He caressed her slowly, his arms gathering her to him like a guardian protecting a treasure. He moved forward, touching her lips tenderly with his, not in heated passion or with an aggressive push but with the gentleness of a breeze, warm and soothing and true. It was a kiss unlike any other Antoinette had felt, even with Edward at his calmest, and she became lost in his embrace, feeling so safe that any thought or fear of ever being hurt again was expelled from her mind.

She was hesitant to pull away, the touch of his lips lingering on hers with a tingle she would never forget. Their eyes remained locked on each other, their arms wrapped around the other's back, longing for a second kiss.

Antoinette was about to become lost again until the door swung open, a panting and panicked Bernie suddenly entering the room and shutting the door behind her. Antoinette and Emmerich both jumped at the entrance, but suddenly calmed seeing it was only Bernette.

"You...confounded...frog..." Bernie glared at Emmerich as she caught her breath. Her hair was unkempt and covered loosely by a hat and her clothes were disheveled and spattered with yellow, reddish gunk mixed with snow.

"What happened?" Antoinette asked, her eyes wide in shock.

Bernie ignored Antoinette and went straight to Emmerich, getting up in his face. "Where did you put your horse?"

"I tied up Waffles in the stables," Emmerich replied, stuttering. "I didn't see anyone there. I thought..."

"YOUR STUPID HORSE ESCAPED!" Bernie seethed. "And guess where I found him? In the outdoor pantry *covered in apple jam!*"

Emmerich gulped as Antoinette hid a snicker.

"HE ATE EVERY JAR WE HAD!" Bernie said. "Broken glass is everywhere and of course everything is splattered and covered in jelly. If your stupid horse gets sick and starts using the pantry as an outhouse, I'm declaring war!"

"You didn't leave Waffles in there, did you?" Antoinette asked.

"Of course not," Bernie scoffed. "I tied him up and put him back in the stable. But you owe me, buddy!" She stuck her finger onto Emmerich's shoulder, giving him a gentle push. "If you want me to keep all of this quiet, you better stop this wedding with Prince Arnold!"

"I don't think that will be a problem." Emmerich grinned as Antoinette held her hand out, showing the ring on her finger. "She said yes."

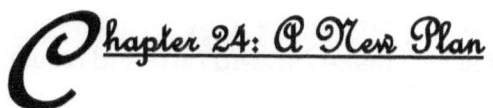

"I see you are feeling well."

Malina looked up to see Vacius standing at the door, his disguise as a servant indistinguishable from the real ones bustling about out in the halls. Malina stood from her seat at the window and drew the curtains shut as Vacius closed the door, locking it behind. She hadn't seen that wicked gleam in his eye in a long while. It made her heart pound with excitement.

"The next king is birthed. All our plans have come to fruition," Malina cooed as she approached him. She stopped, eyeing him from head to toe as if inspecting goods to be bought, and she nearly jumped when he ran his hands through her hair.

"All plans have succeeded save one," Vacius replied as he leaned forward, his lips tickling her ear. "You still have a husband."

"A trifle," Malina scoffed.

"A trifle that needs to be dealt with," Vacius said. "Already he has stood up to you."

"And I stood back up to him," Malina replied. "It was easy to handle."

"But now that Calimus is born things may be different." Vacius sighed. "I worry this will make Edward bold and clever. Already he is attached to the child and seeks to raise him without your influence."

"Darling, of course a father is going to want to influence his child. Whether he succeeds..."

"*His* child?" Vacius stepped back and glared at his lover, his lips curling down into a snarl. "Need I remind you that I have a claim on Calimus, even more so than Edward?"

Malina waved her hand in apathy. "It was a figure of speech. Do not be so easily offended."

"I'm not offended. I'm angry Edward has what is mine!"

"Then do not be so easily angered," Malina clarified. "We shall control Calimus in the long run, and you and I shall have our throne."

"Not if Edward is still alive."

"You worry too much, Vacius." Malina rolled her eyes. "Have I not proved myself able to take care of things? I garnered the treaty and am winning the nobles over and more than anything, I've been able to control Edward. He's as weak as they come."

"You can only threaten for so long, Malina."

"Oh Vacius." Malina smirked as she eyed him with a gleam of her own. "You know threats aren't my only weapon."

Vacius crossed his arms, his voice nearing a growl. "Are you saying you're willing to degrade yourself with this man *again*? Is that why you won't kill him? Because he, too, is your lover?"

"Darling!" Malina laughed. "Are you jealous? You know I only love on Edward when I expect something in return."

He turned his head away and faced the wall.

"You and I have something very special, Vacius," Malina continued as she turned him around to face him. She ran her hands up his chest and fumbled with his shirt to remove it. "Something I have with no other man. Edward is only a means to an end, but you...you are something different entirely."

She tried to overtake him with passion but he steadied her hands. "Then if I'm so special to you, why won't you kill him?"

"What would you have me do?" Malina asked. "Send you, my lover, off in a jealous rage to kill my husband? Will that accomplish all we've planned? Oh, what a silly boy you are, Vacius." She waved her finger in front of him, making him frown. "Darling, we cannot have two kings dead in a month. It's too obvious."

"I will kill Edward for you, then."

"*No*," Malina said firmly, giving him a hard look. "I shan't risk you killing him here in the palace. Not now."

"And why not?" Vacius asked. "I have not failed before. Do you doubt my abilities?"

"It is not that I doubt your abilities," Malina replied. "If the servants or guards find Edward has been killed by a blade, murder will be suspected, and who do you think will be the first suspect? Me. It is too obvious and too risky for *me*."

"Then what do you suggest? Or do you not want to lose your dear husband yet?"

Malina laughed. "He is expendable. I have no quarrel with parting from him as long as it helps me and doesn't harm me."

"If you wish to keep your power, Malina, it is my recommendation you have Edward eliminated!" Vacius interrupted. "The longer you leave him alive, the more chances you give him to undermine you. He will turn the people against you, and we will lose Calimus because he will have Edward's influence."

"I know," Malina said as she stood in front of him. "Which is why Edward must die...but only when the timing is right."

She began to walk about the room, her hips swaying in rhythmic fashion, almost as if she intended them to. "The crown has been mine for such a little while and the power to keep it is fragile. The coming months will be important and must go flawlessly for our plan to work. I do not plan on killing Edward myself, Vacius, and nor do I intend for you to do it. I shall leave that to the people."

"The people?" Vacius asked.

"Indeed," Malina replied with a smirk. "There is more than one way to be rid of a king, Vacius." She turned to face him, coming close and fingering the collar near his neck. "Be patient, my lover, for Edward's demise. After all, I have brought us this far, haven't I?"

Vacius' eyes narrowed as he met her gaze. "Without my help, you wouldn't have left Verloris, Malina."

"Your jealousy is charming," Malina said as she pulled him towards a sofa near the hearth, sitting him down on the cushions and climbing atop.

His hands remained still as she gazed upon his features. "Leave Edward be for now and fret not. My husband's downfall will come swifter than you think."

"When?" Vacius replied as his hands met her waist. She smiled as she moved forward to kiss him, but he stopped her before her lips could meet his own. "When will Edward die?"

Malina laughed as she stroked his chin and neck with her finger. "When the people love me more than him."

"And if they don't?"

"Darling, there is no 'if'," Malina replied as her lips met his neck. "Everyone loves me."

She undid the buttons on his shirt and leaned in close to his ear. "Now, son of the Velori, fret no more and let me soothe you."

Vacius looked uncertain, his mind still not at ease with the threat of Edward's possible rise to power. "But Malina, we should…"

"Sh," Malina said as she put her finger to his lips, quieting him. "Do not use your mouth for endless chatter. It has much better uses besides speech."

She kissed him before he could say any more, drowning out his doubts with lust.

To be continued...

To be continued in

Book 3 of The Ripple Affair series,

"When Dreams Break".

Turn the page for a preview of chapter 1...

Chapter 1: The Man Who Waited

For ten years he waited.

Waited for her to notice him so she could see how much he cared. Waited for her to touch him so they could be closer instead of further away. Waited for her to look at him with the eyes of a lover instead of the eyes of a friend.

For ten years he waited for the woman he loved, and now, after frustration and heartache and thinking the world would look with favor on everyone but himself, she arrived. Emmerich van Ketten's wait was over, and for the first time in his eighteen years of existence, he could say he was happy.

It was morning, just after dawn, when he awoke in the parlor he met her in the night before. The fire had long gone out in the hearth and the air was starting to get cool, but his body felt nothing but warmth as Antoinette snuggled close against him, her cheek nestled in the crook of his neck and her arms wrapped around his chest. He had kept her close throughout the night, wrapped in blankets so she wouldn't get cold, and he held her as she slowly fell asleep. He soon followed, dozing off as his head rested atop hers, and as he slept, his mind was filled with dreams of the future. Their wedding day, as simple as it would be. Their wedding night, where two would become one. A home. Children. A life full of warmth and happiness that made him forget all the hurt and rejection of the past.

For the first time he was thankful, and the future never looked so bright.

Antoinette stirred, experiencing her own dreams as she slept, making Emmerich pull her close and kiss her forehead. He didn't want to wake her. She never was much of a morning person, as was he, but if palace tradition was anything like it used to be when he visited Edeland, a maid or two would be checking the princess' room to wake her for breakfast. With Antoinette absent, the palace would be astir, but with both princesses absent, the palace would be in an uproar. Antoinette's sister, Bernie, slept lopsided in a chair near them and gently snored, but doubtless she would be wakened once the maids came in to find the sisters.

Emmerich couldn't afford to be discovered-at least not yet. Not until after the elopement.

He gently shook Antoinette and she moaned in disapproval. "I'm sorry, my love," he said quietly as he stroked her cheek. "I need you to wake up."

Antoinette's eyes slowly opened and it took her a moment to focus on what was going on. She blinked before offering Emmerich a smile and looked into his eyes. "Good morning," she said.

He smiled back as he watched her expression, his heart giving a flutter as she met his gaze. "Good morning," he answered back. "I'm sorry to wake you, but if tradition is still the same, there should be some maids on their way to wake you and your sister."

"Ugh." Antoinette closed her eyes and swallowed, perturbed. "Forgive me, Emery. I wasn't thinking. Yes, they should be on their way in a little while." She sat up, pulling away from him, his hand wanting to linger atop hers for just a moment longer. He was almost sorry he woke her if it meant her leaving his arms so quickly.

Antoinette stifled a yawn as she sat up, stretching her legs. "For once I wish they'd let me sleep in." Emmerich wondered if she noticed him pout, for as soon as she was done stretching, she placed herself back in his arms and snuggled against him more.

He didn't object. If it meant her touch, he'd gladly face those maids. "It is still early. Perhaps they'll be lenient."

"Mother is planning a wedding. As long as the sun is up, there is time for work."

"True." Emmerich smirked. "But in our defense, we were up all night planning a wedding, too. One that is actually going to take place."

She smiled as she closed her eyes, resting her head on his shoulder. "Today is the day, then."

He hugged her gently. "Today is the day."

"Are you sure the plan will work?"

"Yes," Emmerich began. "You will tell your mother you are going to spend a day with Bernette to enjoy each other's company before your marriage. I will meet you at the minister's at noon. From there, we will have the wedding at the church and go to the inn to…uhm…"

He paused, his face blushing red. It was a general rule of marriages that to prevent annulment, it had to be consummated. To make sure the elopement was legal and to prevent Susanna van Echt from fighting it, they had to cover all their bases.

And that meant moving the wedding night up half a day early.

He cleared his throat, trying to cover his embarrassment and the heat that climbed up his gut, and continued. "To go to the inn and...well..."

Antoinette gave a chuckle, making him turn. "You're cute when you're nervous."

"I'm...I'm not nervous."

"Yes you are. You're stuttering and your heart's pounding like your horse chasing after some apples."

He snickered, remembering Waffles being tied up in the stable. He wondered how the horse fared after eating all those jars of apple jam.

"You have nothing to be nervous about," Antoinette said.

"I know. I'm just..." Emmerich looked away, his face flushing again. "I'm just not experienced...I haven't..."

"You know," Antoinette interrupted softly, touching his chin and turning him to face her. "Some girls don't mind being the only woman a man has ever been with."

"I never wanted to be with anyone else but you." He kissed her tenderly, enveloping her in his embrace. "It's always been you, and it will always be only you."

She could only grin as she wrapped her arms around his neck and kissed him back.

About the Author

Erin Cruey is the author of *The Ripple Affair Series* and finds writing to be extremely effective at five in the morning or when drinking hot tea.   When she isn't working on her next book, she is busy in the kitchen trying to master the art of cooking while not burning the food and pans.   She currently resides in the United States with her family.

For the latest blog posts, news, and book releases, visit http://erincruey.com.

Other Books by Erin Cruey

The Ripple Affair Series

The Ripple Affair

Reign of Change

www.ingramcontent.com/pod-product-compliance
Lightning Source LLC
Chambersburg PA
CBHW030027180626
46810CB00001B/257